D0426039

Praise for Mark Mayer's *Aerialists*

"Mark Mayer writes with a humorous, wistful elegance. His stories are singular, as detached and intimate as dreaming." —**Marilynne Robinson, Pulitzer Prize–winning author of *Gilead***

"These stories are bright and muscular, luminous and generous, nimble and funny, tender and surprising at every turn. They march you to the terrifying precipice of human darkness and relationships and longing and dangle you over the edge. They broke my heart, and I am better for the breaking." —**Carmen Maria Machado, author of *Her Body and Other Parties***

"There's a sense of wide-eyed wonderment in these stories that's truly rare. Mark Mayer may well live in the same world as you and me, but he's able to see beyond it all somehow, and he finds extraordinary weirdness and beauty everywhere he looks. *Aerialists* is exquisite and wild at the same time. How often does one read a book like this?" —**Peter Orner, author of *Am I Alone Here?***

"Through this superb collection, Mark Mayer has built a circus of the normal, has somehow infiltrated the ordinary to reveal the freak inside. These classically constructed stories offer scale models of heartbreak and rage—cynicism and doubt and loss writ so small, then deftly magnified, blown up by tenderness. Mayer shapes the mild, the banal, the picturesque, the sweet, then punctures all that with nothing but reality, a sewing needle in the back of the neck, precise, sharp, unexpected; you go down hard, but know the thrill of being taken out by a master." —**Merritt Tierce, author of *Love Me Back*, staff writer for *Orange Is the New Black***

"Of Stravinsky's *The Rite of Spring*, one baffled critic wrote that the music always went to the note next to the one you expected. That's Mark Mayer's deal: you're bracing for a punch but he leg-sweeps you;

you're still reeling when his boutonniere squirts you; as you start to laugh it off, you realize the blow is fatal. Like a true impresario, Mayer never lets you get bored, and you leave feeling like you got more than you paid for. In *Aerialists'* nine uncanny, perfectly crafted stories, which bring to mind short-form experts like George Saunders and Steven Millhauser, Mark Mayer puts on the greatest show on Earth." —**Tony Tulathimutte, author of *Private Citizens***

"An exhilarating ether of uncommon intelligence inhabits these stories. Mark Mayer writes beauty, writes funny, writes wise, writes awful, writes marvel, writes verve, writes sad. If the emergency exits are everywhere blocked here, even the unbearable incorporates strange uplift, admits fierce grace, and the whole is frequently gusted by truth. This is the real thing: what an exciting debut." —**Laird Hunt, author of *Neverhome***

"Brilliant and wrenching, *Aerialists* explores with great care the struggle to love and be loved, to know and be known. Mayer's worlds unfold with unwavering compassion and vulnerability. The result is revelatory, brimful with the terror and joy of life laid bare." —**Anna Noyes, author of *Goodnight, Beautiful Women***

"*Aerialists* is a work of great imagination. These stories are always in motion, as characters reach for their better selves and touch them only briefly, in singular, exquisite moments rendered in astounding prose. Mark Mayer is wise and big-hearted, a magician of the American sentence. Each story is its own world, inhabited by characters who are painfully, wonderfully real." —**Emily Ruskovich, author of *Idaho***

"A dazzling collection filled with characters who evoke, in their flawed humanity, the strange, sorrowful, and ever shimmering world of the circus. Mayer's bittersweet stories are playful, haunting, and wonderfully inventive. Read them and be transported." —**Mona Awad, author of *13 Ways of Looking at a Fat Girl***

AERIALISTS

AERIALISTS

STORIES

Mark Mayer

BLOOMSBURY PUBLISHING

NEW YORK • LONDON • OXFORD • NEW DELHI • SYDNEY

BLOOMSBURY PUBLISHING
Bloomsbury Publishing Inc.
1385 Broadway, New York, NY 10018, USA

BLOOMSBURY, BLOOMSBURY PUBLISHING, and the
Diana logo are trademarks of
Bloomsbury Publishing Plc

First published in the United States 2019

The following stories have been previously published, some in slightly
different form: "Aerialists" (*Guernica*), "Strongwoman" (*Colorado Review*),
"The Evasive Magnolio" (*Mid-American Review*, anthologized in *New Stories
from the Midwest*).

ISBN: HB: 978-1-63557-217-9; eBook: 978-1-63557-216-2

LIBRARY OF CONGRESS CATALOGING-IN-PUBLICATION DATA
Names: Mayer, Mark, 1984– author.
Title: Aerialists : stories / Mark Mayer.
Description: New York : Bloomsbury Publishing, 2019.
Identifiers: LCCN 2018006312 | ISBN 9781635572179 (hardcover) |
ISBN 9781635572162 (ebook)
Classification: LCC PS3613.A9557 A6 2019 | DDC 813/.6—dc23
LC record available at https://lccn.loc.gov/2018006312
2 4 6 8 10 9 7 5 3 1

Typeset by Westchester Publishing Services
Printed and bound in the U.S.A. by Berryville Graphics Inc.,
Berryville, Virginia

To find out more about our authors and books visit
www.bloomsbury.com and sign up for our newsletters.

FOR MY PARENTS

Barnum had no personal character. In a strict sense, he had no private life. He lived in the midst of the crowd, in the peopled haunts of his great museum, on the road, on the lecture platform, on steamers, in caravans or circus trains, near the smell of sawdust or under the spreading lights of the city. He lived in public; at times it seemed he was the public.

—CONSTANCE ROURKE, *TRUMPETS OF JUBILEE*

Friday I tasted life. It was a vast morsel. A circus passed the house—still I feel the red in my mind though the drums are out.

—EMILY DICKINSON, LETTER TO ELIZABETH HOLLAND

Contents

Strongwoman   1

Aerialists   30

The Evasive Magnolio   61

Twin   76

The Wilderness Act   103

The April Thief   135

Solidarity Forever   198

The Clown   238

The Ringmaster   258

Acknowledgments   289

STRONGWOMAN

A few weeks after my dad moved out, I played a trick on my mom. I asked to give her a hug, and after we held each other a minute I stuck a sewing needle in the back of her neck. I had it taped between my fingers with invisible tape.

She'd been wailing at night. Maybe she thought I couldn't hear her, but I could. I understood she was sad, but the sounds she made in the dark were so gigantic and horrible I didn't know where they came from. There were glow stars above my bed, moons and shooting stars with their tails peeling down, and I watched the yellow light they stored drain out. I hated myself for how I'd stuck them there. They were all clumped in one corner of the big empty ceiling, too close together to make any constellations. I tried to restick one, but you can't, they just fall. What helped a little was to pretend there was a black hole over the bed. That was what had sucked them together there.

I never said anything about the sounds. I did my homework well and made sure my teachers liked me. I was a good kid, basically, I think, for an eleven-year-old. I loved my mom, but sometimes I would pester her to tears. It was easy to make her sad, but she only wailed like that after she thought I was asleep. She would be up early cooking breakfasts she clipped from the paper. "How's my man doing?" she would say if she saw me staring off. Then she'd hug me. She was getting fatter and I liked hugging it all. There was a good white pad of it behind her neck. She didn't have a talk with me about the needle. "Ow, crap!" she said. She looked surprised, then sad, but she didn't make the sound.

A few days later, she told me I was going to spend the summer in Denver with my dad. Maybe it had been the plan all along.

I wanted to say I'd done it by accident. First I'd taped my middle finger and ring finger together, only because there was some tape. And then I'd seen the little needle hole of light between my fingers, so I put a needle through. And there. I'd figured out from one of their fights that I was an accident, which was okay. What it meant, though, was that maybe everything I did in the world was also an accident, that I was a way for more accidents to happen. I liked that. All the rocks I kicked down the sidewalk, which weren't going to move on their own, all the cars that stopped for me to cross the street. The invisible tape was part of that, and the needle.

It was an hour drive to Denver from Fort Collins and we hardly talked. She tried to dance a little to the radio, then quit. I watched the neat lanes of traffic, the millions of cars that were supposed to somehow never touch.

My dad had quit being a lawyer and said he was a property magnate now. He had two apartment buildings and a bowling alley he was fixing up. We spent most of the summer at the alley with his different girlfriends and a handyman named Gus.

"Junior," my dad said the first day, "start loving it."

There was a claw machine I could play without paying, a spot-the-differences video game called Titty Match-Up, and boxes of Sour Belts that were expired but tasted the same. The smell wasn't the shoes or the shoe spray or the beer spills or the burnt motors in the ball retrievers or the broken popcorn machine. I couldn't figure out what it was, but my dad strolled around breathing deep like we were in a garden.

He was so excited to see me, I realized I wasn't going to see him a lot. He called Ling-Ling Palace from the lanes at ten in the morning. "General Tao's breakfast. We got a special occasion here. What? Look, employ your expertise." He plunged the antenna into his palm.

The fancy, sagging business shirts made him look like a sultan, and he was learning to talk like one. He had a thousand keys now and he was always throwing them from hand to hand. If they dropped, he would leave them on the floor until it was convenient to pick them up. He didn't nick his mole once all summer. It looked like an ornament on his jaw.

He was trying out names. "Kingpin's," he'd gesture, his watch sledding through arm hair. "Would you grow your gut at a place called Kingpin's?"

I missed her. We talked on the phone, but we didn't say anything. She asked was my bowling game getting good, even though I'd said the lanes were broken. "Can I come home yet?"

"You have two homes." She explained divorce like I'd never heard of it before.

"I have two gnomes? What am I going to do with two gnomes?"

"Both your gnomes love you, Junior. Even when you tug our beards."

"I grew a beard. You wouldn't recognize me. I have a shark tattoo now and a big forked beard and I crash motorcycles."

"I'm thirty feet tall and I eat lightning bolts and juggle tigers."

"We're stupid, Mom."

"I love you back, Junior."

"How's your momma?" my dad asked at work. "She all mended up?"

I thought for a second she'd told him about the needle, but he just meant the divorce.

"Mr. Zenichek," Gus said—we were watching him repair a ball retriever—"my social worker says not to put the children in the middle." He was going through some kind of divorce too. On Wednesdays and weekends, he would bring his three little daughters with him. They played Titty Match-Up together, clacking the screen with their bright, fake nails while I tried not to look.

"I don't know," I told my dad. "She's running a marathon."

"No doubt," he said. "My social worker tells me not to lie."

The roof of my mouth was starting to bleed from the Sour Belts. It wasn't a lie. She said she was going to.

"Junior," he said, "don't pretend like I don't care."

"I think she's really sad, Daddy."

"You darling boy," said my dad's girlfriend Dolly. Her eyes turned shiny on me, and her hair spray or lotion smelled like jam. Through his silk sleeve, I could see her fingers rubbing his arm where the skin was like an old balloon. With her other hand, she tried to touch my ear. "She'll be fine. We've all been there."

"Darling boy," he winked at me. "Well. Well, well, well."

My dad said Gus had almost become a lawyer himself. He'd done correspondence courses, and then, just when he was going to take the bar, a crazy woman had thrown a twenty-five-pound bag of birdseed from her balcony and knocked him stupid. "This guy," my dad liked to say, "has the best manners of any man I've ever known."

"No," Gus would say. "Don't tease. This isn't so."

Gus kept cocktail napkins with cartoons on them folded in his shirt pocket, but he used a bandanna from his back pocket to wipe his forehead or blow his nose. He washed his hands every hour and was always saying how grateful he was to have his health, even though we all knew he was brain damaged. My dad said he'd pay Gus extra to teach me some etiquette while he worked. He called it my Mexican finishing school even though Gus was from Colombia. I ate my lunch with Gus, and he would tell me to eat more slowly and put less on my fork. Soft bread should be chewed eight times, meat eighteen times. We each had to make a toast with grape soda before every meal. "Look there," he said and pointed with his insulated mug at the irides- cent pink storm on a bowling ball. "Richard Junior, please give a toast to this."

Once he brought frozen leftovers and at lunch, when they were thawed, he took a bite and cried. I couldn't believe it. Maybe it was something his wife had left in the fridge. It was orange and oily with peppers floating in it. "Try this," he said. "You must absolutely try."

The claw machine had stamped leather wallets, and I finally retrieved the one that said VIPER on the side. "You son of a dog," my dad said. He was proud of me. Then he said we would have to put it back. I had to cry in order to keep it, and after that I didn't want it anymore.

"Nope," he said, "it's yours now. Bitch like that and you have to keep it."

I did keep it. I hated it, but I have it.

He said he left my mom because he didn't love her anymore and that that happens. He never said anything about how she'd gotten fat—maybe it had nothing to do with it—but his girl-friends that summer were all very thin. They seemed to like him, so there was no reason not to be happy for him. We would all watch Gus working on a ball retriever, and my dad would reach into the seat next to him and work his heavy tanned fingers over their small thighs into the narrow where I didn't let myself look. "What can I say? Your mother is a beautiful girl, a beautiful woman." He looked next to him. "All women are beautiful, and all men are ugly, and the most beautiful thing is that they might love you in spite of it. That's what it is, Junior—your momma loved something very ugly."

He was full of lessons for me.

"Junior," he said, "you're turning twelve. It's Summer of the Boner. Time for a man talk."

"Richard," said his girlfriend Alayna. "You're embarrassing him."

"Subject one," he said. "Objectifying women. This is serious, you can really hurt somebody with this stuff. You have to always see the whole bird, not just her cuts."

"Richard, stop." I thought I liked Alayna better than Dolly or Kim. She tied her scarves like a pirate and liked thumb wars, but I didn't like it how she was grinning now.

"Your stiffy isn't going to state its reasons and your job is to never figure them out. Because the reasons are hurtful. As soon as you think, *There's a set*, or, *Those can walk*, you're turning women into objects. Women should be mysteries, not objects. You get what I'm telling you? Always tell a woman you don't understand why you want her. 'It's beyond reasons, baby.' Except ugly girls—you can tell ugly girls they're beautiful."

She slapped his thigh. "Dickie! Look how embarrassed he is."

He was so happy and handsome in his alley. "Here we are," he said every morning when we got there. Here we are—like this was who he'd been waiting for us to be.

"Gus, Junior, good news," my dad said at the end of the summer.

A dancercise place back in Fort Collins was going out of business and would sell Kingpin's its disco balls and light machine on the cheap. Gus could take me back to Mom's and pick up the goods. One trip, tidy.

Gus's old pickup smelled like Christmas candles. "Leather seats need oil every year," he said. "These are imitation, but true leather you must condition."

I spent the car ride watching the cars and programming my new watch. It had eight buttons. "Detonation complete," I said when an alarm went off. "One million people just exploded."

"Richard Junior, you know that is not funny at all."

The dancercise studio was on Lemay next to a Flowerama and across from the hospital. It was locked, and Gus had to pat the glass door with the band of his class ring for a long time before a woman came.

"Sorry," she said. "Potty."

She led us into the empty studio. There were posters everywhere of women in vibrant spandex, and long panel mirrors, but with the lights off it was like the inside of a cardboard box.

"I guess you talked with Miranda," she said. "I'm Celia."

"Mucho gusto. Soy Gustavo," Gus said. I could see how helpless he was. She was smiley and curvy and creamy brown. The big dark room should have made her look sad, but it didn't.

She laughed at him. "And you?"

"I'm Junior."

She laughed again. "Not for long."

Gus and I carried two disco balls and the light machine to his truck. She followed with a box of cords and papers. Gus counted out the bills on his tailgate.

"Okay," she said. "Hasta la pasta. Bowl some strikes."

Gus looked as if he would cry again. He sat in the driver seat, wiping his forehead with his bandanna and staring through the dash. His door was still open and the cab was dinging. Finally he got out and walked next door to the flower shop. He came back with a polite bouquet. He sat holding it in the dinging for a minute, then handed it to me. "Bring these for your mother," he said.

The door of my house smashed the wrong way against the frame, then swung back, but it was not my mom.

"Mrs. Zenichek?" Gus said.

A tremendous woman stood there. The sinews of her neck filled the doorframe and tugged as she turned her brawny eyes. Her shoulders and arms, even the muscles of her expression, were all partitioned. She looked like a butcher chart. But it was a woman: she was wearing pajamas; I could check. She took in Gus, the flowers, me.

"Mom?" I tried to call past her.

"Oh, Junior!" My mom appeared behind the monster and pulled me into the living room with a long hug, but it was different. She did more hugging—more holding and squeezing—but somehow it felt like less hug. She wasn't as soft, which was maybe healthier, but I didn't like it. I felt her arms, not her. "Welcome to Mom's house!" She laughed, and it was long and watery and bright. She held me back to look at me. Happiness rashed around her eyes.

Two sleeping bags were on the floor of the living room. A box of wine balanced on the arm of the couch. Her Shiva statuette on the bookcase had a pink and green ankle sock over its head.

"This is Klara," my mom said.

"He's a dumpling," said Klara. "And flowers!"

I extended them nervously. "Keep 'em," Klara told me. "I'll grab your shit."

She did, and the flowers I know ended up on the table, but by then Gus was gone already, and for all my manners training I hadn't even wished him goodbye.

Her name was Klara Loyzaga. My mom and her had spent most of the summer together. Klara—sometimes she pronounced it the Spanish way with two flicks of the tongue, sometimes she didn't—was a professional bodybuilder and strongwoman. She had competed all over the world and on cable television, under the name Klara Belle. Our living room was now full of videos of her shiny brown body in exhibitions of strained perfection and strength.

We spent a lot of good time that fall with Klara. She had a brother who'd died rock climbing, and she made a big deal about enjoying life. She bungee jumped and cooked her own hot sauce and supported important causes I'd never heard of. The Zapatistas. The Tutsis. Fair trade. She read a special newspaper that came once a week from France. Klara and my mom had already been to the Medicine Bows and Escalante and Telluride in Klara's Eurovan, and we went all over together, like a gang. We went to Elitch's and Klara paid the upcharge for the XLR8R, and they strapped the three of us together and towed us up to 182 feet, then dropped us. My mom sobbed the whole way up, but it was different than before. *I hate it! I hate it! I hate it!*— but then she loved it most. After that I wasn't shy. We watched *Deep Space Nine* and Walt Disney Classics and Klara's tapes in the living room and ate stove-popped popcorn with nutritional yeast and cumin and did massages. We took Klara rollerblading for her first time—she drove over with a Tweety Bird pillow taped to her butt. She left a guitar, which I was allowed to play, behind our TV. She tuned it to open G so I could slap the strings and bonk my knees like Elvis. Her face muscles made her whistle dangerously loud. A couple times we had sleepovers in the living room, the three of us. I explained Dutch ovens and she wanted to make it a competition, but Mom wouldn't have it. If I buried my watch in my sleeping bag, it woke only me, and I could roll toward my mom and listen to her breathe and watch the nylon of her sleeping bag tucking in and out with her breath.

In September, before it got cold, Klara had a beach party. A ditch ran through the back of her subdivision, and she trucked in sand and dumped it ditchside and invited her friends over for daiquiris and sun. There were squirt guns and hulas, Jamaican ginger ales for me, and sidewalk chalk for a watermelon-seed-spitting contest. "Do you know how hard it is to find a watermelon with actual seeds in it?" Klara told me. "Monsanto wants to neuter my melons!" She drank her margarita out of the paper limeade tube.

"Come on, Rico. Gas it!" her friends yelled when I got up to spit, but I kept laughing and screwing up.

They were all accomplished women in their thirties or forties. Potters, lawyers, a judo sensei, a professor of avalanche science. Somehow my mom knew them all. One had taken bass lessons from Gene Simmons. They balanced me on a surfboard and I tried to float down the ditch. When I passed one of them dangling her feet in, she said, "All right, Marlene. He made it: honorary Gorgon."

They all asked me if I had a girlfriend, then pretended not to believe me. Klara spent all fall teasing me about it.

Say we wanted to go to a movie. "What do you think?" she would ask into the paper. "Should we see *Unstrung Heroes*?"

"I don't know," I'd say.

"'So touching the heart almost stops,'" she'd read. "Rico, baby, women love that shit."

I tried, but I couldn't look at Klara without seeing anatomy. Muscle overhung her. When she moved, it was an exaggerated demonstration of movement. *This is how the body holds a steering wheel between two fingers like a cigar. This is how the body scratches a chin with a shoulder. This is how the body cuts through a burrito with a fork.* She had a trick where she wiggled her fingers to make her fat veins pop back and forth over her tendon. Her skin was as firm, tan, and finely wrinkled as an earthworm's. Her gold necklace barely reached her collarbones. Her chest was large, and I watched and tried not to watch to see how much of it was muscle. Her hair was hard black, wavy, and not as long as it was trying to be. I didn't know—didn't know how to know—if she was beautiful.

She sold my mom a weird black health tonic called KM/Matol, which I pretended to find delicious, and she wore a magnetic bracelet that balanced her blood flow.

"That's made up, right?" I asked. Often it was just me and her in the living room, making up stuff on guitar, waiting for my mom to finish whatever she was doing. My mom was trying to be an event planner now.

"Total bullcrap."

"Why do you wear it then?"

"Ancient knowledge, man. Bullcrap will balance your blood flow."

"What do you mean?"

"I mean it's SOP to lie to yourself a little bit."

She said her father had been a strongman, and her grandfather had been a strongman, and her great-grandfather had been the strongest man who ever lived. He could restrain four draft horses, two in each hand.

"How do you know?"

"What's up?"

"How do you know he was the strongest man who ever lived?"

"We're talking big-ass Budweiser horses."

"But how do you know no one else—"

"The fuck, Rico? Because my grandma told me."

I didn't know adults got bored, but she was bored in minutes. "Let's *do* something," she'd say. She was up for anything.

"Let's make toasts," I said. "I'll get Capri Suns."

I stood on the ottoman and tried to remember what Gus had taught me. "Pick anything," I told her. "Then tell a little story with a compliment at the end."

"Take it away, toastmaster."

"Friends, when I first met Klara's bicep I thought, holy flipping moly. Danger ahead. But since then, Klara's bicep has become a close personal friend of mine, and I can tell you, he would never even—" I froze.

"*He* would never even *what*?" she said with her jaw cocked.

"Hurt a fly?"

"That so? All right—hear, hear. We'll see about that." She lay back and crushed the couch beneath her shoulder blades. "Let me tell you a toast about this couch. Once upon a time, there was a little puppet named Pinocchio, and he was made out of a chair Geppetto smashed on the ground one night in a drunk. This Pinocchio got his shit into *all* kind of trouble. He did everything wrong. Turned into a donkey. Joined a circus. Got swallowed up by a fish. One day, he turned into a real boy, but he kept feeling like there was still a splinter in him, and probably there was. 'Help me, Blue,' he kept saying to the fairy. 'Help me, Blue, I don't feel right,' but there was no help. That's the deal with being a real boy. Sometimes he wished he could just be a chair again, but he couldn't. So, here's to my favorite couch, which—thank god—will never turn into a boy." She jabbed the little yellow straw into her Capri.

"Okay," I said. "Weird."

"What," said Klara, "that's not how Richard Senior says his toasts?"

"I liked it. It was good."

"Gracious Dickie, making toasts and sending flowers." She sat up and looked over the couch back at Gus's flowers, dried by now into dull clumps of color, like panties by the road. "*My dear wife, Marlene,*" she said in a voice, "*take these flowers from my toady as token of my deep ruefulness.* What a mensch—and we never even sent him a note. He's a better man than me."

My mom seemed happier. I didn't hear her crying at night, but I don't think she slept as much as before either. She watched more TV and talked to Klara on the phone. She was getting healthy, she said. She ran every day. Her voice was different, more cackling and bright.

She had this new way of teasing me.

Like one night she said it was boys' choice, and I wanted Chubby's for green chile.

"Fuck yeah," said Klara.

They put on their straw cowboy hats. "Look at you," my mom said over her shoulder in the van. "You're embarrassed! Your mom's embarrassing you! I guess this is the beginning of it." She was taking a shrill joy in something.

"Of what?"

"Dudehood, dude," said Klara. She turned up the NPR.

"Pink. Socket," said the radio.

"Eye!" said Klara.

"Cold. Loser," said the radio.

"Sore!" said Klara.

"Eyesore!" my mom cheered. They high-fived. I was confused.

A girl I knew from school, Janey Collins, was at Chubby's with her mom and dad and older brother. She was silent and beautiful, and I'd known her since the first grade but I hadn't talked to her since fifth.

"It's Janey!" my mom said, and Janey's mom and dad and brother looked up. Janey did not. "Go say hi."

I tried to direct us toward a booth.

"Come on, Rico," she said. "Quit being so cute."

I gave her a pleading look. Janey's family was watching.

"Need me and K to hold your hand?"

I went over. The red in my face was blinding.

"Hello, slut," I said and walked out the jingling door.

❖　❖　❖

15

My dad got a call about that one.

"Power play," he said when my mom handed me over. "Here's how it's going to go." She stood above me watching my face as I tried to hide my sniffling from the phone. "She'll hate you for a few weeks—don't apologize, just pretty much leave her alone. Sometime after Christmas, you tell her you want her to be your girl."

"I'm embarrassed, Dad. Her—"

"Don't let her see it," he said. "Look, who doesn't like to be teased? Now your mom's going to make you call her and apologize, but I want you to dial me instead."

My mom's face was so worried it was like I'd been called away to war. "I *want* to apologize," I said.

"Good, good. Your mom's eating that up, no doubt."

"I feel really bad."

"Perfect. Okay. I love you, son. I'll talk to you in a minute."

Sometime that fall Klara stopped coming around, and my mom wailed again at night. The sound was as strange and hideous as before. It was so loud, but also choked, like it clogged her throat getting out. I didn't know how it could come from her. It seemed like it didn't. I heard it in the bathroom at school or loading the dishwasher—not really, but I'd remember and it would chill my skin the same.

During the day she was her same new self. We didn't meet Klara Wednesdays for Buffalo wings, but my mom would take me to TCBY or the juice bar at Wild Oats. After the thing at Chubby's, I was grounded from going out for real food, but I didn't care. "That's just your diet trick!" I said. "Don't take your fatness out on me!" We spent a lot of time just being quiet with each other.

Finally I asked where Klara was.

"She fell in love," she said.

"With you?"

"No," she laughed. "With a man."

"Oh," I said. "That's all?"

"I guess," she said. "I guess that's all."

Nights, while she cried, I sometimes snuck downstairs and watched Klara's videos. She competed in a league called Babes of Brawn and represented the Philippines, where she said her family was. In one of her videos, she pulled a pickup truck across a parking lot, while the judges stood in the back with a keg. In another event, she heaved sides of beef onto meat hooks that swung through a slaughterhouse. For each feat, she had to wear a different bikini and different boots and gloves. Sometimes, I would pause the video on her grimace and look: her whole face snarled back behind her teeth. I tried my weightlifter's face in the bathroom mirror.

Once, I left my mom's rubbery dumbbells on the bathroom counter.

She brought them into the kitchen. "Practicing your clean and jerk?" she said.

"Mom," I said. "Don't." I was coloring Africa for Geography.

"You're right," she said. "I'm sorry. That's private." She started pumping the weights. "Didn't used to be private. I remember cleaning your little thing."

"Mom, don't."

"The little birthmark."

"*Mom.*"

"You used to try to push it back in—"

I let my voice go cold. "Yeah," I said, "we were pals. Guess what? I wash my own dick now. Go slit your wrists. I'm busy."

I wanted to be nice. I was trying. I told myself, *Be nice. Be nice. Be good. Be good.* But maybe I knew it didn't matter and we would never be close again. She would always love me. I got that much. It hurt her to, and she would anyway.

She cried that night, all night, and in the morning she said, "I forgive you."

"For what I said?"

"Yes. I forgive you."

"I'm sorry."

"I know."

I was finishing my maps. I had them all spread out and she stood behind them at the kitchen table. She looked huge and strong and far away. She didn't hug me or tousle my hair. "Junior," she said, "I'm not going to tease you anymore."

The marathon started at five thirty in the morning, and she told me I should just stay home and pour myself cereal and she'd be home by lunch. I heard her get up. I heard her sniffing at the early air and the teakettle filling with steam. When the car was gone, I got up and washed out my eyes and fried two eggs in her new butter stuff and made toast. The route was on the fridge. The 10K cheering section was at City Park.

It was just a tent stand that some high school kids were manning, handing out water cups and energy goos. There was a guy in a visor and hiking shorts and a Harvard windbreaker that barely zipped over his belly who kept mumbling announcements from his stopwatch and two pairs of college-age girls sitting under fleece blankets so their knees looked like knuckles, like the blankets were two green and yellow fists. I looked at them for a second. *Darling boy, well, well, well,* I thought, but I just sat in the grass next to my bike. It was cold. Klara wasn't there. No one said anything to me.

She was going to be happy to see me. That was as much as I knew. She'd be tired and then I'd be there and she'd keep trucking, still tired but with a boost. I thought about hiding and springing out, but the college girls might think it was weird.

The Harvard man yelled everybody on: "Forty-nine forty-three! Keep it moving! Keep it smooth!" The girls jumped out of their blankets and ran alongside their friend Bridget, hollering her name. They returned carrying her sweatshirt. I could see steam coming off of it. But they all moved on to the 20K cheering section before my mom appeared. The distance between the runners grew longer, and each looked redder than the previous one, until they started looking pale. They didn't look happy to see me when the path turned them toward the tent.

I heard her before I could see her. There was something of the night wailing in the sound she made when the weight of her stride forced out her breath. The day was starting to get bright and it seemed wrong that I could hear it now.

Her eyes looked blind, and there was a strange smile under them, clinging there, like only the smile was holding her up. The shake in her legs was more violent than just the jiggle of her thighs.

"Twenty more miles, miss!" the high school boys yelled. "You can do it! Grab some water! Do some goo!"

She groaned. The pores on her checks were red.

She didn't see me till I went out to her—and she stopped groaning and stood still.

"Surprise!" I said. I hugged her. "You can do it, Mom. I know you can!" I whispered it so the high school boys wouldn't hear. Her sweat smelled bright and normal, and I waited for her to hug me back, but it was like she couldn't reach.

"I have the map. I'll be at 20K. I'll be at all the tents."

"I can't," she said. "I'm not going to make it."

"I believe in you," I whispered, but she sat down on the path and looked down at her thighs.

"Ma'am, we can't let you sit there," said one of the high school boys, coming over. "We'll need to get you into the grass."

"Get up," I pleaded. "This is only six miles. You did three times that in training." I dug my arms under hers and tried to pull her up.

"Give her a minute, little man." Without asking, he touched her neck for a pulse.

"Please. You can do it." With all the strength in my arms and legs, I picked her up, but I wasn't ready when her weight shifted forward. I stumbled back and landed on my butt, my hand in a splotch of runners' spit. I watched her knees fold and hit the sidewalk, her forehead swinging into the concrete. She skidded a half inch on her scalp.

"Oh snap," the high schooler said.

There was blood already. "Get up," I whispered. "Please, Mom."

A walkie-talkie beeped, "We're gonna need the paramedics to City Park."

She was quiet. She didn't even lift her head up from the blood. I was going to cry.

"Fuck, dude," the boy shook his head at me. "You can't mess with them when they're like that."

It was like I'd thrown her down. "I'll go for help," I said, but I didn't. I got on my bike and raced away.

She had stitches, then a scar. It wasn't my fault, she told me when she caught me staring. I'd told her I'd waited till the paramedics got there, but she would have forgiven me for leaving her. It was her new way of being gentle with me. I could have smashed lightbulbs in the oven door or mowed over her basil plants, and it would have been the same. I was becoming something that couldn't help itself, and all she could do was love me anyway.

But this was the difference: when Klara came back, finally, my mom would not forgive her.

It was a Sunday morning, around Christmastime. We were doing the windows like we used to for the holidays: ugly clay medallions I'd made, stamped with tiny thumbs, god's eyes with yarn that changed colors, a chili pepper in a cowboy hat, a Rudolph with menorah antlers from a magazine glued onto cardboard with a hole punched through, a stained-glass *shalom*, holiday cards my mom had hung from string. We kept them all year above the laundry, then put them up with suction cups on the windows, and it wasn't a big jolly deal—no cider or cookies or old LPs. I would lick the dust off the suction cups and fart them onto the windows and my dad had never even helped—but it was different this year, I could tell, because she was crying. Not hard or loud or with any sound, but in the daylight, where I could see.

"I can reach the top," I said. "Look." But that didn't help.

Her face wasn't like mine when I cried or like Klara's in the videos. It was relaxed and still, like she was watching something and the tears were just a part of seeing it. I didn't think it was my dad she missed, or Klara, and there wasn't anybody else except me. It was quiet and I waited for the suction cup farts to make her laugh, but they didn't.

That quiet stayed until Klara knocked on the kitchen door. She had a paper plate of long purple Filipino cakes.

"Where have you been!" I was excited to see her.

"How's Duke?" my mom said.

"What up, Rico. Merry Christmas, Marlene."

We looked at one another.

For a second, Klara's face relaxed and I could see how she was sad. It was proof of love or of something she was here to restore. "Sweet gash," she said. Her jaw cocked into a smile. She looked at me and landed the plate on the counter.

"Hug?"

This time I was the one in pajamas. I tried to hug her fast and sit down, but she held me tight.

"Missed you, dude." She strapped her arms around me.

"Whoa. What is this?" my mom said.

"Rico's my bruiser. I'm giving love." She shrugged and kept holding me.

"Easy, Klara." I could feel her magnet armbands digging into me.

"Ain't gonna crush him."

"Klara, let him go."

"It's cool, momma bear." She let me go and stepped back.

There was no way for me to hide it. I couldn't even try.

My mom sighed, looked away.

"You can't just reappear with cakes, Klara. You know what we're going through. You don't treat people like that."

I was there in between them with it. I didn't know what to do.

"Look, M, I—"

"You 'got all the love in the world,' I know, and we need it."

"Marlene, you're not the only—"

She stopped. They looked at me, at it.

"Junior," my mom said, "why don't you go have some cake."

I ran up to my room with the plate and stared at the purple cakes, fat fingers of sticky purple rice. They fought for an hour, longer than she and my dad had ever fought. I couldn't hear what they said. I didn't feel like trying. But I could hear their heat and venom. I heard them laughing too. I heard their noses blowing.

Maybe they were kind to ignore it, not to make any cheap jokes at my expense. My mom didn't raise her eyebrows and say, "Happy to see her, Rico?" They didn't embarrass me, but I wasn't dumb. If I were one of them, they would have teased me and I could have taken it. But I was something else, something they could excuse, and I'd been excused, to my own room, where I had no idea what to do.

Klara left and my mom came up to my room.

"I forgive you," I said.

"For fighting?"

"I don't know," I said. I was angry. I didn't forgive her.

"She said to say goodbye and she'll see you soon."

"So you're friends again?"

"We don't know. We're going to try."

"How come you didn't think that I might be angry at her too? Don't I get to yell at her?"

"I don't think it works like that."

"Why not?"

"You can tell her—you can tell her how you—"

"You got to yell."

"I know."

"I don't understand."

"I know," she said.

"I don't understand!"

"I know," she said. "I'm sorry."

I had all the blinds down in my room. At the window's edges, cold lines drew sharp boxes on the wall. She pulled a cord and let in some white December light. Backlit, she looked gray and false. I wanted to kick her out of my room, but I'd been waiting all that time for her to come.

"How're those cakes?" she asked.

I could have said, "They look like dildos," and she would have said, "Like dildos, huh?" And I could have said, "Yeah Mom, you should try one." And she would have laughed, I think, and said, "Go to your room," and laughed again because we were already there. But I shrugged and that was all. I hated her then. Hate was my last way of holding on. She could've choked and I wouldn't have missed her, not for a while. But I knew I couldn't hate forever. I would forgive her, soon, and that would be all. We'd have to love each other at a distance after that.

They got coffee sometimes. I know they did wine and ceviche, some happy-hour thing, pretty regularly. They were friends, and I was fine. Mostly I left them alone.

I saw my dad for Christmas at his new apartment. He asked me again how my mom was.

"Terrible, Dad. She cries all night."

"Cries?"

"Cries and moans."

"Really?"

"Yes sir. Just can't get over you, I guess."

"You little shit," he said.

"I mean, you must be one hell of a guy for her not to be able to get over you like that."

He laughed. "You're turning out, you know that? You're turning out."

Among other things, he gave me a big electric belt that would rapidly sting me until I grew abs. I was supposed to wrap it around my stomach for fifteen minutes a day. The card read: "To the ladies of Preston Middle School, from Santa."

When presents were over he said he had some sad news. He was selling Kingpin's. He had to.

It was a long story, he said. In October, he'd gotten a full-page glossy photograph of this hideous she-man in some vile G-string thing. It was signed in Sharpie, *Thanks for the flowers, Dickie dear.* He was confused, he hadn't sent anyone flowers, especially not some tuck-dick beef queen, but he hung the photo in the staff shitter at Kingpin's just for gags.

"A few days later, Gus comes up, all nicey, and says, 'Do you miss her? Is that why you hang the picture of your wife?' 'That is not my wife,' I explain to him most cordial. 'But I *see* her,' he says. 'I *see* her when I drop off Yunior. You miss her.' This is your mother he's talking about. '*Hell no,*' I say. 'That roast piggy is nobody's wife.' But he just gives me this great wise somber look and says, 'I miss my wife too.' Then I start to figure out who sent the flowers. I should've known him for a pervert. I ask him, 'Gus, honey, did you buy Klara Belle flowers?' And he blushes up like a chubby."

The smile slackened out of his stubble.

"So Papa fires the mongoloid," he said. First, however—he raised his eyebrows and thumbed his mole—he'd allegedly slurred Gus with one or two ungenerous and perhaps insensitive labels and thrown a can of XK-12 rental-shoe spray in his direction. There was a suit against him. He'd had to shed the alley.

I tried to tell him it was all right about Kingpin's, but he wanted me to mourn with him, so I did.

"Titty Match-Up!" I cried. "Our guts! Where will they grow!"

He smiled. "All she wrote for Gus's custody bid, I'm afraid. You sell an unemployed, brain-dead Mexican to an arbitrator. Plus, he forgot he'd filed for a character reference from me."

"His daughters? Gus lost his Wednesdays and weekends?"

"You dog," he said. "See, you got to move in quick on that shit."

The belt hurt. The whole idea was you could just lie there, doing nothing, and it would work out for you, but it was exhausting. Lying there was exhausting. I would lie on Klara's favorite couch at Mom's and sweat and gasp and feel little shocks punching muscle into me.

In the spring, I asked Janey out and she said yes just like my dad had said she would. It was easy. I had a girlfriend and a discernible six-pack. I hadn't had to do a thing. "Sure," she said into the phone, and the panic spiked.

I didn't tell my mom about Janey, but she found out somehow. "Be nice to that girl," she said from behind me somewhere.

I promised myself I would be nice to Janey, but actually it was all I knew how to do with her. I didn't know how to kiss her. I didn't know how to go on a date. I didn't know how to tell her she was beautiful. I'd always thought she was. I just made myself small and embarrassed around her, and then at night, in bed, imagined the brave and evil things I should have said or done. I could tell she'd be bored with me soon.

We met at the food court one weekend—her, her friend Reina, and me. Mostly Reina talked while I kept us supplied with fries.

"Hold your arms like this," Reina said. She flexed two fists over the fries.

I did what I was told.

"Yep," she said. "That's your jack-off muscle. You're a right hander."

Janey didn't laugh.

"Janey, tell him something dirty and it'll be bigger by Monday."

"No, it's not. I'm learning guitar."

"Wow, that's beautiful. Let's go to the music store then. You can play Janey a song."

That night, under the peeling stars, I would treat myself to the million things I might have said or done. *Well, if they have a capo, I can play "Drink My Stick."* But I just jabbed a fry through the rubbery gaps in the table.

"So never mind, I guess," Reina said, retrieving her gum from her cup lid. "Not like Janey's gonna *wah-wah* with the first guy to learn his chords." But later, at Zumiez, Reina brought me a stretchy shirt and told me to try it on.

"Why?"

"So you can be like, 'Yo Janey, feel this shirt.' She really likes you, you know."

"She does?"

"Put it on. She's a total pervert once you get to know her."

Janey was my girlfriend for a couple of months, and then she called me one night and told me she wasn't anymore.

"Okay," I said. "I'm sorry."

She laughed. "Why are you sorry?"

"I don't know. I'm sorry," I said.

She told me not to be sorry.

Sorry? I thought once she'd hung up. *I'll show you sorry.*
I wrenched her pretty hair and tried to make her wail. I could
hear my mom, at the opposite edge of the house, cackling on
her own phone, "I love it. Tell the whole thing again." *I'll show
you sorry*, but I couldn't. I let go and lay back on my bed and
stared between my stupid stars. "I told you!" my mom was
roaring. "Too many is too many!" I listened hard, but I couldn't
tell what she was laughing about.

AERIALISTS

My brother finishes his deployment the summer I enlist and wants to play he's gone full PTSD. "Lock up this feeling," he tells me. "You won't be coming back so sweet."

He's standing behind the couch with that navy posture, watching me and Trina's staring contest. I say, "Don't worry, Harris. You were never sweet." I can see him with the side of my eye drinking one of his green drinks. Takes him a whole bag of groceries to make those things.

Trina's cheating, walking her fingers on my knee. The staring contest is for who chooses the DVD, but Harris has to leave the living room before I'm watching anything.

Something traumatic's happened, at least to the way he talks. "When we're erratic, depressive, whatever—we're who we've got. You know I'm there for you down the line."

Trina's eyes are green with little sunflowers. "You were a line cook on an unsinkable aircraft carrier," I say, staring in. "You wore the same paper hat they wear at KayJay's. You had grease popping at you. That was your war." She doesn't blink.

Harris describes in his new vocabulary how it feels, how you come home, and your house, your neighborhood, no one knows you, how you don't belong any more.

"So take your GI to college, baller. That's what I'm going to do. How often did you get your dick wet on the USS *Truman*?"

Trina doesn't flinch, just mouths it back at me, slow and silent (*dick . . . wet . . .*) and I roll backward off the couch. *Breakfast Club* again.

Harris reaches to help me up, but I slap his hand and stay sprawled. "I promise to stay away from the griddle, don't worry."

"Did you even read my emails?" he says.

"And you turtle-waxed the drones? Harris, I'm here for you. You're my brother by all reports. But tonight—every night till Trina leaves for school—is date night. So, remember what you said about feeling like you don't belong?"

An hour later Harris is back in the living room and says the reason he made his little speech was that he's taken a job as third engineer on a Dutch cable ship, running fiber optics along the Indian Ocean floor. "I bus out tomorrow," he says.

I wish Mom or Dawn, or Amelia even, would come in and cry about it—that's probably all it would take to make him stay. The way my heart is, there's only RAM enough for one thing at a time. All it can feel is Trina leaning back on my chest. I swear there's a soul of some kind making loops through our two torsos. Out my chest into her back, down, and back up my belly through me, like we have our own inner northern lights.

"You can have anything left in my boxes," he says. "My army surplus is in there, my telescope." Then he takes the painting he made of me when I was a boy off the wall and hands it to Trina.

"I remember this little man," she says, but it has that sound of when, more than speaking, you're listening to yourself speak.

Harris says, "You take that. For your dorm. While he's serving." I can feel the northern lights getting nervous somewhere. "Look at it sometimes for him."

"Harris, you know Mom's not letting that out of the house."

"You're lucky if Mom notices you're gone." He laughs, he knows he's right. Mom loves us, but she's basically asleep.

The painting's from when Old Max—that's our dad—ran off, not even a month after Mom and him adopted Amelia and Dawn, and Harris and I spent the year pretty much outside, in our yard or next door at the Golds'. In the painting, my hair hasn't curled yet and I'm sitting still as I can for Harris, a sad piece of candy in my mouth. Harris said, "You keep moving, I will take you up and throw you off the roof," but you can tell he spent forever on my hair.

I wait for Trina to say, "I shouldn't. I can't take this," but something happens in me when she does. I say, "You're a mean little pecker, you know that, Harris? You know *exactly* what you're about. You want me to feel sorry for myself or something?"

The northern lights freeze, shade out, I don't know where they go.

Harris says, "You'll need someone thinking about you, Corbin."

I say, "Trina can think about whatever the fuck she wants," but my heart's pounding her on the back, like *Help, help, let me in*. Trina's looking out the window, and Harris is almost smiling at me. I think maybe now he won't have to go. We're all frozen like that, DVD on pause, till Gold's plane comes in over the house and we look at each other—Dr. Gold is going blind.

We listen for a crash, anticipating it together, but he lands on the runway and pulls the twin-prop into its hangar. We know every whine of it by heart.

Mom, Dawn, Amelia, and me take Harris to the Greyhound the next morning, and he hugs us without compromising that navy posture and steps onto the bus that takes him to his plane. I've never even heard of cable ships before, but how else would an internet get built?

He really leaves.

We go for drive-thru—no one cries—and scatter for our rooms when we get home.

Harris used to threaten to throw me off the roof because I'd told him I could fly. I thought I could. I could remember it, not jumping off of anything like he assumed, just slowly floating up over my bed, the house, sustained by something in my chest. It seemed like I'd done it often, but when I went to try it on purpose—stood in the yard and held the hose so I wouldn't float away—I guess my heart had gone weak.

It wasn't blind Dr. Gold flying his plane. I'm over at Gold's for work that afternoon, all ready to chew him out, but he says it was the CEO of some spice company taking a test flight.

"What do you mean?"

"I mean a company that runs stores that sell cinnamon sticks." Gold admires himself as a pain in the ass.

"You're selling the twin?"

"Seemed not, not the way he was talking. I had to throw in the Cessna too."

I don't know why I thought he would keep them, but the whole neighborhood feels different with them gone. "Didn't I tell you I'm taking a plane for if I'm on the *Truman*? So I can duck home to Trina, land on the quad, like *Oh hey, girl. Wanna get malts?*" I say *Truman* because it's the one boat I know.

I'm Dr. Gold's assistant for fifteen dollars an hour until I report to RTC in October. I also get him pot and mark it up about one thousand percent. Gold's main career was land survey, but he's done aerial photography longer than I've been alive. I'm organizing the photos for after he's fully blind. I scan them and retitle them something descriptive his computer can read back to him—*Toxic Reddish Sinkhole*. Gold doesn't understand tags, so I copy every photo into five or six files, by place and date if I know them and by anything else I can think of to help him find it without his eyes. His drives are clogging up with folders like *Landfill Fires* and *Quilty Looking Fields*. The photos aren't really about what they're of, but I wouldn't know how to file them by feeling. I'm also building him a better website. Gold thinks I'm the Pelé of HTML.

When I was a kid, Dr. Gold let me and Trina draw chalk floor plans of our mansions on his runway, life-size swimming pools and home theaters. I'd fling worms and the rest of it, but I loved her already. I was always like, "Naw, I don't need to draw mine. I can just draw a room at yours . . ."

Gold's place is the original farmhouse for Cedar Farm. Once he paved his runway Gold sold the rest to a cheapo developer. Kit homes, ranch grass, and planters. Gold's place has a whole bedroom for framed insects he collects through the mail. And he has so many fish tanks you don't even need to turn the lights on with the glow—especially a blind man doesn't. Sometimes he'll give me some piece of clutter that was Mrs. Gold's to give to Trina, a compact mirror or a quartz watch. She died, slow and dry mouthed, when I was six, which I wish to god they hadn't let me see.

I'm scanning pictures of pit mines all afternoon, and Harris is out of sight, out of mind. I can only think about three times a minute how I'm wasting it not with Trina. It's already late July.

Gold's at the other computer, which he has speaking to him from some game or something he's playing. "You are in The Desolate Citadel. Crumbled glory surrounds you." It's not like him, and I've been hearing crap like that all week.

"You slaying dragons?" I say.

"I'd be happy just to meet a dragon. I'd be happy to meet a lizard. There's nobody in the whole place." He shakes a toothpick from the shaker and says, "Come see," but he sounds kind of slugged.

Gold dresses like a cowboy, except instead of a pistol he wears a mini radio on his hip and instead of a Stetson he has a shiny, bald head. He likes sheepskin collars. He limps from an infection he had in his knee. When he raises his eyebrows at you, which he likes to, the wrinkles make him grow a half an inch.

I get the stool and look over Dr. Gold's shoulder. It's some truly ancient internet. No browser—just a telnet connection running in Terminal. "What's this, a chat room?"

"It's a wasteland," he says and types *east*.

>east

>You travel east on the crumbling aqueduct wall and enter The Frog Garden. Croaking fills the air.

>look

>You see a small pond formed in a ruined corner of the citadel wall. The mud at your feet jiggles with tadpole tails. Frogs balance on old stones and croak in rhythm.

>@look frogs

>You see brown frogs with green spots and green frogs with brown spots.

>say, Hi frog

>You speak to yourself.

>east

>You travel east on a mud path, away from the ruins, and enter The Bowling Green.

>look

>You see clean thin grass extending in all directions. Balls, pins, croquet mallets, and glasses of Pimm's are discarded all around you. A hammock hangs from strings extending endlessly into the sky.

>who

>You are the only Territorian here.

"Somebody stand you up?" I pat him on the shoulder.

"This was a thing Ella liked. She would chat with people and build new rooms or what have you. It was beyond me. I'm just flying survey."

"Empty?"

"No survivors."

I say it without thinking. "You're not looking for her, are you?"

He looks back at me. I can see the white clots roping over his eyes. It scares me sometimes how smashed he seems. "I'll use my headphones if you'd prefer."

"Your house, you be pathetic as you want."

Back at my desk, I write DONT BE A ASSHOLE with ballpoint on my arm. Then I change it to DON'T BE ANASSHOLE, which looks stupid, so I go to the bathroom and scrub it off. "Fuck you," I say to the mirror and screw my face up.

At my computer, the chat's popped up.

TRINA: I've eloped with a beautiful Spaniard

I stretch the window so I won't have to see Gold's desktop picture, a black-and-white of barefoot Ella Gold walking on mud.

DIRTBIRD: aw shoot

TRINA: His chest hair is tight black cursive

TRINA: His ass is as hard and round as Dr. Gold's head

DIRTBIRD: he has genital warts

TRINA: We're making love on his horse right now

DIRTBIRD: his dick is cheddar cheese

TRINA: as the horse gallops us on I cling with my thighs to his

TRINA: resolute manhood

TRINA: Oh, how the pampas are trembling!

DIRTBIRD: Please dont

TRINA: Give me the riding crop, Antonio!

TRINA: Now faster, Estebancho! Fly, fly!

I sign out. From Dr. Gold's desk, I hear, "You are in the Dungeon. Cold iron manacles hang from the stone walls. You are the only Territorian here." I breathe the blood out of my ears and sign back in.

TRINA: You OK?

DIRTBIRD: Trina wins

DIRTBIRD: Sorry. I'm at Gold's.

TRINA: I know. I usually can't get you that easy. Are you freaking?

DIRTBIRD: naw

TRINA: Here. How Shall I Love/Bone Thee? Let me count the ways:

TRINA: 1. Internet phones. 2. Internet texts. 3. Internet emails.

TRINA: 4. Nasty Skype.

DIRTBIRD: i know

TRINA: Sexy patience?

TRINA: Are you scanning photos right now?

DIRTBIRD: Supposed to be

TRINA: . . . so? Get me going

DIRTBIRD: lol i'm not scanning it for you

TRINA: bawk bgawk

I get back to work, watching the scanner squeegee across a photo, scraping off what it needs—not a rock beach, not an image of a rock beach, just a measurement of changing light.

"You are in the Bubble Chamber. Strong pink bubbles large enough to lie in lift you up." Gold's holding his face inches from the screen even though the computer's speaking to him, like he's waiting for Mrs. Gold, twelve years dead, to lean out the monitor and kiss him.

"You do realize that place has cyber-semen all over it."

He looks over.

"Just seems you should know. The giant lily pads and hot tubs and torture chambers? People built those for, you know, doing the dirty qwerty."

"You're worried about me?" he says.

"You're sniffling the sheets, Gold. It's making me sad."

Gold sighs, pushes up from his desk, and takes the aviators off his bald scalp. I decide if the calcified bastard wants to kick the crap out of me I'll let him, but he limps off to the other room and comes back in a minute with something in his hand.

It's his bowl. He hits it and stares at me.

"Goddamn it. I'm sorry—" I start, but he interrupts: "Harris didn't stay home long," he says.

I'd rather talk about Ella Gold than Harris. "He's just pissed. All those years and he's not a hero or something."

"He okay?"

Gold's stare still pushes on me, even if it's blind. I say, "Harris would rather be missed than happy." Meanwhile, the phone in my pocket is filling up with more of Trina's texts.

Gold asks if they're going to drug-test me, and I tell him there are tricks. We pass his pipe, wood stem and stone bowl, listening to the computer fans. It takes all my willpower not to peek at my phone.

"Did you write letters or telegrams or what when you were air force?"

"Mostly I dropped bombs." He faces back at his computer for a while. "I wish," he starts—it takes him so long to say what he wishes I figure he's not going to. "I wish just one of my photos could've had some *air* in it. I wish I could've taken one picture of the actual air."

Some moments are moments, others are the whole summer passing. I ask and he says Trina can come over to help me sort through his boxes of prints in the storage shed. I text her and she walks down. They tried to make Cedar Farm Road look like real suburbs—sprinkler, doghouse, trampoline, shrub—but there's also Gold's runway running through the back of it all and no city to be suburban to. Gold's storage shed used to be a chicken coop, and there's a root cellar, a rusty tractor, a few other eroding remainders of farm.

I watch Trina through the windows, coming around to the back door. The pockets on her jean shorts are so small, her lip gloss is sticking out. You can tell from the way Dr. Gold says hello without getting up that he'll be leaving us alone.

We smoke a little, in the storage shed, blowing it out the chicken ramp. I can taste Trina's lip gloss on the glass piece, and for fun I imagine we've never kissed and I'm stealing a taste of her lips already—but somehow it's a sad feeling, I don't know.

We find a box marked CEDAR and start laying out aerials, trying to make a map on the floor. Our houses, the town road, the river, some from lower or higher—we mosaic it with coop dust peeking through.

"I can see us," she says, pointing.

I take the print. "Where?"

"Right there, under my trampoline. See the outline? My back, your legs . . . remember?"

I remember it under the trampoline—the mat not really shielding the rain, just slowing it into fat black drops—but I can't see any—

Then I hear the game of it in her voice: "The Andersons' backyard—see your shoulder blades in the tree house window. That was bad of us. And there, in the bed of my dad's truck."

The town spreads as we open the box. I point to the swings at the elementary school. The middle school roof, where I scuffed my butt black on the tar paper.

Trina takes a photo from a different box. "Here we are at—whoa—at a big hot-air-balloon expo."

"Yeah?"

"We're in that pretty blue one there, making the basket swing."

"Oh, how the pampas are trembling?"

She shrugs.

River islands, rice paddies, peninsulas of ice—we travel a few.

I wait till I know it's time. "And here"—I point—"here's us in the photo storage coop. What exactly are we doing in there?"

"Well," she says, and she comes and sits over me, the lip gloss pushing even farther from her pocket. The skin on her thighs is smooth and tan, sun warm.

I find all the brads in her cutoffs with my fingers. I lean into her breasts, to feel sad, just one sip of sad where she can't see. Then I breathe at her neck till it quivers.

It's the whole rest of the summer passing. I watch Trina's lips, not pursing, just their shapes getting soft and full. I watch myself waiting forever for them. And when they finally touch mine, I watch the play of it slowly turn till we're saying something through it, something easy and soul-spoken moving torso to torso between us. The more we say it, the more urgent it is to say, and the more urgent, the slower we move, so slow that the whole summer passes. I'm there and I'm high overhead in a single-engine plane, watching it go. My little self, barely eighteen, not a hope.

Sex lets you know there's an outside to the human body, but it doesn't let you get there. Like how they say the northern lights are sliding through everything all the time, but only certain skies will let them show. It doesn't have to be dark or even far north. I guess it comes in where it wants to, weather from a star.

Cool, Trina's skin is as smooth as well water, but the heat makes it grab. I wait for that. I don't do anything, just wait for it to grab my hands and take them. Or sometimes it grabs hers. I love that, her one hand on my chest, the other on herself, while I just keep her close. The lights draw their big bamboo-brush calligraphy between us, letters I don't know. When she comes, I can come too, without one touch if I want. I'm not embarrassed. I think it's magic—like, *See, I'm there where you are too.*

I'm with her, but I'm also high where I can see my whole life passing. The tree house, the pickup, the storage shed. The USS

Truman in the Persian Gulf. She's leaving in two weeks, one week. Tomorrow. She's gone. Her smell's on all my shirts. Then summer done, laundry run. And I'm back in this body here.

The first time we manage to Skype, Trina's already through orientation and into her second week of classes. She didn't want me to help her move in, but she carries a laptop around 208 Alpert Hall, shows me the room, the roommate, Melody. "Mel wore pants with stirrups to a party last night," she says. "Got more attention than she knew what to do with."

"It's because 'stirrups' is one of the words guys know," Melody explains to me, landing next to Trina. "If they can say, 'Are those stirrups?' they think they're flirting with you. You pretty much have to write their lines."

What am I supposed to say? She has curly hair crowning out of a headband and a chin that, no offense, belongs on a climbing wall. She seems like a fine roommate, but I wouldn't flirt with her.

"They were just working me to get to Katrina, but"—Melody draws an *X* on her heart—"she responsibly declined all male attention."

I try to tell Trina the latest—my mom's back on narcotics for her hip thing. Dawn smells like menthols. Amelia's been kicked out of school already.

"What? What happened?"

"It's okay. Never mind." I can hear Melody opening a coke. I wait for her to get the hint.

"Should I eject for a while?" she says offscreen. "Maybe I'll go rape Cameron."

I wait while the door with its fire-escape map swings closed. "She's special."

"You'd love her. What's up with Amelia?"

The camera's weird—my face feels self-conscious. "Back on the spectrum. She was touching it in class," I say. "They couldn't get her to stop."

She laughs. "She wouldn't stop?"

"She would, but then she'd do it again the next day. She didn't realize she was doing it." I grin. "In Ms. Reglind's class."

"Oh my god, Reglind," she says. "She'll tweak! She'll end up back in her neck brace."

"I miss you."

"What's a hand down the pants anyway? It's comforting." She pats. There's a photo of us parrying milkshake straws over her bed. I look like anyone's idea of a high school boyfriend.

"Show me something," I say. It sounded sweet in my head, but aloud I can't tell—it sounds maybe hurt or demanding.

"Show you something?" she says. "Like what"—coy—"my new hole puncher?"

"Okay. Start with that."

"*Oh*, you mean like a *boob*?" she says. "But I really shouldn't. It's Melody's laptop. I forgot to tell you the camera on mine definitely doesn't work."

"Fine," I say. But then she does it anyway, automatically. Pulls her shirt up, folds the cups down, and I get a lonely sick feeling I don't understand.

She bounces them in her hands. "The boobs," she announces. "The boobs say Amelia is just getting to know her body."

She's happy and beautiful and herself, goofy and real and not even so far away, but I can't sense her. She covers up again.

"We haven't been doing stuff," I say.

She smiles, but I know the one. Usually it's for other people's moms. It's hard to get privacy, but, well, what would I like? She says it warm and natural, locks the door, and kneels on her bed with a book. "Total genius, by the way," she says, pointing at the cover before she slides it under the laptop. She settles back onto her heels.

She squeezes herself, half joking, trying to be generous with me. But it only gives me a lump in my throat.

"What do you want?" she says again. "Rule: I'll do anything, but you have to ask for it. You have to say it first." She does arm stretches, neck bends, pretending nothing's weird. "Shorts off," she says. "I want to watch that dick get hard."

I alt-tab into a different window where I won't have to face her.

"Uh-oh," I say. "Can you hear me?"

"Sure," she says. "Did you say something? Did you ask for a little—"

"Can you hear me?" My voice cracks. "You're frozen. I think the Wi-Fi's maxed out."

"Yeah, I can hear you fine, but—"

"Can you hear me?" I say. I don't think I've ever lied to her before. "Hello?"

"Hellooo . . . ? Earth to cocktease . . . ," she says.

I yank out my wireless card and the call fails. I'm in my room again. Ella Gold's quartz watch, Harris's flint and steel, yellowing surge protector with half the room plugged in.

I power off my phone, wait five minutes, and listen to her voice mail. "Hello, this is tech support. We're horny."

Call her back. But I don't. I turn on the TV, five hundred stations, and not one is on the war.

Mom finds a half-day public school program Amelia can go to in Quarter Horse and goes part time at the bank so she can be there in the afternoons. I try to be there for my sisters in the meanwhile. I read their mermaid stories and tell them, yeah, I like it, it's good, which makes them so happy I wonder how mean I am most of the time. "You going to miss me when I'm on the *Truman*?" I ask Amelia.

"On *The Truman Show*?"

"On the dang aircraft carrier."

"On the dang aircraft carrier, starring Jim Carrey?" She giggles like nuts.

I find the cigarettes I've been smelling on Dawn and chew her out. "You're twelve. You think grapefruit juice tastes bitter. You're not credible with a pack of Camels."

"So? Why shouldn't I smoke?"

"Oh, you haven't heard that part?"

"You're not Harris. Stop trying to be Harris."

"Who's that?"

"Don't be a dick," she says, like an expert.

I want to ask Harris if I'm supposed get a physical or anything. Do I cut my hair or do they do it? I want to do it so I can hear Mom mourn my curls. She keeps reminding herself to sign me up for life insurance through the bank. I look at the USS *Truman*'s Facebook page, but it's boring. Talent-show pictures interspersed with all-caps OPSEC reminders: *POST NOTHING ABOUT WHERE WE'RE GOING OR WHERE WE'VE BEEN.* I email Harris *what's up on the indian?* He sends me back the weirdest emails: *The cable spools and all day splits the wake. 13% pornography. 3.5% salt. One could grab the line and swim forever. I was checkers king in Durban, electric, incorruptible. They drank in every language, which gave sobriety a holy bleakness. To Gwadar, if I make it. To Corbin, via satellite.*

I tell Mom Harris is cracked or at least wants me to think so. She says, "I had a dream about Harris. He was so much taller than me." I write him to be careful and he doesn't write me back.

Trina is taking the maximum load they allow first-years and joining everything there is to join, like yoga that meets in the courtyard of the commons, and auditioning for a play about the Irish Republican Army. She's busy when I call, but I'll wake up to texts about how much better the weed is at college or weird excerpts from her night, **TREECLIMBER OF THE MONTH!** or **Well hi there Corbin**, which means someone else was playing with her phone. **Trina is hot.** And her, I can picture it, wrestling with the guy, angry and smiling, to get her cell phone back.

On my lunch break from Gold's, I ride my bike in to see Mom at the bank.

I put my finger in the belly of my hoodie and say, "Teller, this is a robbery."

Mom looks at me like maybe it is. "Do you need something, Corbin?"

"Gimme all your Dum Dums."

"You need lunch money?" She isn't listening to herself. Banks are supposed to look like you couldn't just blow them down, but hers is all plasterboard and kooky cat clocks. Mardi Gras beads are still in the nylon ferns.

"I need you to wake up," I say.

"What? I'm at work, honey."

"I know. We're not on the phone. I'm here too."

"You're funny, Corbin. But," she whispers, "don't stick your finger under your shirt like that. There might be silent alarms."

I tell her I need the car. I can make it to State and back in eight hours, plus a one-hour visit, I'll be home before she's in bed. "Can you take my bike home today?"

"Your bike?" she says. "Someone has to get Amelia." She smiles. "Want to see the new hundreds? They're counterfeit-proof."

I ask her if she wants to at least do the salad bar, and she says, "I do my eight-hour shakes, honey. You know that."

Back at Gold's, I watch him bumble around his basement, feeding his fish, shaking the flakes by his ear to distinguish them. I think of asking him what's wrong with Harris, but I don't. I drive him to the grocery store so he can reload on pizzas, hamburger, coffee beans. He announces our progress from the passenger side. "Lisbon Street? Brick house on the left? Three elms and two chimneys?"

I ask, "Do you picture it from here or overhead?" He nods, like there's no difference, and catalogs everything we pass—KayJay's All Day and Night Diner, the water tower, the Mormon church.

That night, far below, the young man in my room texts his girlfriend.

8:45 PM   I'm in Drew Barrymore's Airstream

8:47 PM   she wants me to hump her tits

He strips naked, does a hundred push-ups to get pumped. He lays his lamp behind his hamper to get the lighting right.

9:25 PM   soft as flour

He takes pictures of himself in his mirror. He deletes them. Takes new ones. Puts the new ones in an email. Deletes the email. Deletes the new ones off his phone.

11:01 PM   still humping

11:13 PM   starting to chafe actually

He goes to the bathroom and spits into the sink for a while like he wants to yak. He stands up, sailor straight, holds a salute. The northern lights feeling keeps refluxing in him, but there's nothing to puke. She texts him back:

1:42 AM   Sorry! Was taking a nap.

He waits for her to add *with the rugby captain, with my history prof* but she doesn't. She isn't playing. Trina wins.

The room goes dark when the phone goes dark, and it might as well be his gray, painted-metal berth. There might as well already be warplanes parallel parked overhead. He searches the dark for something to assure his body of where it is, but it won't be convinced.

1:44 A.M. the room returns:

Miss you too.
>where
>Your room, 3:37 a.m. Two and a half weeks before you leave.
>look
>You see Ella Gold's quartz watch, Harris's flint and steel, a yellowing surge protector with half the room plugged in.
>get up
>Sweatpants, flip-flops. You leave your room. You leave your house.
>east
>You walk through the clod grass till you stand on the runway that cuts through your neighborhood.
>look
>You see long edges of dead landing bulbs. Weeds in the concrete cracks. A lot of sky.
>look
>Back fences, TV dishes, a lot of dim sky.
>look
>There isn't any more. There's a Gatorade cap.
>@kick cap
>You kick the Gatorade cap.
>@kick earth
>You kick the fucking earth.

A hundred stalls line The Imperial Stables. A high, circular window lets moonlight down on the horses' backs. I pat the Percheron and the Bay and try talking to them and riding them, but they're not set up for anything like that. It says, "Don't try that again!" or "Wanna take that back?" when a command does not compute. In The Mud Baths, I wade into the cloud of purplish steam, listening to the mud bubbles' loud smacks, and descend through the hot mud into Gob's Headquarters, a dim underground poker lounge. I blow out the gas lamp on the table and the room, it says, goes dark. From Gob's, The Diminishing Tunnel runs north till I tumble out of a laundry chute onto a mound of tablecloths in the basement of Lala's Dollhouse. Lala's Furnace leads nowhere. I climb the basement stairs and exit the dollhouse living room to a pea patch that seems normal sized. North of The Pea Patch is a charred launching pad. North of the launch pad, tetherball.

I hit the ball. I hit the ball. After I hit the ball six times, I win.

At the edge of the world, I build a runway. I put the blue landing bulbs along the length and build the old chalk mansions room by room.

The commands are easy to learn, but it's tedious. I build Gold's hangar and planes. The Andersons' north of Trina's, the Kellys' north of them. I walk through the yards, jostling up the lightning bugs. My mom's old tank is in our driveway. Inside it smells like melted Carmex. On the back dash, there's her pocket guide to American fauna. The floor is covered with Dawn's and Amelia's bobby pins and hair ties, snagged with shiny, loopy knots. I walk around the house. I build the scrub of red currants next to the garbage cans. Raccoons maraud the bins. Driveway gravel is sprayed all through the front.

I need no sleep or food here. I log in and find myself standing where I left. Welcome! You are in The Irrigation Ditch, it says.

I walk in the dry ditch south, past Gold's sandbags, over bleached wood boats, under the plank bridge behind the Kellys'. Standing low in the weeds, I look beneath the fence slats into Trina's backyard. I see the trim green lawn her dad keeps, the trampoline he drags ten feet each week to spare his grass. I build the fence, choose its verbs—*climb, jump, squeeze through*. Barefoot on the grass, I build the trampoline and crawl beneath. It's raining, fat black drops are dripping through.

```
>@look phone
>You see no new messages. Last text to Trina: nvm
yr nasty skype. i made us something.
>@text Trina, call me
>where
>You are at Gold's, not doing what he pays you to.
You hear him upstairs creaking the floorboards
back and forth. The higher pitch as he nears the
edges of his rooms. Familiar sound of a house
ached by its bodies.
>look
>You see Territoria's rectangular cursor waiting.
Behind the small window are folders of Gold's
unsorted scans. Stacked TIFF files still named with
the eight-digit string the scanner assigned them.
```

In there somewhere, Comstock Road giving up dust, the L—shaped roof of KayJay's Diner, the baseball diamonds, home plates locked in dry mud.
>close computer
>say, Yo Gold I'm going home!
>north
>You travel through the side door and across the dirt to your backdoor.
>who
>Dawn is blaring her workout dance videos in her room. Amelia is at the unlit kitchen table looking at a glass of milk.
>say, Not thirsty?
>sip milk
>It's room temperature, tastes glum.
>say, Little sister? You there?
>Amelia leaves the room.
>say, Bye then
>up
>You travel upstairs and enter your room. Your same junk. Dawn bangs around below you. Your laptop fan wakes, complains.
>@say Dawn, STOMP STOMP STOMP!
>Dawn sings, ". . . into the groove . . . prove your love to me."
>@look window
>Out the window, you can see the raccoons have gotten the garbage again.
>@look phone

```
>No messages, no calls. You see the date and
subtract. Ten days.
>down
>You travel downstairs and out the front door to
gather up the blowing trash.
```

In Gold's Photo Coop, I brush the warm dust from a box and flip through—river islands, rice paddies, ice coasts. It's quiet. The old cardboard feels soft and smells sweet. I enter The Hot-Air-Balloon Expo and hunker in the swinging basket as the flame plows upward through some ripple in the air. Blue air passes straight through the wicker. The blast valve spits out its measured roars and the red balloon plumes up, twisting slow. Lying back, I watch higher balloons rotating around the bright baffles overhead.

I drift, maybe I sleep, and waking, I stand to see what's now below. The USS *Truman*? Its endless complex of valves and dials? Or The Trembling Pampas? The Quad, The Chem Lab, Mayner Hall? No matter how weak the navy internet is, it could have handled this. There's a fog beneath the basket. The wicker is slick, and it's dark enough to permit some stars. I lower the balloon and sink through the haze, squinting at the unbuilt space that now comes rising.

A car, a shiny blue Acura I've never seen before, is pulling in.

```
>who
>Trina. Trina is here.
```

>You are standing on the front porch, facing west.
Grackles pick seeds out from the dirt in the front
yard. Towels are hanging on the rail because Dawn
and Amelia were doing the Slip 'N Slide, which
is still in the grass. Box elder bugs are stuck
together on the planks.

>@look Trina

>Hard to say. You haven't heard anything about a
blue Acura. She gets out and shuts the door like
a TV cop, tired and decided.

>say, Whose car is that?

>Trina says, "Maybe let's talk in your room?"

>@look kitchen window

>Mom and Dawn are in the window, stricken already.

>say, You didn't need to come home to do this.

>Trina says, "I know."

>Trina says, "Let's go to your room."

>say, But that's how it's going to go?

>Trina says, "Let's please go to your room."

>say, Just answer me.

>Trina nods.

>say, I think you should go.

>Trina says, "Don't you want to know?"

>say, Do I?

>Trina says, "It isn't like that."

>look

>You see a few cheap homes on foundations that go
a foot or two into the dirt.

>Trina says, "This is our chance. I want to leave
things right."
>say, Everything's right. It's fine. I'm fine. I'll
be ten thousand miles away.
>Trina says, "Be safe."
>say, Fuck. Just go.
>say, Just please go.
>
>Wanna take that back?
>She leaves.
>look
>You see the blue Acura drive past her house and
continue.
>
>Don't try that again!
>go
>You need to specify a direction.
>who
>You are the only Territorian here.
>

The day before I ship, Dr. Gold says he'll take me out anyplace
so long as it's KayJay's. I'm the one driving his Range Rover and
it's noon, but he leans at the windshield and says, "Might got a
headlight out." I don't laugh.

KayJay's All Day and Night Diner closes at 2 P.M. The coffee
iridesces because the plate grease gets into the mugs in the
steamer. There's a strip of something sandpapery at the edge of

all the booth seats because the old folks slide off the vinyl. "Do you actually like KayJay's?" I say.

"It's what we have," he says. He's memorizing the jukebox— 17-01 for "Walkin' After Midnight," 08-01 for "The Year That Clayton Delaney Died."

He gives me a dollar for "Corrina, Corrina" and "Talkin' World War III Blues." "Heart medicine," he says, but I'm not in the mood. I walk away, put the bill in the leukemia jug, and return. "Might be a lot queued up already," I say.

He asks what Mom and Dawn and Amelia are doing for me tonight, anything special?

I say I think we're watching a movie.

"What movie?"

"Whatever's on. *The Truman Show* and some pizza bites."

He nods. He orders us dinner-plate cinnamon rolls.

I tell him I'm sorry I haven't finished his website yet. I can do it in my down hours, no problem, so long as my laptop holds on.

"So's it feel like the end of the world?" he says.

I poke my coffee a couple times and wait for him to keep going.

"Like she neutron-bombed you?"

I say it's all right and tell him look out, she's refilling your mug.

He waits awhile for me. Then he says, "You're going to war, Corbin. Have you realized that yet?"

"I'll probably be at a computer the whole time. I doubt they'll even bother teaching me guns."

"They'll teach you war one way or another." I see him thinking whether or not to let me in on some Vietnam shit, how it feels to lift the latch that drops a Mk 81.

"I thought you just wanted to buy me lunch."

"All I know how to do. But I did want to say—" He stops for his voice to pitch back down. "I wanted to make sure you knew you didn't fool me, writing that stuff into Ella's internet thing."

I don't know what to say. I couldn't explain anyway.

"For a second or two, yes, I thought she'd wrote all that. And for a little longer than that, I was going to murder you for starting my heart up. But it lets me see the neighborhood again."

"In case you need a map," I say. I don't care what he thinks. I'm never logging in again.

He gets his breath back. "Funny to see it how you do. You show Harris? It might be a care package for him out there, whatever's going on. Let him add on how he remembers things."

"Fuck Harris." I'm surprised how hard it sounds. "Seriously. Fuck him whatever he's got." I get glances. I look out the window at the cabled-up patio chairs.

"Think about it." He smiles. "How many years has Harris been sleeping on water?"

I'm sweating. "I'm sorry. I know you feel like talking."

But he doesn't let that stop him. He yarns one out about the time he couldn't land because while he was gone a snowstorm had buried the runway. "You didn't even have your learner's permit, but you did a handsome job with the plow. I remember watching you, thinking, I'll be damned, the good-for-nothing neighbor kid wants me to make it home."

The CSS *Ariadne*, where Harris works, is a big slow ship that holds four thousand miles of communications cable in coil tanks. It floats on giant rotating thrusters, and as it goes, the cable works its way up from the tanks, through a bell mouth, and off a pulley block at the stern. The cable's a little thicker than a garden hose and toughened up for seafloor pressure— polyethylene, then steel wires, a copper tube, petroleum gel, and I forget what else, but the inner core, barely a centimeter thick, is a two-way stream of pure light. That's your World Wide Web, zapping along the bottoms of oceans, unless an earthquake breaks it or a fishing trawler drags it up. Then they have to patch it. There's Harris, I think, third engineer, a.k.a. turd engineer, sailing New London to Penang, laying line. Sky and ocean a calm steel blue, half moon sinking. He's watching his coffee totter between the sides of a Styrofoam cup, trying to picture how the moon pulls on the water, and the water on the ship, and the ship on his coffee and him.

That's how I imagine it. There haven't been any emails for a while.

The yard is mud when I go out for one last look before I ship away. Dawn and Amelia are already in the car, and Mom's yelling through her cracked window that I'm going to be late . . . and the girls have to get to school . . . she has to get to work. "What are you doing?" I pretend I can't hear her over the rain.

As if I could guess what I'm doing anyway. I'm trying to see something as well as I can see it, but I don't even know what it is. Gold's open hangar with no planes in it. The chicken shed, the trapdoors on the root cellar and the well. The runway, the driveway, the dirt I used to draw in, the place the dog picked out to die, the junk alcoves where I'd go off to sulk.

"Corbin, we gotta move it," she's shouting.

I stood right here with the garden hose the time I tried to fly. I wrapped it around my arm and held on as tight as I could so that when I drifted up over my life I'd be able to hand-over-hand back down. And when I couldn't float up—when I just stood there, beating my heart, my feet stuck to whatever there was to lose—I still squeezed the rubber in my fists. "Please," Mom's shouting, "let's go."

THE EVASIVE MAGNOLIO

The old prize elephant died with his head in his trough one night in late November. The peach farmer saw him there at sunup, foul water raising a line of grime on his open eye.

Stony stood a long time watching the trough. Then he stared a long time at the blackened sky and the blighted land and the cold light sifting dust. And when he looked again to where the blight showed curved and polished in the elephant's eye, the thought came to Stony that maybe the elephant wasn't fully dead. A little dead, but not the whole way through. He felt almost a conviction.

Stony splashed till he'd cleared the dust like it was just a clump of sleep. The farmland, brightened in Maggy's amber eye, seemed ready to come alive again. It needed rest was all. Impossible then that an elephant could die forever. But he watched the creature's sunken head till there was no other conclusion. Even then, he walked around Maggy trying to nudge him up with a few hard leans. Maggy smelled the same as ever, like a paper bag of crickets, but there was no deep twitching beneath his claps.

He went for help, unsure what help he'd need. All Carnation, everyone in the town and outlying farms would need to know. But already out his gate and twenty strides toward town, Stony realized that, if Maggy wasn't gone already, he was leaving him to die alone. He walked back, unchoked an apology, and tucked his hand into the elephant's armpit. He'd wait there till the warm was gone.

The November wind whipped, but it was like wringing stone. Life-heat drew slowly through muscle so dense. All these winters, he'd pinned Maggy in blankets to keep the cold out, like cold was an unwelcome guest, but cold of course was the host all along.

Stony pressed the armpit for some last of its old mugginess and when he found none walked through the late-morning darkness into town. It was an hour's journey, but he didn't feel the time. Another season, the light off the crops would have tinged his sleeves green, but this year, like the two before it, there were no crops at all. At both sides, naked land stretched off too straight and flat to fit a rounding planet. No vehicles lumbered the road; none had in weeks. The commerce the town survived on was the winter kind: they'd peddled to themselves from pantries and cellars since their last real harvest, its memory nearly gone.

What could they do to even halfway commemorate their elephant, grand finale of his tent circus, for god's sake? Here lies the Evasive Magnolio? So called because he once stood before thousands, continents over, and nightly vanished into air? Their soil might have been worthy of him once, not now. The cemetery hill rose indistinctly beyond the homes. The dust slouching against the grave slabs showed which way last night's storm had finally gone. They might not have bagpipes leading the march or a reception with ice cream in their punch, but they'd all come out and wish him off. He'd need every single one of them for a pallbearer, of course.

It seemed the town was already in mourning. The center square was empty, and the houses facing in on it were boxed up against the gales. He knocked first at Jonah Hames's, that young stalwart. Hames had always treated him like next thing to an uncle. "Elstone here—favor to beg," he said.

But the latch didn't lift and the porch boards didn't transmit any hum.

"Anybody home?"

Anyplace other than home? If Hames wasn't home, he'd be out there in the center where Stony would see him or around back on his smutted land, where he'd stand out like a steeple.

Well, no need to be a perturber, Stony thought.

Every house in Carnation had been outfitted in its day with a weathervane. The founding mayor himself had drawn and cut the tin, and sixty distinct creatures crowned the sixty homes with a crowded local zodiac: a weathercock, weatherpig, weather-wolf, weathersquirrel, all the way around to the mayor's house, where a weatherelephant pointed his nose with the breeze. Stony thought he'd try the Elkharts next, but when he looked up to confirm their address, he saw that most of the vanes had been lifted off by some gale.

He'd noticed too that the Elkharts' truck wasn't parked beside their cabin, and looking around, it appeared many others were gone on some errand as well.

The shreds that remained of the last night's gale were twisting dust into provisional shapes, white warps that traveled partway around the camp of farmhouses in silence and fell. From horizon to horizon a pure quiet held the air. The statue of the founding mayor stood bird-shat and tarnished, staring off to where earth and air wafted into one.

Stony worked through the town, looking for any tracks but his own. The Pooles, the Karstens, the Coopers, they'd taken their curtains with them. He could see their empty rooms from where he stood. "All right," he said. "That's all right." He turned back to Farm Road B.

Dust rose up from the footprints he'd left on his walk to town. The path before him swayed like a row of ghostly corn.

There was a folktale to the effect that you should give an elephant to your enemy, because what might appear a generous gift had the appetite to ruin him. That might have been why—as a boast about the stamina of their soil—the founding mayor had bought Maggy when Maggy's circus sank. He rode him trumpeting into the newly chartered town, everyone out to greet them, and led Maggy around, and anyone who wanted to could reach up and have his hand shaken in that strong and nibbling grip. Stony had been shy. He'd thought—forgive him—that a king bull elephant might not adjust with kindness to farm life, but he saw right away that the beast's heart was vast and tired. Maggy would droop his head and track you with those amber eyes. The mayor led him through town those first weeks, till he knew every housecat and everyone had had the chance to touch his hairy sides.

"He's big," Stony said when the mayor brought him out to the peach farm, too dumbstruck for a subtler observation.

"That's the last thing about him," said the mayor, beneath an ear like a sheet of moon.

"He looks a hundred years old," Stony said. And maybe he was, no one knew, but the mayor explained that they all looked that way.

"Would he like a peach?" he asked, and with the mayor's permission Stony fed the giant his first peach, a heavy O'Henry yellow, sleepy in its fuzz.

"Well, look at this," the mayor said, watching Maggy's face. "He likes you now." Maggy wasn't doing much, just gazing down at him, his trunk flirting after a damselfly, but Stony took the mayor's word. "He'll remember that peach forever," the mayor explained. It was a famous quirk of the elephant mind.

Before he died, the mayor declared their elephant would live at Stony's. He'd be happy there, among the peaches. Stony had done his best to make that so.

Stony had never been to a circus, though through his decades as the elephant's caretaker he'd learned to imagine it, more or less. A caravan parading wonders all but perished from the earth: lions, tigers, talking dogs, a man with a throat like rhubarb who ate and lived on steel. Anything you could picture in advance a real circus would have to beat. He'd wondered tormentingly how Maggy's vanishing act could have worked. It must have been something great—an elephant gone straight into air. "Could you ever look at the air the same after that?" he used to say to Maggy's visitors. "No," they'd all say back, "I suspect you couldn't," and they'd all look at the air, his air, the shiver in his trees.

If he'd thought about the elephant's demise at all, Stony had idly imagined Maggy expiring back into air. He'd head out to the pen one morning, and the great haymow would have evaded them once and for all. But Stony, stumping back through his gate, saw how unevaporable an elephant was. There Maggy lay, an acre of their good dead ground balled up into a beast. He rested on his knees in an outsize posture of prayer, as he might have in his heyday to let a lesser elephant climb his back. His mouth and sawed tusks were sunk into his basin. Its rim jammed his throat. Stony considered the size of the self that had lived inside Maggy and that could, with nothing more than will, straighten those oaken knees and raise an elephant up like a barn.

Stony had never traveled, never married. It seemed he was born already settled down. But his elephant had seen the capitals of every continent. He'd seen the eyes of every family in every city large enough to fit his tent. The horses, the dogs, the roustabouts, the band; greetings from governors, flowers from their wives—and none of it forgotten. They kept him at spearpoint, the mayor said. Maggy remembered the whole globe; every room of it was bright with knives. No wonder he was weary. He was armored in weariness. The wrinkles held him from the teeth of the world as if he'd long ago cringed a safe inch inward. Stony never goaded him with anything meaner than a pat. He kept the pen open so Maggy could wander the orchard, never mind if he nearly cleaned it. Nothing was better than watching him forge his way down the narrow rows, peaches dropping behind him from branches that rebounded as he passed. No doubt there was plenty out there Maggy would have liked to forget. He looked now, in his dust, like a dry-cured brain, a jerky of every memory in the world.

Maggy had been in his care since the mayor died, and that was many years. Maggy was family enough for him, and that was not a thing he said for consolation. Summers, Maggy used to haul around a swimming pool on two rows of tractor wheels, and kids would plop in from every side. They gathered when he bathed Maggy, gawking at the edifice of suds. One Christmas, mad with festivity, they put wings on him and stood him in the pageant—the angel, annunciating a kingdom with no end. That was long ago, a dreamtime. Stony had fetched Maggy every cast-off husk and root that he could manage. With the cows and pigs all butchered, there was plenty of silage left-over, as sour as it was old, but Maggy never whined. He hid his affection for Stony some days, but Stony sensed it there.

It was hard to say how long Stony waited on his step for some idea for how to carry an elephant himself. There ought to be bugles lining the way to the cemetery, the whole town circled at the top of the hill, but it wouldn't be. It seemed a day, if not several, that he sat, running his sweating thumbs over the stair, polishing the gray stone brown. He watched the dust warps gathering and dispersing, certain he couldn't stand if he tried.

Then he was standing. And he was walking back to the pen with his wheelbarrow. And he was oiling its axle for the long push to town and dragging his box crates out from the shack. The day was active again. He could feel his determination, but he had to observe himself to see what he'd determined to do.

He pried off the short ends of the box crates and joined the crates in pairs to make leg caskets. Eight crates in twos for the limbs, four together for the head. He got his rags and the step-ladder. Then the knives and the saw. He stood the ladder at Maggy's shoulder. He washed the great neck with a cloth.

He felt unsteady. He sat atop the ladder with the saw across his knees and leaned back into Maggy's hard-crusted dough. He waited again for time to seal against him, but it would not.

What was the use of a gravestone on a low hill at the back of the world? Whatever memories the town had of their elephant, they'd taken with them when they'd fled the dust. However light you traveled, there was room for those. Why carry an elephant a mile just to have him join their honored mulch?

But he wouldn't let himself be tricked. He turned on the ladder and chose with his eyes where to cut.

He pressed his peach knife into Maggy's neck, but it only pushed the tough skin back. He tried to punk it quick and hard, but it made no difference. He lacked the strength. He wiped the neck again with a rag and waited for the shame to pass.

It took a pick to break through and all his will to bring it overhead. Stony opened his eyes in time to see the head bob against its trough. A strong elephant smell escaped behind the spike—mud, the bruised green juice of leaves. He hadn't smelled mud, real joyous mud, not mere wet dust, in a long time, and it braced him some. The knife wobbled in its handle as he tried to widen a way through the inch-thick skin. Beneath the skin, the bright lodes of fat seemed the cleanest things in the world.

His gummed hands were sore and cold, but he moved the ladder to Maggy's other side, repeated his work, and tried to shuck back a collar of skin. Dry lime sloughed from the old spear scars. The fatigued tonnages of memory and muscle clasped in that skin didn't want to let it go. But they did, with a little work, no grudge.

He felt about in the meat and deliberated where through the titan spine to aim his saw. Dragon meat could be no redder. It was a red more densely hued than black, richened from a lifetime of straining against that weight. The saw slid and hawked, then stuck and bucked at Stony. He had to catch hold of Maggy to keep from falling back.

Part imagination maybe, but after so many nights listening to dust storms sweep, Stony could discern his farmyard from their sound.

When the storms first came, the spray against his roof had been just the blunted wind. He'd heard its direction and speed from how it strained the tin. But a dust particle striking tin made a bright sound, and each sleepless night the pinpricks grew brighter till he could make out in their sparks the slant of the roof, the corrugations, the tin quavering against half-extruded nails. So when the storms seemed sure to lift the farm and shack and fields themselves away, that was when Stony's ears learned to see it all there glittering brightest. It was a comfort as he lay in bed waiting out the nightly barrage to see his well, his long lines of crackling trees, his elephant, and sweeping over it all, the storm's sparkling cloth, much like the one a circus magician snatched out of the air, once to disappear an elephant and a second time to bring him back.

But this midnight, the elephant beside him in the storm was half decapitated and cold. Stony could hear Maggy's choked neck dampening the metal basin, the soft dust striking the soles of his feet, catching and sifting in every crevice of the inglorious slump, skimming every one of his bullhook scars. He heard the dust spray quivering the saw blade set in Maggy's neck and going silent as it landed in the dampness of the wound.

It didn't help to cover his ears. He and Maggy lay under the same cloth. No matter how he burrowed under his pillow, Stony could feel the cloth pushing up over his bedfellow's tall back, snagging in the awful slice. All night the magician to their east pulled and pulled and the sparkling cloth flapped overhead, till every lump and billow took elephant shape.

Stony permitted himself to wait in bed till dawn. He rested his sore hands in the cool atop his quilts and watched the peacock feathers in a jar on the nightstand, their color drained off by the dark. The feathers were from Maggy's old headdress. They drooped. Their feelers joggled, which meant a leak somewhere in the shack wall. With the first shear of sunrise, when he could tell the green in the feathers from the gold and blue, he swung his heavy knees off his mattress and returned to the elephant's side.

The saw was nipped tight in the spine. He took its stained handle and worked it free, the head shaking, the trunk waggling through the trough water as if the elephant were coming alive.

The blade was old and his hands and elbows ached. The wide, cold bone had rubbed the saw teeth nearly flat. If he winced and kept a fast pull going, the heat of the stroke still did something, but not much. And after the head would come the legs, which would go no faster, and then, somehow, a limbless mass of lavish gore. The box-crate coffins lay empty in their row. It might be all the work he completed the rest of his life.

Long ago, Stony had overheard a girl, one of Maggy's frequent visitors, instruct her sister that the elephant could hear you whisper from anywhere in town—and he'd adopted that superstition for himself. It wasn't the big ears: the girl said Maggy could listen through his feet. A grumble every few country miles—chore songs, half prayers, the gut-muttering you spoke when you were all alone. *I don't know, Maggy. I just don't know.* Stony had never considered that he might actually believe in it, but they were desolate sighs that hung in him now that earshot extended so many miles.

He tried getting angry. "Boil that girl," he said. "Boil you, Isabella George!" It was her married name he yelled, and he knew her children's too. He'd carved them whistles. Peachwood and leather leashes, every kid got a whistle, but boil Anna, and boil Neville with his croup. He coaxed up his anger and drove the saw fast enough to blister dead meat. He took up the hot saw and smacked it down in the cut, like a hatchet, like a sword overhead, and a sick whey jumped into his eyes. But Stony knew he was only hoping to snap the handle or bend the saw beyond use. If he could hate them for leaving him, if he could just conjure up one ounce of perfect hate, it would be enough to live on till he died. But he didn't blame them, no more than he blamed Maggy for being big.

He patted him. A pat had used to mean apology, as well as goodbye and hello.

He told himself he was going to look for sharper tools. He washed his arms past the elbow, changed his clothes, and walked to the abandoned town.

He surveyed the little place, but it was as empty as it seemed. The dust had been driven up against the doors—he tried a few of them and let himself through those that gave.

He was interested to see what besides himself they'd left behind, and walking in the Gants' back door, he was surprised to find it wasn't just corn dolls and tacks. It was beautiful stuff—a tablecloth that must have taken years to stitch, still spread on the table, and candlesticks, dust clinging to the polish, a shelf of well-thumbed paperbacks.

He walked out the front door and across the square. The school building was locked, but through a window he could see the desks still demonstrating order, the large globe peeling, some indispensable fact of history still written on the board.

He thought of the town in its heyday, never a stop for a train circus, but rich enough once to bring a traveling air show to town. He remembered the barnstormers, duded up after their flights, illustrating their stunts with the ruby swirl of their cigars. Their hats hadn't let a patch of sweat seep through, not all day in their sun, and one fellow saw Stony staring and let him try it on. The fellow said Stony was a lucky man because the largest elephant and the sweetest peaches and prettiest women in the world were right there in his little town. He guessed the man was only aiming to be overheard by Kimmy Poole. Stony had imagined her to be a local beauty at best, but he had no way to know.

He watched a gust flesh itself in what it could find as it crossed the center square—husks, dust, the down of long-dead roasters. He had some joke notion of elephant heaven. Wide grassy plains, of course. Not in the clouds, but on a good, solid tramping ground. Long mucky rivers. Banana meat sunning on every rock. And, more than anything, the numbers of them—hundreds, thousands of elephants, called to herd by instinct. It seemed a sufficient view of paradise.

He let himself into Isabella George's and walked through the rooms the family had left. The cabinets still had some cups. The bedding was gone, but there were mattresses and frames still in two rooms, even a nightstand where his peacock feathers could sit. The lamps had porcelain bases and still some oil left. There were a couple clean knives in the kitchen, but he didn't test them on his thumb.

He made a few trips around the town, trying not to think about what he was doing. He took some pickled corn from the pantries, the remaining preserves, and carried them back to the Georges'. He took some blankets, an old clock and busted radio to tinker with, a paperback novel, *The Sunken Argosy*.

He fed. He cleaned the flue. He took open the clock and stared at it awhile. He moved room to room, sweeping out the dust, holding a lamp to the walls to find the seams where it blew in. He tried resticking the wallpaper with some shoe polish he found. He was in bed—not Isabella's, one of the kids'—before it was even dark.

In *The Sunken Argosy*, the first mate wakes from the horror of a shipwreck to find he can breathe so long as his feet are on the ocean floor. He walks through the glowing water, the corpses of his sailors floating overhead. There were mermaids on the cover, an underwater cave filled with red eyes, but Stony's attention wouldn't keep.

He knew what would happen. It had started already. He'd seen a few flies at the slice in the neck, eager to learn what had been under that thick skin all these years. More would come, digging here and there, pawing the meat with their eyelash legs, licking up their spit and toddling on. Soon it would be thousands. Maggy, as ever, would draw a crowd—bluebottles, greenbottles, blowflies, burying beetles with red inkblots on their backs. They'd parade across him, a fertile new frontier. Eggs laid thick as foam would sizzle open. Larva would bore through the giant, enraged with inborn hunger, their slick creased bodies graying as they gathered cold flesh inside.

He squeezed his eyes. It was dark now, not one lit curtain anywhere in town, and he could feel it was the same cold dark that settled over his orchards every night. He waited for the dust storm to sweep from the peach farm toward him, revealing everything it held. The wind would pull across Maggy's bulk and the wave an elephant left in its cloth would billow higher as it rolled toward town. The elephant, taller than a circus tent, wider than the square, the dome of him pouring upward through the night. He'd hear the maggots busy in his meat, their frenzied hunger the writhing of the storm. He supposed he'd know it when Maggy had vanished, hatched wings and filled the sky.

With every blast of wind, he saw the hungry carnival arriving. *Behold! Behold!* He closed his eyes to listen as it rose.

TWIN

can thank my resemblance to Reese, the Groovy Girl doll, for my twenty hours a week at Kid Genius Toys. The owner hardly looked at my application, just held up an organic-felt ten-year-old, who, in her miniskirt and bangles, looks like a shop-girl already. My other job, Quiznos, has the black company polo and visor, but here, where I wear what I like, I can feel the customers not seeing me. I'd been waiting for someone who knows me to come in.

There's a boy, Matthias, the owner's son, eight or nine years old, who's always here and, of course, far more interested in me than any toys. But he's all right. He hates the children's music his mom plays. She leaves him here with me, often for hours, while she runs errands, god knows what, and he'll switch it over to my songs as soon as she's gone. He likes me to sing—"Jimmy Jazz," "Alison," Stevie Nicks. He doesn't even know how in love with me he is.

He always has trivia, which I always believe: Did you know that in a one hundred percent silent place you can hear the blood inside your ears?

"What's it sound like?"

"I don't know."

"Does anybody know?"

"Actually everybody, we just don't know it," and we both catch each other listening to our ears.

Who did you see when you saw me today? Nineteen years old. Two jobs, an apartment, a forgivable roommate, a little less than a thousand dollars in my account. Reese, according to her tag, wants to defend the environment. Her favorite food is grapefruit, favorite activity hanging out with friends. I have a few friends, a boyfriend I plan maybe to break up with soon. Matthias, true authority, says I have a wonderful voice. Less sugar in it now, but despite myself I hear it sweetening up for the Kid Genius moms. "Don't you love him?" when they pick up a plushy bear. I can more or less imitate anything Matthias wants, but I have no actual talent I'm afraid. Don't know about you, but when it's just me I don't sing.

For weeks this summer, Maple's father has been Sunk Dad, they call it, lying in the living room, clawing raisins one at a time from the box.

When he surfaces finally, gets up from the crumpled couch, there's something different about him. He stands in the living room brushing his teeth, looking at the air.

"Daddo?" Maple says. A weird smile cuts his stubble.

"Hey, my girl," he says, toothbrush tucked in his cheek. He gathers the newspapers, spitting his toothpaste in the yard, takes a floor lamp from the living room and sets it up at the kitchen table, where he sits late into the night sorting through a stack of marble-green file folders, signing notes and making stacks.

"What are you doing?" she says. He's busy. A tuft of his hair bobs along with the pen.

From bed she hears him on the phone: "Peggy, could you take Maple for a couple days? No, feeling much better actually. It's a, what do you call it, a retraining thing. If I do well, maybe they hire me back." This is a lie, she can tell. "Pete's? So bring her. Take her with you to the falls."

He comes into her room, watches her a second, starts putting clothes into her duffel.

"I'm not asleep."

He doesn't say anything. He packs two shirts, two pairs of underwear—then throws in a handful more of each.

"You lied to Ms. Woljson."

"Call her Peggy. You're almost a teenager."

"I'm eleven."

He twists a pushpin in the giraffe print where they pencil off her height. "You're the most beautiful, strongest woman I've ever known. Okay?"

When she doesn't answer, he says, "Wake up, there's something we have to do."

He sits beside her with his guitar and the tape deck on his knee. "This one's the studio version," he says. He nods and strums once. She watches the wrinkles in his neck. "We're doing all the hits."

"We have to do it now?"

"We're ready. I'll go copy off a few."

She wants to pinch and wake him. "What's the falls?"

"Me, my, mo, mull," he sings, but there's no humor in it. "Warm up for your solo."

Sasha's parents come at dawn. At the curb the open van looks like an eye. Maple drags her duffel down the walk, smears an earthworm through her hopscotch and her moons.

Sasha's straw hat is on her face, the brim slick from breath and brightened. Maple sets it straight, covering the length of the scar, as she climbs by.

"Morning, Maple," says Ms. Woljson. "Look, Sasha, look who it is."

Sup, Lefty, Sasha says to Maple, mind to mind.

Hey.

The seat belt has lanes in the weave, dry red jam on its buckle. "Good morning, thanks for taking me," Maple says aloud.

"We should be thanking you. Sasha, you get a whole weekend with Maple! Yay, exciting!" Ms. Woljson tickles out a little squeal.

My mom's an idiot, Sasha says.

Totally, Maple says.

No, you fucking love my mom.

Not really.

Liar. It's going to be fucking extra boring at my uncle Pete's. Sasha is two years older; everything bores her exquisitely.

We'll have to write like a hundred new songs, Maple says. She tries to say it with no enthusiasm. She's never actually bored when she's with her best friend.

Mr. Woljson presses a button and the van door skates closed, crushing a tissue pack that rolled into its track. They pull forward and a Saint Christopher medal swings from the rearview mirror, child god glowing on Saint Christopher's back.

It's quiet. Ms. Woljson turns to say something to Maple or to check if she's asleep but changes her mind, turns back with parted lips. Sasha has her bear tucked under her thighbone, its fur sharp with old spit. When the van brakes, her leg squeezes down on his face and the eyes go loose. Sasha's key chains swing against the back of her wheelchair. Her arms lock up like chicken wings and she hunches around them, her chin not quite propped on her wrists. Her beach hat slides forward and the scar, a pink come-hither, curls out from the hat's back brim. Ms. Woljson puts her hand on her husband's and smears around his knuckle skin. The van ferries its load of humming air.

Band practice? Their band, most recently, is called the Dead Ringers. Only original compositions now. Their latest singles: "Lobster Blue Bruises," "Supercuts," and "Hate You 2," all by Sasha. Maple's songs, "Bullhonky" and "Slap Bracelet," still sound like gay birthday party music, Sasha says.

No. I'm gonna sleep, Sasha says.

Rock-a-bye, assholes, Maple sings. It's from one of Sasha's old tracks, but Sasha doesn't laugh. Whatever she's so annoyed about, Maple can't guess.

Maple fakes sleep. When no one's looking, to see if Sasha's really sleeping, Maple pushes on her eyes and looks hard right and back at the node that connects their brains. The halo is gold and fiery and swells a little in pattern with her breath. The thin light squeezes and flares as Maple pushes on the channel that leads through to her.

You could have just said you were feeling like a needy little bitch, the node says. *You want some atten-ten?* Sasha laughs. *All right, fine*—and she sings lead, Maple harmony:

You took me to a late-night movie;
I fell asleep and dreamt of you.
I know I'm your best distraction—
Hate me once, and I'll hate you too.

Maple wakes a hundred miles later to the sound of gasoline glugging into the tank beneath her head. It's a Sinclair truck stop with two retired army tanks and a helicopter out front. A POW flag droops above a plastic dinosaur. Sasha is gone.

"Peg's changing her," Mr. Woljson says, sliding the door. He's tidy, smiley. He's got the tiniest butt. He probably would've been scoutmaster if Sasha were healthy and a boy. "Pac-Man? There's an arcade inside."

But inside there's no Pac-Man. Zombies splatter and fuel tanks explode in the dark. Mr. Woljson grumbles and feeds his quarters into a game called Fog City Pandemic. They lift heavy etched-plastic guns as melted-down faces moan and encroach. Wailing pipes out of the black speakers that overhang the screen. A fragment of the Golden Gate Bridge forks up at the game horizon.

"So how're things in the Palensky household?" he says. "Your dad seemed to be doing better." He levels at a zombie, fixes his aim, and shoots again.

"Uh-huh," Maple says.

"Shoot offscreen to reload," he reads. "Dang." She is dead already. He fights off another zombie and drops his gun into its rubber holster, wipes his palm against his jeans. "Look, Peg and I want you to know you'll always have our place when his bummers hit. You're really sweet with Sasha—if fair was fair, we'd be paying you—but it's okay if you're not there to see her. This year's middle school, and Washington doesn't do special-needs inclusion. She'll have her track, and you won't see her so much. But really, come hang with us whenever you like. Spin some records." They've rounded on him, a herd of the Fog City dead.

Maple can't help it. He winces and grabs her a stack of mostly unused napkins from on top of a discarded pizza box. "I'm sorry, Maple. It's okay. He's getting better. Hey, let's get back to the van."

Maple watches from her seat as Ms. Woljson and Sasha back out of the finger-smudged double doors. "Chuck? Everything cool?" Ms. Woljson says when she elevates the chair.

What a surprise, says Sasha. *It's Maple in tears.*

Shut up.

"Tender times is all," he says. They drive by the tanks, the POW flag, the dinosaur. PLEASE DO NOT CLIMB ON DINO is printed on the dinosaur's side. "Did you hear they did the fossils wrong?" he says. "No such thing as the brontosaurus after all."

"No?"

"But if it didn't exist, then it's not extinct, am I right?"

Ms. Woljson reaches over and thumbs a skin flake from her husband's ear. Two brothers fight for who gets to stand with the tank's gun to his head. Dino looks up with happy squints.

Okay. What is it, Sasha says finally.

If she stares hard enough at the boys, the tank, Dino, maybe she won't say it, but it comes anyway. *They're splitting us up.*

I do love to watch the Kid Genius moms try to figure out who Matthias is, when he's sitting there on the counter—my son, my brother, my ward. These rich young boutique moms have placed their all-in bets, and anything that doesn't abide by their code now threatens them. At least that's what I tell myself as I chirp, "Right this way," and scurry to show them the Lilys and Laylas and Lolas and Reagans, mothers' ideas of daughters' ideas of late girlhood. You'd be surprised how many can't stop themselves from asking. "Is this your big sister?" they ask him.

"She's my daughter from the future via time machine." We decided we needed a reply, and this is what he composed.

Me: "Da-ad, you're embarrassing me." They, the rich moms, flee.

Matthias, as far as I can tell, has no dad. Dead or absentee—he doesn't seem plagued by it. He likes the idea of being my dad; he keeps making new attempts to turn it into a game, but I don't know. He wanted me to tell him his future, but I wouldn't tell him about Daddo. I stirred his staticky hair with a sparkle wand and said, "Thy fate is thine to discover." "I want to be a life scientist," he said.

The first five years of her life, Maple lived inside someone else's manic episode. She was lucky. They had her mom's life insurance to spend out, so why not go for it? They named every fish in the library tank. They blowfished at each other through the glass.

"I didn't miss you or anything," Daddo said when he walked her home after her first-ever day of school. "I worked all day on my business plans! I could drive a Thanksgiving food truck? Lady Maple's Turkey Tank? Or make my line of savory chewing gums? Lady Maple's Chicken Chews?"

He said it was her vote. She sucked on her name-tag yarn.

"I see. You made so many best friends you don't even talk to me now?"

She told him about the one girl, the special deaf girl in her special chair.

"That's Siamese Sasha. You've met her before. I'll show you something amazing."

He showed her online when they got home. The article's picture showed the Woljsons, still young and blond, looking with strong, worried love at the baby, or two babies, in their arms.

"Sasha and Hannah, before the surgery," he said. "Connected at the brain." Two baby girls fused at the fontanel gazed up with symmetrical wet grins. Their long skull made a pink tunnel beneath four happy eyes. "The cookies baked together—as the cookies sometimes will." He scooped Maple crossways onto his lap in the swivel chair and pressed his forehead, his long eyebrows, into hers. "'Sorry, Boss. Either she comes to work with me or I go to kindergarten with her. We're joined at the nog!'"

His sour man-breath puffed into her mouth.

He hoisted her in front of him, their skulls still connected, and wobbled elephant-style into the kitchen. It hurt her armpits. "We are Palenskys if you please. We are Palenskys if you don't please! Hey, Honeybuck, Maple and me put our minds together and determined—"

"Daddo?" Maple said. He'd fallen quiet. "Who's Honeybuck?"

It was like a fly had hit him in the face. He blinked and put her down and used the kitchen window to erase the warm spot on his forehead; on hers, a splotch of his panic remained.

When he couldn't, or didn't, find work, he collapsed. He lay with sunk eyes, on his bed or the couch, his stubble pushed into the cloth. Maple missed school. She threw the volleyball against the living room wall. Plaster shook down into his hair.

For four months, he hardly spoke. He got her meals, got her dressed, got her into bed—all from afar. He was unreachable, but when he cried, she cried too, like they were connected behind the eyes. He tried to hide it, went to his room, and she, automatically, went to hers. She pressed on her eyes to keep out his tears, pressed till she could only hear them straining and that was all, the oily inside roar. That was where she found the node. Orange, black, a ring of blue, she tried to see where it led.

That fall, Sasha's mom arranged for every kid in kindergarten to have a playdate at their house. Sasha had a big-screen in her bedroom, Madonna posters. Ms. Woljson had a glassblowing studio with a furnace and a long blowpipe. "Sasha loves the colors," she said. "She loves orange."

"Me too," Maple said.

"Talk to her. It's okay to talk. She's very thoughtful in her own way. Maybe you'll connect."

The two girls watched from across the studio as Ms. Woljson blew a cooling drop of glass into a sphere. An aperture in the hot glass opened and closed, and the orb sealed in her breath.

Are you there? They said at the same time, inside.

Jinx.

Sasha's house was a knight's hop from Maple's, two blocks over, one up, and Sasha's parents never asked. She'd kick her shoes under the bench in the entry, run back to Sasha's room. Pretty soon they gave her the code to the garage. This was childhood, right? A tin-can phone line, out your window into mine? Best friendship, which has always been equipped with exactly the powers it needs?

Maple sat on the edge of Sasha's queen bed and watched MTV, muted and taller than her. *I can't believe you're allowed to watch this*, she said.

I watch whatever. I can tell you all about everything, if there's ever anything you want to know. Do you like the Shamblers?

I don't know.

They have that song "Sucking on Ozone"? "Crash-landed in your stepmom's pool, I remember you from the middle school"? Her voice was so clear and close.

I don't really know about anything, Maple said.

Most people don't.

Will you sing it again? Maple said. *Do the whole song.*
I'll do it once, she said. *Then we'll try it together.*

On the interstate, Mr. Woljson puts in Maple's dad's tape and
his voice comes on: "Hi Grandma, hi Woljsons, hell-o the future,
ha-ha. It's Maple and Brian here, August 2004. Studio cut. All
songs were written by Maple Palensky, my beautiful daughter.
First some oldies, then our hot new set. Ready, Maple?"

There's a pause while he waits for Maple, last-night Maple,
to nod. She remembers his weird calm face lit by her plug-in
globe.

"We don't need to play this," she says. The van has speakers
back, front, high, low. It feels like panic to have his voice all
around.

"Come on, chanteuse. Don't be shy."

"Maple wrote all the songs," her dad is saying. "Well, it was a
collaboration. Here's what I mean."

The pinwheel turns loudly. The guitar lets out the bronze gust
of a major chord. "It's always the same. She thinks it's a . . ."

"Game." Her little voice barely made the tape.

"I start out a line, I'm doing just . . ."

"Fine."

"But every dang time, I can't find the—"

"Rhyme!" Ms. Woljson sings out.

"This is so sweet."

It's idiotic. Maple knew it was, but with Sasha here it burns
worse. "Kangaroo Soup," "My Fallible Mailman," "Invincible
Tim." Her dad is loud and flat and idiotic, she is squeaky and
faint and idiotic.

You tiny ho baby. It jets through the node.

I know.

And your dad sounds like moldy balls.

We both do. I hate the sound of my real voice.

Your real voice?

Not like that. I meant—

"Oh, Invincible Tim never learnt to swim," Ms. Woljson sings along. "Drowns and clambers out again."

"This is really rude," Maple says, "but is it all right if we turn it off?"

"No way. You guys are rocking it. Brian sounds so jolly."

Is this what you do all day? Fart away the college fund?

"Now the new set," Daddo is saying. "Here's a little number Maple and me cooked up."

I don't have a college fund.

Well, we got thousands stashed away for me. Sasha is turned away, watching the trees slice by.

You're really good at sarcasm.

No, you're really good at sarcasm.

"Peg," says Mr. Woljson. "She said she doesn't want to listen."

"Okay, okay," she says and hits eject, but it's too late. The first lines have already played:

You took me to a late-night movie;
I fell asleep and dreamt of you.
I know I'm your best distraction—

The node goes to ice.

You did not.

I'm sorry. I'm sorry, I'm sorry. I couldn't tell him it was our song.

I wrote it.

Your song, I meant your song.

Mr. Woljson glances at Maple in the rearview mirror. He taps down the cruise control.

"So want to play a game then?" he says. "Suitcases? I'm going on a trip, and I'm bringing my atom bomb. That's *A* and *B*."

I just wanted to hear it out loud and then he wanted to tape it and—Sasha's anger swells into her skull.

Out loud? Sasha says, disgusted.

"Sure, I remember that one," says Ms. Woljson. "I'm going on a trip, and I'm bringing my atom bomb and my Christian Dior."

"Oo—very nice."

She tries to silence her mind, but the interrupted song skips and earworms, the incomplete line floundering and replaying without its second half: *I know I'm your best distraction . . . I know I'm your best distraction . . .*

Are you trying to kill me? Sasha says, her anger trembling.

"Maple?" The Woljsons are consulting each other in their silent way. "Your turn, Maple Candy," Mr. Woljson says. "All riders must play suitcases."

All riders—Maple can feel it gouge Sasha. All the time, in little ways like that, they forget she's there.

He doesn't mean it like that, she says.

Just stop.

He—

Stop! Sasha shrieks—the scream, the airless scream that doesn't pause for breath. The thin node sears and rips. A migraine blooms at the back of Maple's skull.

"Maple? Maple, it's *E* to you."

"Maybe a little Ebola fever?"

"Oh dear. Maple, what's wrong?"

She pukes on the side of an exit ramp and Sasha quits screaming and switches to the silent treatment now. At a gas station, Ms. Woljson gets Maple a Fresca and a straw. "I got migraines bad at your age too," she says. "Just awful."

They arrive at Uncle Pete's houseboat at sunset, and Maple remembers that this has been advertised, a houseboat, a night in a houseboat, but it doesn't look like a house or a boat, no pitched roof or glass windows, no paddle wheel or furled sail. It's a storage unit, floating beside many others in a harbor—a flooded parking lot—along the flat course of the Erie Canal.

Uncle Pete welcomes them from his roof with a quick sideways spit and a big wave. He helps Mr. Woljson carry Sasha across his gangway and up the spiral stairs that lead to the small roof porch, the only space that can hold them all. He hands Maple an old Super Soaker with a brownish reservoir and squeaky pump. "Maple, was it? Will you take gull patrol? It's Rolling Thunder around here."

"Where's Jeremy," Ms. Woljson says.

"He'll be back soon. He's out drawing dicks and balls on everything." Maple has only heard whistling laughs like Pete's in movies, old whiskey-faced men who die clutching their chests. He mixes a few drinks on the top of a mini fridge whose orange extension cord she traces back down the stairs. He rolls the cap of the tonic water off his finger and into the murk, slices a lime with the pocketknife he keeps on his hip.

The houseboats are lined like trucks at the truck stop, only enough water between them for garbage to collect. No steering wheels or braking levers that she can see. An American flag slaps its backhand at the other boats, atop a four-foot pole.

"You like my flag? If I'm not mistaken it's the flag they fly on the moon," Pete says. "It's a moon flag." He leans back and swigs wisely. "The lonesomest flag in the world."

"What happened to your old Jolly Roger?" Mr. Woljson says.

"Don't ask if you don't want to know." Pete laughs his whiskey laugh again.

They talk about money, about Lockport, Pete's little town. Sasha's wheelchair is pointed off at the sunset. At her knees, a slingshot is bracketed to the gunwale. They talk about Niagara Falls, how Sasha starts cawing there, every single year, as if she knows. They talk about pituitaries, CAT scans—"I hope they don't make you pay," Pete says.

"Why's that?"

"Why? They lost your kid."

"Christ, Pete," says Ms. Woljson.

Mr. Woljson says he's going to go unload the van.

Ms. Woljson says one year she'd like to visit the ashes without a blowout.

"What blowout?" Pete says. He points at a gull for Maple to shoot, but she misses.

"Pete lives here all year round," Ms. Woljson says to Maple. "Even after the water freezes."

"If I seem deranged, she means." He tosses her an Otter Pop.

Alexander the Grape. Maple has purple on her lips when Sasha's cousin Jeremy climbs up the stairs and nods hey to his aunt. From the corner of her eye, Maple can see the rip in his pants where his knee sticks through. He's drawn on it with a pen. He sits and takes a big can of iced tea out of his cargo pocket, cracks it open confidently, but he doesn't know where to put his eyes.

"Hey, Jer," said Mr. Woljson, coming back up the stairs. "When'd you sneak in? Meet our Maple?"

"Not really," Jeremy says. As he drinks, his pale black mustache gets wet and sticks to his lip. It's just a bluff of a mustache, as soft as the hair under his Big Dripper Plumbing cap, she can tell.

"Well, you should," Mr. Woljson says. They all sit there.

My cousin's pretty much a Neanderthal, Sasha says. *He's going to be one of those forty-year-old guys on BMX bikes, you can tell already. He won't even look at me.*

He's the freak. I bet he stole that Arizona.

I wonder if he's in love with you. Wouldn't that be gross?

Disgusting, Maple says.

The adults resume their conversation, but she doesn't listen. *What would you do,* Sasha says, *if tonight you wake up and he's trying to kiss you—if it's even possible for him to kiss, with his big teeth.* Maple hides her laugh. *Is there a type of girl, some-where, who would find him cute, the way some people like those skin-disease dogs?* But they decide they cannot even bother with him and have band practice instead. They sing "Lobster

Blue Bruises" and "Supercuts" and just to prove they're past it they sing "Hate You 2" and swear they will never, ever fight again. And they never do.

Jeremy takes a tin of Vienna sausages from the same cargo pocket, fits a half inch of preserved meat into the slingshot on the gunwale, and aims at a neighboring boat. There's a wince in the air and a seagull perched on the boat falls back in a spasm of flight. Jeremy whoops. The sausage bounces but stays on the roof, and the seagull lands again and examines the lump of meat.

"Eat it," he whispers. The bird feints twice and devours it in four quick nips.

"Dude," says Pete. "I told you, don't feed the enemy." He takes the water gun and squirts nipples onto Jeremy's shirt.

Maple watches the Woljsons look down. She watches Jeremy set his jaw and turn red. He wants to spit or swear or storm off, but he's trapped. It doesn't matter how much he hates his dad—there's nothing to say and no one to say it to.

Maple wakes that night when Jeremy jumps onto the bunk above hers. His ankles hang down in front of her face. He brightens his bug bites with three fast claws, flicks his rubber flip-flops off, and pulls his feet out of sight. His hand drops down but swings away from her toward a tackle box on the stand. The hand opens the box and takes a pack of cigarettes, a lighter, a paper-towel tube with a dryer sheet rubber-banded over one end. The lighter scratches, he exhales aloud, relief and mock relief. She can hear his wet lips squished inside the cardboard, and she can tell how terrible it would be to kiss them, his long and flappy lips, covered with that weak black hair. She thinks about them rippling toward her, water leeches, and shudders. He reaches down, and she scooches away, but he just takes an iPod from the tackle box, dusts it carefully with the overhanging sheet. Soon miniature screams tunnel through his earphones above. It's too soft to hear the words, just the tiny rage.

She turns and touches her forehead to the plastic wall beyond which Sasha and her parents sleep. She pushes in on her eyes and tries to listen in on Sasha's dream but remembers Daddo's voice coming on from all sides in the van. She pushes harder and plunges up a glimpse from the dream across the plastic wall. A dark school hallway. Or the hallway of an office or apartment building. *Where is this?* she whispers, but Sasha isn't there. She runs down the hallway looking for her, pressing her forehead harder on the plastic wall. The farther she runs, the darker, and the less real. When she gives up and opens her eyes, her bruised vision swells with dizzy, addled lights. Jeremy flicks the lighter just for sparks.

Balled in her cot on the other side of the wall, Sasha, as always, is the first to understand. *Don't go,* she says. *Please. Even if it is a lie, don't go.*

Maple jams her fingers into her eyes again and bites her blanket. She calls to Sasha—it's not a lie, it's real, it's real, I'll never go—but the words circle and make no sound.

There's no one else for me. Please. I'll be alone.

Maple pleads back identically. Please. Stay. She echoes back—it is how the game is played. Don't go. She digs into the node, calls down the long hallway, but it doesn't make any sound. She listens. The lighter stops scratching, the iPod dies out. With some imagination, she remembers they're afloat. Her own little voice will be hers to keep. Maple does not even say goodbye. She fakes sleep by faking dreams, from which, in the morning, she wakes.

Niagara Falls: Uncle Pete and Jeremy ride with them in the van. Pete, in the way back, digs his knees into Maple's seat. The tires strike a long note from the asphalt. No one talks. Daddo's tape sits there in the console above the Woljsons' hands.

In the parking lot, young couples sunscreen their thighs, old couples hurry each other, sort through little taupe backpacks in their trunks. The noise of the falls is there already, air and crushed air and air rising. They follow the crowd. A woman in ranger greens hands out blue ponchos from a box, a waxy bag of French fries on the table at her side. A German man photographs the Woljsons slipping Sasha's poncho on. "Wonderful," he says twice. "Wonderful."

A simple labyrinth of ramps and rails shapes the waiting crowd, which shifts leg to leg, a single twisting sheet of plastic blue. From a few feet off the ponchos look opaque, but up close Maple can watch the hair on her arms lift against the plastic. The Woljsons, Pete, and Jeremy, pushing Sasha up ahead, merge with the strangers. Maple stops to tie her shoe and the crowd pushes around her. When she stands, she hardly needs to walk. The crowd walks for her. They've already moved aboard.

She can't see the Woljsons, but she's okay. The blue crowd wraps around the main deck and spreads up two sets of stairs. The wind on the water is shaky. The crowd's plastic cloak flicks one way, flicks another. Then the ramp is up. The horn has blown. A murmur rises all around.

She tells herself what she has told herself since, and it is true: you are alone but you will be okay. She climbs the stairs to the upper deck—*Pardon me, excuse me*—the crowd parts without a word.

She can't see, but she doesn't care. A man struggles with the camera strap under his poncho. A boy, hoisted on shoulders, kicks blinking sneakers into his father's chest. The crowd points, makes dull, awed sounds.

Somewhere on this boat, she imagines, the Woljsons are searching for her: *Maple? Peg, where's Maple? I think Maple is lost.*

Finally they are close enough. Water rises over the crowd, and there is not one world: a higher earth crashes down on this one. Maple closes her eyes as the boat enters this place of constant rain.

Under the mist she can feel the burst world quaking. This is why they come here every year, she realizes. Not to visit Hannah—these forces dispersed her cupful of ashes long ago—but for Sasha, who once could hear and understand and move like any other child, before she was cut halfway out of the world and trapped there. In her guts Maple feels a planetary purr, its slow singing. This is the place where Sasha remembers sound.

Then the ferry turns and the roar shifts through her belly. Slides away. The deck talk starts again.

She finds them on the dock. "*There* she is," they say, mostly unconcerned. Jeremy pretends not to notice her. They all get clam rolls. Life goes on.

"Shotgun," Jeremy said back in the parking lot. Your mom said nothing, just went and sat with her brother in the back. Your dad raised your chair, and Jeremy climbed in up front, surprised.

I remember him showing off his legroom, playing with the locks—bored, nervous, feeling watched. He flipped through the AAA maps tucked into the door, fingered the phone charger, the glove box latch, took Daddo's tape out of the console, flipped it over a few times, and pushed it in.

At first there was nothing recorded on side two. For ten minutes the van speakers just breathed. Then, beside a Christmas tree farm, my dad came on: "Hi. Hi Maple. Hi everyone. Hidden track, ha-ha. I hope it's a good surprise." There was a long pause. I remember your dad smiling at me in the mirror. "Who knows when or if you'll hear this or how long it's been. Maybe it's ten years, twenty years later, and you just put the tape in to hear my voice and remember. If it's been long enough, maybe you could play this for her. I just wanted, especially for Maple, to explain. It'll be an accident, but I think you'll know deep down. It's better for you. I'm bad for you. I see you sometimes, your teacher said it too, slipping off into some dreamlan—"

Your dad pressed stop and pulled to the side of the road. I watched him dial 911 on his cell phone and step out of the van. When he returned he took the tape and put it in the pocket of his shirt, glancing at your mother with tight lips. "It's going to be okay," he said vaguely and drove fast.

What they don't tell you is that, even at its worst, when your body seems uninhabitable, depression makes you believe in a comfort, in you somewhere, that your attention is retreating toward. Geoff, my boyfriend, called this morning around ten and could hear I was still in bed. "You must like it there," he said.

"I tried. I can't get up."

"You can. You just don't."

"I could toast a strudel. There's a strudel I could toast." I lay there striving for the intoxication of actually being stuck.

What got me out of bed finally was a conversation I imagined myself having with Matthias. I'd go in to work and I'd teach him about "I Feel Fine," the Beatles song, how, before Hendrix or the Who, it was John Lennon who invented feedback by leaning his guitar against an amp and being bighearted enough to realize there might be something musical in the squawk of trapped sound. I'd tell him my dad told me and tell him he had to tell his daughter, so that she could go back in time and tell him again—

Get it?

Maple, you're weird. I might have talked to him half an hour in my head, long enough to wonder about myself.

My dad, so far as I know, made no suicide attempt. He would have had plenty of time. He changed his mind? He lost his nerve? I didn't ask. It was assumed collectively that I didn't know, that I had not understood, and I could go along with that. Our tapes disappeared, but I know we made them. I remembered what I'd heard, the extra underwear he'd tossed into my bag.

Matthias brought a friend to the store today. A friend his age—a girl, no less. They sat on the floor together playing some high-speed card game that had them slapping at each other's hands and giggling. I left them alone. Finally there's time to sort through the receipt drawer—that's what I told myself, but I didn't. I played my own game, one I've been practicing lately, in which I concentrate on the simple sentence that describes me at present—Maple is making a turkey melt, no mustard, or Maple is discounting a coloring book with a bent spine—I concentrate very hard and try to sense my life taking place in that sentence. Look, I am smoothing out crinkled receipts, I am smoothing receipts with the heel of my hand.

I texted Geoff under the counter and told him to stop by.

So that was the scene when your mother brought you into Kid Genius Toys this afternoon: Matthias sitting barefoot on the counter, his girlfriend gone, and Geoff eating his lunch. He brought me—who works at Quiznos—a Subway sub. "Thought you might want some variety," he said.

Geoff. He's been about to start his lifestyle magazine for two years now, about to fix up the motorcycle his brother gave him, elaborating the same business plans, sketching the same tattoos. No real strikes against him. Maybe he talks a little too loud. I suspect I don't love him, but sometimes I honestly can't tell.

The bell jingled and your mom backed you in. "I heard a rumor we might find you here," she said. She parked you under the stuffed-animal tree.

Geoff gets earnest when it's good-manners time—"Such a pleasure to meet you, Mrs. Woljson. I've heard great things about you . . ."—till his notion of himself is the only thing in the room. Your mom made sure to tell me in earshot how impressed with him she was—anyone with any pity can see how he needs to impress.

Do I need to tell you about you? You looked like an old lady. You were lying back in your jogger, your old pink headband holding the hair out of your eyes, bandanna around your neck to keep your shirt dry. An Animal Planet octopus show playing on an iPad strapped to your chair.

"Hi, Sasha," I said, out loud. I petted your hand like I'd pet my grandma's.

"Oh my god, she's smiling, she totally remembers you," Geoff said. "Look at your great big smile for your old friend." He almost poked your face.

"I don't know. She just sort of smiles like that."

He said I could trust him. He said he could tell.

And then what? We watched the octopus special on your lap, the giant creature squeezing itself through tubes. Geoff showed you the plushy mosquito puppet. You didn't stay long. Geoff had to go too, held the door, thumbs-upped. "Sasha loved Maple," your mom said to him on the way out. "I never saw anything like it."

I might as well admit I was scared—of something, of you, the twenty-one-year-old with diapers and armpit hair, the real person I abandoned when, in the name of reality, I abandoned you. How are you?

Me? I ride the bus from Kid Genius to the Quiznos. I listen to my songs, watch the high school boys listening to theirs. I collect my paychecks, take them home, Swiffer the kitchen, feed my roommate's cat, settle in with some cereal and my roommate's HBO. I don't hear voices. I feel fine.

Matthias didn't say a thing the whole time you were in the store. He's often quiet with the customers, but I don't know. At the very least he could tell there was something between me and the handicapped woman in the special chair.

Tell me something, I thought at him after you left. Ask me, did you know humans are the only singing land animal. That birds can't survive in space shuttles because they need gravity to swallow. Tell me if we ever need to leave the earth and start a new planet, the birds will be left behind.

But he couldn't hear me. Or I couldn't hear him.

Finally, when the quiet was too much, I went to the back to turn the kiddie music on. I put my sub into the unused mini fridge, and a butterfly fell out. It must have flown into the ancient fridge years ago, baited by the light.

"Look what I found," I said, hardly breathing. A sign, a gift, from the universe, from you. The golden eyespots trembled in my palm.

"Can I have it?" he said.

No, he couldn't have it. Ten bucks an hour and no one paying me to be his sitter. But I could tell it was his already. Once upon a time, those wings had stared down birds a hundred times their size. It worked until it didn't. It worked enough.

I get my paycheck, the money's mine. "From me to you," I said.

He placed it gently on his knee.

That's me. A grown-up by any measure. I'm taller, smarter, more sensible. I have work, I have a plan, I'll be okay. We knew it even then—I would have friends and boyfriends and a husband someday, and you would not. I would, with relative ease, live among the living. I do. And only very seldom does the scream rise up: *Where is Maple? Where is Maple? Maple has been lost.*

THE WILDERNESS ACT

Pussy shopping, he should have said—*that's what you're talking about.*

That was what he should've said. *From the comfort of your own home.*

Three weeks later, Rainey was replaying it still. "So, Will," he'd said when the pub noise idled, "how did you and Cheryl meet?" They'd invited him to come toast the kid. The interim director—the Ultimate Frisbee himself—had knocked on Rainey's desk, said the office bachelors were going to take Will out to the Hungry Toad after work and mourn his passage to the other side. But next thing he knew the whole booth had turned on him.

"You ought to get out there, Rainey. Get online, get looking, get laid."

"Match.com is snatch.com. I'm telling you." Even the Ultimate Frisbee was straining his eyebrows and nodding along like he did in his performance reviews.

He could think of nothing to shut them up. For the next half hour at least, they—a staff supposedly dedicated to the preservation and protection of nature—rounded on him and praised this website, that website, the techniques and technologies Silicon Valley had engineered for scoring poon.

Actually, no one had been so vulgar, and it might have only been a few minutes of cajoling, not a half an hour, but in the weeks since the Hungry Toad, over the course of the referendum he'd hosted in his mind as he putzed around his house, commuted, exercised, their true thinking had been revealed. They wanted nothing less than a revolution against nature in which the ancient, mysterious, deep-dwelling workings of mutual desire were to be replaced with shopping. *Get out there.* They wanted the species to actively commodify itself, and who, historically, had been victimized by such logic? Women, obviously . . .

He could feel his lips moving. He was on his morning run, on the mountain trails behind his house. The trails were busy, even this early in the day. The gravel scuffed pleasantly underfoot. The trail, wide as a bike path, switchbacked up the east slope of Prospect Peak. Prairie dogs hustled for cover half-heartedly; they knew these humans didn't have teeth. To the east, the city went about its business, as cities are wont to do.

Maybe his coworkers thought forty-eight (you wouldn't know it from his pace) was so old he needed e-dating explained, but in fact he was just old enough to see how it was part of something broader in the culture. Thirty years ago, when he moved to Prospect, it was a disregarded midsize town that happened to be where it happened to be—at the edge of where Colorado topography began. If you wanted a hike and knew which side of a no-trespassing sign was which, you could follow your nose: hug the stream till a patch of wildflowers caught your attention, chase them till you made your way to a view. But those days were long gone. Doctors and lawyers and tech entrepreneurs, the kind who biked to work with carabiners on their backpacks, had started buying up the mountain land and perching mansions in Brazier Heights, not because they hated and wanted to destroy nature—believe it or not, they claimed to love nature, but in this confused day and age, no one knew the difference between loving something and owning it.

That was why he was proud to work for Open Space and Mountain Parks. Prospect had pushed back and passed a sales tax so the city itself could purchase mountain land to keep in its natural state, and as the wealth of the city had grown, so had its reserves. With his help—he did the books—city nature stayed natural.

Rainey could smell the sagebrush, the warming sap, the dew-damped gravel dust, and could sense the animal in him responding to the smell of the day. *There's no stink online*, that was what he should have said to them. *More power to you*, he should have said. *But I'm old-fashioned. I need those phero-mones. I need the smell.*

"You hound dog," they'd have said. "You nasty old hound."

He burned through three pairs of running shoes a year.

Rainey frowned and nodded at the other runners. The girls—the women—he went for eye contact, made sure his pace was strong, but he couldn't really smell them, even the ruddiest, not with his modern nose. Ancient man had scrambled the earth on all fours, torso caked in dirt, and navigated, knew the world, by smell. When he stood, he'd traded scent for sight, and the trouble started there. Dawn of crunches, now that anyone could see your tum. Dawn of the loincloth and all the consequent deceptions. Descent of man.

He'd made some exploratory profiles on a few of the websites. Not his real name or face, of course, just his researches into how the new world spun. It seemed a very formal world, with its private messages, the various visiting cards you could leave. The height of civilization, no doubt. An endless mall where women pursed and posed in windows that arranged themselves before his eyes according to algorithms whose ultimate motive was, of course, to keep you in the mall. He'd chatted experimentally with the women behind the glass, but the more interested he was, or could imagine himself being, the less likely he was to say hello. What if it worked? What were you supposed to tell your grandbabies when they asked how you fell in love? "My womanly wiles, of course," Grandma would twinkle. "A *lady* knows how to crop her tits."

The candidates were pretty, though, some downright inspirational. Prospect was looking fitter every year, especially online. The trail runners worked up a nice blush, but online, lady limbs reached across rock walls and curled against ballet bars, focal-pointed, retouched, viciously lit, single drips of sweat like those on smoothie-label nectarines. If their real-world counterparts were even half as toothsome—but he pitied them when their profiles disappeared, pitied their new boyfriends too, with their eyes pinched tight, trying to hump a photo. Because if you were desired *as* an image, desire would reduce you *to* an image. Till your real body and breath and thoughts and speech were only the media in which your lover sought your image.

The trail ended at Devil's Scapula, the mountain-long rock slab that stood over the town. His turnaround, halfway up, was an overlook, a railed wooden platform from which he could see his house, down, down, alone on the edge of the city's designated mountain land. As a structure, the house wasn't much, but it had trail access, and no neighbors, and his view of the Scap was unblemished by any other house or road, not even a telephone wire. Smartest thing he ever did was buy his acre before Prospect boomed and the mountain parks closed in around it.

The overlook where he paused and confirmed that his house still stood was a popular spot for profile pictures, he'd observed. It telegraphed a certain Colorado-ness, maybe: this is me and my mountain, me and my valley, my sunshine, my drippy Camelbak, my hiker's ass perched on the guardrail. VitaminDeena, Nature-girl89. And wasn't that precisely the problem—they thought of love like they thought of their environmentalism and their fitness routines: an important feature of the lifestyle they aspired to.

He took yesterday's flyer down from the guardrail and unfolded the new one from his pocket. MEETING OF THE PROSPECT CERVIDAE SOCIETY: COME OBSERVE THE MULE DEER'S FALL RUT. ALL WELCOME. It gave today's date and his address. The tape had enough stickum to reuse.

That would make a better story, wouldn't it? Your grandma came over to watch mule bucks fight for screwing rights out my back window, and, well . . . look how she still blushes after all these years.

Would he tell the whole story? How he'd seen her profile on some dating website, this pretty young woman, an environmental studies PhD candidate it said, with a dissertation on the mule deer, and he knew from her pictures there was a hike she liked to do, so he did some targeted outreach. All fall he hung posters on the overlook till finally . . .

But he was merely leaving love notes under stones. No tender knuckles ever knocked at dusk. "My name's Nicole? I'm here for the rut?" Not in any universe he knew. *Come right in. I'm just setting out the crackers. Make yourself at home.*

Then one evening a woman of his own age, perhaps a few years older, and a bit more wind-blown and sun-browned than the environmental studies PhD, came to the door with binoculars around her neck. He couldn't very well throw her out. "Attendance has been down lately," he explained. "You might be the only one."

She didn't seem bothered by that. Her name was Janice. His name was Tom Rainey—Tom or Rainey, you could call him either one. She wore a purple fleece pullover with the snaps unsnapped, smudged glasses, a halo of brown frizz over her thick hair, but when he shook her hand, he felt his prostate pulse with intuition.

"Wow. Did you shoot that?" she said, pointing up at his wall.

"I hunted when I was younger," he said, turning, but he was confused. He had hunted as a kid, but there was no trophy taxidermy on his wall. She was pointing—what had he been thinking?—to the photograph of Ayers Rock above his woodburning stove.

"I know exactly what you mean," she said. "Bag Australia, bag Fiji. I used to travel like that, like the world's something you can drag home." He couldn't tell if she was covering for him or not.

Love at first sight, probably, was just a contrivance for ennobling the decisiveness of the sex drive, and yet the assent his lower chakras were sending him seemed hardly related to sight at all—not that she was unsightly, he would never have said that, but there was something knowing and impatient in the brightness of her eyes, something in the immediacy of her hiking shoes weighing his carpet, that suggested she, the woman he sensed, was hidden somehow, or that she'd made herself visible to only him. She smelled like . . . he couldn't smell. He tried to glimpse what animal his mind had briefly mounted on his wall.

He shrugged. She shrugged. She had nice shoulders, muscular. They knew what a shrug set down. "Have you traveled a lot, then?" he said.

"I don't know, it's all travel after a while."

Was she enlightened? She looked unlikely enough to be a Buddha.

But would she like anything? Tea? He'd baked some sourdough bread that afternoon? The gazpacho wasn't too old? The refrigerator light was blinding.

"I'm impressed," she said. "You look more like the beef-jerky sandwich type."

Because of his jaw muscles? he wondered. His skin? She was making fun of him? He couldn't tell.

They sat on his back porch and watched the deer make their usual evening trek along Bald Creek and across the leeward flank of the Scap. He lifted his bonsai off the railing, kept their teapot full, cleared cobwebs, swatted moths. "Sit," she said. "I didn't come to make you tidy up. If a room gets tidier when I pass through, then something's being wasted."

He wasn't sure what she meant by that. It sounded promiscuous, maybe—which was exciting and disappointing. Or maybe it was a spiritual comment of some kind. Her dense brown twist of hair, the sun marks in her skin, they did suggest someone who would waste none of life's energy on illusions that entropy could be stopped. A lover of *actual* nature, in other words. For such a person, of course it was all travel. What was a home? There was no way to step out of the world.

Head of the supposed Cervidae Society, he worried he'd have to display some zoology, but she said, "Now, these are *mule* deer, is that right?"

Indeed. The same you found munching flowers all around town. He couldn't guess why she was here.

Any mammal larger than yourself was a reminder that we'd rigged the system. The deer were faster, stronger, pointier, more massive; there might have been some mutual regard. Instead, their walleyes wobbled nervously at the drain grates. They lipped the ground for trace salts and hurried to catch up with each other. No one wanted to be ditched. "They know how to nature-watch," Janice said. "Nature-watch for your life."

But she was commenting, he sensed, on his porch, its posts, with their pretense of a framed view, and his teak seats watching through the frame. For a lover of *actual* nature, there was no inside-outside and there were no pretty scenes. Nature's threats moved even on his porch. She was changing him already. He worried he would let her down.

They visited into the dark. The rival bucks never showed. When he mentioned his job, OSMP accounts supervisor, she shook her head with what he took for disappointment, which was strange—Open Space had high approvals. Every so often something in the wind turned on his porch light, and she had a different face each time: her eyes blacker, wetter, more fixed. "Weren't you wearing glasses?" he asked.

They were in her hair, she said. She'd adjusted the binoculars to her eyes so she could see the does perfectly. "But it's true you're a bit of a blur."

He never found the moment to admit he hadn't been to Australia and hadn't taken the photograph himself. She'd been everywhere, had lived in New Zealand and Brazil, had taught businessmen ice-climbing and leadership skills, tried emetic—and he assumed hallucinogenic—rainforest teas he'd never heard of. All of it by accident, it seemed. It was not a date of course, but he felt assured of the moment when it would retroactively become a date. It was late and dark and they were alone.

She sniffed her tea. Herbal steam parted around her chin. He imagined he could smell her wet neck skin, the cool air that grazed it. He could taste already the large freckles on her chest. He looked closer than he might have since she'd said she couldn't see.

"Are you even interested in deer?" he said finally.

"You know, not really." She laughed. "Confession? It might make you angry."

Angry—there was invitation in the word.

"I've always wanted to see a mountain lion. That's why I'm here. Your deer are just my bait."

The sex was challenging for Rainey. He would serve one of his soups, maybe some savory muffins, and tell Janice about the latest quandaries at Open Space and Mountain Parks—did Oklahoma trail gravel corrupt Colorado geology? Should a Prospect rap duo be allowed to shoot a music video on Everett Mesa? Then, equipped with mugs of tea, they'd move to the living room, settle in before the woodstove, where she'd built a fire, and make love. When it was done, she would offer to help with the dishes and leave. He would dump out her cold tea, lock his doors, and make sure the fire was out. "Of course you're welcome to stay," he said aloud, an hour or more after she'd gone.

She'd say it was obvious: OSMP should analyze the market trends of various gravels to see which would add the most long-range value to their geology. And maybe folk-rock videos could be allowed but metal and rap were clearly too pollutant. He didn't know what she had against OSMP and might have defended his department if he hadn't sensed that she, in a code he couldn't yet break, was actually making fun of him, his home, the routine to which he'd subjected their sex.

What she was saying, probably, was that the contradictions of managed wilderness had infected his passions, which were as nervously overseen as his parks. And maybe so. Maybe he kept it all too properly zoned. Maybe the spread of his kisses from lips to nipples to hipbones was too predictable, too reasonably paced. But it was daunting being with a lover of actual nature, who probably expected some kind of pure animal love. He tried to spring the wild man for her, but his established personality wouldn't just shed on command. It hovered and admonished the wild man's performance, his hoots and hoists and bites, which were obviously too tentative and embarrassed to convince. She was a world traveler, after all. She'd climbed Aconcagua. She'd broken her back riding a horse.

He tried trying harder, roared hopelessly, but it was only a show of effort, which was to say a show of strain. One night in a spasm of bravery, he pulled open his shirt, a good work shirt, and a button flew into the open woodstove where it made a hissing green flame that watched him scornfully, as if it knew something he did not.

The fires she made every visit were his best evidence of what she wanted from him. She built them as soon as she came over, a kind of private foreplay, it seemed. She brought over firewood, in excess, piling the extra out back, and gave him a handsome copper pot to put on top of the woodstove—to soften the air, she explained. As a sexual compulsion, it was new to him, though it'd probably been around as long as fire itself, the species' most ancient way of saying, Let's come together and survive the night. That must be what she wanted, he reasoned with one knee on the carpet and one aching on the tile that surrounded his stove—an old-fashioned Cro-Magnon thump by the embers, his sex in contest with whatever lurked outside their ring of light.

She told him to relax, but a conscientious person made love conscientiously, and, especially in view of the relative simplicity of his own orgasm, there was nothing wrong with wanting to discern her subtler cravings. Still, when his soup, his muffins, his porch, his living room, and so on all went without compliment, he began to resent—not her, he didn't resent her, he resented himself for worrying so much, for being so naked and fearful and tame. It left him enraged.

Janice made sure to achieve her orgasm, flushing beautifully, the wood fire bright on her skin, but by then his characteristic kindness had turned on him. Bitter noise cycled through his mind. He gripped the skeleton that jerked underneath him, angry at the inscrutable pelvis out of which his cavebabies would scream.

"Tell me a fantasy," she said, after, smoothing down his brow. "What goes on in there?"

He tried to laugh, but it came out curt and scoffing. "You're my fantasy," he said.

"No. I'm flesh. You may have noticed." Sex relaxed her, like it was supposed to. She sat up against the foot of the couch, draping her nakedness across herself like something hard earned, expendable, ultimately fictitious. A tattoo, an eye, a hieroglyph, among the freckles on the side of her breast.

He said maybe he didn't know how to fantasize. Did that sound pitiful? In his mind he was prying the melted button from the stove with a knife to see if it could be saved. "What's yours? Did you have one? Something buck wild?" His face blanched or steamed red, he couldn't tell. "What's wrong with me?" He said he was sorry if he was being weird.

She was kind. She said he should think about it for next Friday, was next Friday good? She said maybe they would play with it, get to know each other a bit, and meanwhile, she would enjoy thinking about him thinking about it. It was all for fun, right? They'd both be looking forward. So make it good! Now, did he want any help with the plates?

Even before he met Janice, he'd seen himself mentioning her to the office, not boastfully—she was a human being, not an accomplishment—but then also not so casually as to risk understating the authentic depth of his affection. He imagined the office bachelors chewing their rue as he described the fires she built in his living room, and he imagined the eavesdropping women of the office perking their ears and reconsidering Tom Rainey when they heard the passion in his voice. One or two might even visit his cube for an afternoon pry. But come Monday, all talk at the office was of the Arsonist.

Arsonist was what the Ultimate Frisbee called the vandal, or team of vandals, who had painted a four-letter word of some infamy in giant letters on Devil's Scapula, where all of Prospect could see. "Arson, people! Conference room! Worse than arson! Worse!"

Typically, Rainey didn't mind all-hands meetings. There were bagels and paper boxes of coffee, problems to solve, and not much expected of him participation-wise. He took his notes while secretly playing poppy-seed hockey: you had to pass the seed down the page with the nib of your pen without making stray marks. Arson they had contingencies for, but what was to be done about a hundred vertical feet of graffiti that could only be reached on belay? It would take a series of pressure washings to scrub the word away, but the rock was so high above the grid they couldn't reach it. They'd lose half their psi pumping the water up the thousand feet, and a pressure wash might scar the rock in any case.

He was as concerned about the vandalism as anyone, to be sure, but all thought returned to Janice. Pumping, pressure, psi. Even the letters on the rock wall called her heatedly to mind. Sexual, violent, what other word could label actual nature? Nature warmed wordlessly against his thigh. He wanted to . . . he would . . . his brain burned, but nothing resolved into a storyline.

"Could we introduce a lichen that eats paint?"

"Lichens don't eat. They breathe. They're breatharians."

"You not likin' the lichen, bro?"

"Licking the lichen and likin' the licking." Jed and Jazon clapped fives.

Ayers Rock? The outback? Some pitiless rock ledge from which he and Janice look out over their dangling feet and perceive what annihilable nothings they are? He lowered his head over the conference table and cautiously covered his eyes. Say they met that day in the cabana. Say together they took this climb, and now on this ancient ledge . . . but the voice of a travel promo began to play over the fledgling seduction scene: "The beautiful spectacle of Australia's Red Centre resides in the deep, spiritual power of the landscape." It might have been the voice of Crocodile himself. "The Anangu people of the land say their first ancestors . . ." Meanwhile, up the hill behind them came a parade of tourists, zinced retirees in safari do-rags, pointing their trekking sticks at the same sunset he was urging on. Warm red dirt, creaking hammock—it was all prefab.

Next to him, on what looked like a hundred-dollar notepad, the intern was drawing the Scapula, the four letters prudently replaced with dollar signs and question marks. The Ultimate Frisbee was cleaning the screen of his laptop with a fingernail. "Tom," he said, "do you have any estimates to associate with removal procedures?"

"How about lemon juice?" Arturo, the volunteer coordinator, said. "Lemon juice strips paint."

Rainey said he didn't have any numbers for anything like that.

He wondered what Janice would have them do. Leave the letters? Every human habitat had its markings, a tradition old as petroglyphs—was that the enlightened view? A view of the Scap increased the value of your property by five to ten percent—except not now it didn't, not with those letters there. So figuring twenty thousand homes averaging five hundred thousand dollars—that was half a billion dollars vanished overnight. Five percent of the gross municipal product, somehow robbed.

An accounts problem—where was that money now? Transferred to a world where it bought nothing.

He'd planned to go to Australia decades ago. If there was just one person in the world for you, as some romantics believed, then he could be sure his was on the other side. Instead, he'd bought a photo of Ayers Rock and invested his inheritance in his house, his acre. Across the ledger from his real estate were the debits on which its value was based: his parents' deaths, his years in this office, the hours spent dragging mulch around his yard. Somewhere in that column was the woman, whether or not she existed, whom he'd left on the other side of the world.

The poppy seed was rolled in ink and sticking to his pen. Now Janice was here, and his house was worth fifty thousand dollars less.

That Friday, he trimmed the coronas of hair around his nipples in the shower and watched the thin brown pinches chase to the drain. He vacuumed the living room and put a throw on the arm of the couch to lay down in front of the woodstove when the moment came. Her fires left splinters in the carpet, and you wouldn't want to get out of your jeans without something down. He thought about stashing condoms somewhere. You didn't store condoms in a living room, but he felt like a twit jogging to the bathroom with his little springboard all abounce. He tidied despite himself, started a soup—chili oil, lemongrass, an adapted tom yum. The lemongrass, crunching under his knife, had more personality than him.

"Tom yum?" she said when she came over. "If you expect some pun from me . . ."

Pun soup! "I never thought of that!" He laughed too loud, but kept his eyes down as he fussed with the garlic skins, anxious she'd ask about the fantasy as soon as he looked up.

He planned to demur—*fantasies weren't his thing maybe, and things had been so crazy at work . . .*

But he never needed to. She went out to the back porch to untangle the wind chimes—"How can you not hear that? They're being strangled"—and returned immediately, beckoning in urgent silence.

He followed her out, unsure.

It was dusk. The wind was full of birds—gray jays and shrewd crows riding their own feet like brooms.

She pointed. Had she somehow not seen the graffiti till now? "Right there," she said. "No. *There*." Finally he saw. In his walnut tree. Only fifteen yards out, its eyes shocked in the porch light, autumn muscle slinking along the limb—a mountain lion. It took a second for the smoky caution and power to cohere into a cat.

He was impressed with its invisibility and equally with her eyes. She'd only gone outside an instant. The solemn cat watched them, or smelled them, or regarded them with some blood sense in which sight and scent were not distinguished, and then, with affected confidence, lay down.

He called Animal Control.

"Does he make your spear arm tingle?" she said. He couldn't tell if she was teasing him. She was standing—was that so smart?—at the close edge of his deck.

"I suppose I wouldn't be much with a spear."

"Come on," she said. "All your back-to-nature talk and no survival reflex?" He could see the cat's ears responding to her voice. He wanted to go finish the soup, but she wouldn't let him go, like the cat might dissipate if he stepped in again.

"It's just lying there," he said.

"Watch. Don't be scared. This means something to me." She put her arm around his hip and squeezed.

Now he began to understand. She was warming, as she did before the woodstove. The lion's gaze, with its halted fire, was making her want love. The cat poured its strength between shoulder blades and relaxed along the limb, its dominance as complete and assured as its sense of peace. Janice and the lion returned each other's gazes while he shifted foot to foot. His choked wind chimes twisted on their string.

"Think he could get us from there?" she said. "One long pounce?"

He said he doubted it, but it was obvious to him she wanted to believe it, wanted to make love here, on the porch, within the lion's reach. His lover of actual nature saw sex for what it was, nothing more than the tussle for life, meat's crude method for whipping up more meat. Love was dishonest if it forgot that the only alternative was death.

At the very least he should take her inside, smear her against the glass while she eyed the wildcat, but he couldn't.

He looked back through the sliding glass door into his kitchen, more visible at night than he'd quite realized. Through his window he could see circles of the red chili oil joining into larger circles now that the boil was off.

But Animal Control will be here any minute.

Animal Control, ah well.

The khaki team came and tranquilized the cat. It was amazing how quickly it was over. They shot it, caught it in a tarp, caged it, and took it away. The tree was empty. He'd failed her. She'd be done with him now, he supposed.

She said they needed to talk. She had not built a fire, the soup had been inferior, he'd disappointed her in front of the wildcat, which was all she'd come for in the first place. She hadn't asked what fantasy he'd prepared, she'd known not to ask, and knowing that, she must know his incapacity.

They sat opposite each other at his kitchen table, but he couldn't look at her. He watched the window where his walnut tree, and its constant reminder, would reappear as soon as there was sun.

She turned his chin toward her and said a word.

He didn't understand.

"I could be wrong about you, but I have a feeling." She said the word again, a common enough word, a silly word; there was no context for it.

He said it back, inflected it into a question, and she nodded. He said it again, and she nodded again. "It's a safeword, dummy."

Rainey burst out laughing. He apologized and steadied himself, but he was helium light with relief. She kept talking—an experiment, some stuff about him—but he couldn't really listen, his ears were too full of relief. He looked at her. He hadn't looked at her all night: she was wearing a brown leather jacket and eyeliner and had—he counted them—four silver bracelets on. She'd cleaned up for him. He was still laughing. She was very beautiful in her way.

"I thought you were going to break up with me," he said.

She nodded. "Don't you think I ought to get to know you first?"

He felt like weeping. "I love you," he said.

She kissed him between the eyes. "Enough excitement for one night?"

He understood. He bound her wrists with kitchen twine and pushed her against the glass.

❃   ❃   ❃

So that became a dimension. It was easy to worry. He didn't want to hurt her and didn't think he could recover if she had to use their special word. At the same time, he felt he'd be letting her down if the word wasn't somewhere within reach. Like the lion, make her feel her mortality without fearing it—that was the trick—but it was a lot to negotiate internally as he reached for a fire poker to press hard but not too hard across her shoulder blades and yanked her jeans down but kept them high enough to shield rug burn.

He worried as he threw himself upon her that there might be real assailants in her past—these things were common— whose attacks he might inadvertently recall, or other lovers who'd played similar games. He imagined them forcing the same acts on her but meaning it better, men decades younger and stronger and less eczema afflicted, their aggressions uncompromised by sensitivities like his. He hated her theoretical villains, but—this was the magic of it—once worry became anger you could use it. When he worried she was disgusted by his panting or unconvinced by his grunts, he could convert it, with a little anger, into fuel. Cuff her over, press her into the rug, and it was generous. Truthfully, he felt present in the act for the first time in his life.

She seemed happy too, to judge by how her orgasms recoiled. The one thing, though he could never mention it, of course, was that she was a little bit lackluster in her role. He wanted to remind her that they were out on empty land where there were no neighbors who might be troubled by her screaming. It wasn't that he was a critic, or disappointed, he just wanted to give her everything to the utmost, so if she wanted to run and make him take the closet door off its hinges to get her, he'd do it. He'd do anything for her. If the lion came back, he would not be so shy now.

He wished it would.

The chances, he bet, were better than even that the lion would revisit his walnut tree. He asked the Division of Wildlife colleagues with whom he shared Prospect's E Building. "Hey Candy, hey yo, Dale, hey do mountain lions—quick question—do mountain lions like to return to the same places?"

They seemed surprised to see him outside his runnel of worn carpet. They told him to call over to the Front Range Wildcat Survey. "Gotcha, gotcha, thanks a bil." He tried to carry the call off like business, leaned back in the office chair, made his voice loud and professionally relaxed: "Tom Rainey calling from OSMP, I'm inquiring about—"

"Tom Rainey on Brown Briar?" the guy said. "I was just looking at your paperwork this morning. Jenga's back at rehab, hate to tell you."

"Jenga?"

"Yeah. We tried a release with the GPS collar, but he ran straight back to people-land, and we had to pick him up. It can take a while to get the pet out of them. He'll spend the winter, at least, in Cudsburg."

"Jenga?" He examined the pattern of holes on the mouthpiece of his phone, the map of the proposed open space expansion T-pinned to the cubicle fuzz.

"I didn't name him. Did you talk to the a-hole in Brazier Heights who had him? There ought to be jail time for that shit. I'm sure this guy didn't even feel the ticket. You know how Jenga got out, don't you? Fell down a dumbwaiter shaft. They had him in an indoor pool room, like a spa they didn't use. I'm like, you're going to litter-box a mountain lion? What's wrong with a beagle? See if Cudsburg can remind him how to pee straight."

He didn't tell Janice. He sensed it might revoke something if she knew their lion was in truth high-end merchandise. The red-clawed beast in his tree, purchased from some meth-town breeder—he couldn't help feeling that it reflected on him.

A coincidence he would have liked to share was how closely the mountain lion's name resembled their word—three letters in common, the same springy mouthfeel—but of course he couldn't let on that the lion had a name.

The silence of the safeword—there was something more than the word itself inside that silence. On his morning runs up toward the Scap, it replayed in his mind, gaining inner volume as his breath grew loud. His body craved the word, a sugary itch on his tongue, an erogenous absence in his ears, and as his strides, coming fast, shook the word inside him, its froth thickened his sweat and collected at the corners of his mouth. He suspected he would climax at once if he heard Janice say it—a theory he supposed he could test anytime. But of course he wouldn't. He did not even mumble the word to himself, not on the wide-open flanks of Prospect Peak, not even back in his home with the sound of the shower surrounding him. He didn't know the limits of its power to dispel.

So when Janice stopped calling him and didn't return his calls, at least he knew it was not because he'd disappeared her with the word. Beyond that, he wasn't sure where he'd gone wrong.

For a couple weeks, he prepared for her on Friday nights in case she decided to just arrive as she had in weeks before. He stacked firewood on a few sheets of newspaper by the stove and vacuumed the living room carpet till it stood tall; he cooked a soup or a curry, something aromatic, as if she would find her way by smell; he rehung the wind chimes along the short end of the porch so they'd have a wider, less impeded view of his walnut tree; and when he caught himself making such preparations on Tuesday and Wednesday and Thursday nights as well, it occurred to him that these could be expressions of heartbreak. He saw himself from outside his windows, toweling his cutting boards and pots.

It was strange. He'd been practically studying her, but he realized he didn't know where she worked or lived. He didn't know where she liked to go. He didn't even have a picture of her for the office bachelors. The copper pot she'd left on the woodstove was the only material proof.

He ran. It was supposed to be a kind of folk remedy, being on mountain land. Mountains provided scale. The endless repetitions of pine cones and grass provided scale. The muscular, iridescent fish, briefly thrilled by his shadow. One afternoon, running on the piney shore of a small lake, he nearly stepped on the head of a fawn. The rest of it had been dragged away. He looked all around, but saw no predator, just bands of shadow on the water, the wind's weight on the lake. A ponderosa soiled in its honey. A bronze-eyed horsefly ducking through sun. The fawn's weak dead eyes begged and accused him. He thought he should bury the head, so it would not be waiting for him there, and waiting in his memory, but the ground was too hard and rooted to move without a shovel. He thought about throwing it out into the lake, but it would only bloat and float to shore. Finally he found a soft, swarming anthill, which he opened with the heel of his shoe, and buried it there.

He ran on, and a few steps down the trail realized this was not the order of things. Nature didn't bury. *You're tidying again, Rainey*—but when he turned to dig up the fawn's head, he could not find the anthill again, so he ran back home, blind eyes everywhere underground.

If it was heartbreak, a website on heartbreak anticipated angry phases. On a run before work, he saw a handsome young couple walking their dog, a dystrophic-looking labradoodle, both of them holding steaming mugs of coffee, actual ceramic mugs, which was typical Prospect idiocy. They could afford an addled designer dog but disdained to-go mugs as, what, too rat-racey?

"He's not supposed to be off leash," he said as he passed.

"You're free, Opie!" he heard behind him—"I release you, Opie! You're free!"—the woman laughing, the dog huffing and jumping at its name. *I have a name! I have a name! It's my birthday! I have a name!*

He picked up a rock—not that he would really belt it at the dog or the couple, just to squeeze until his heart calmed down.

He slept very little, reported punctually to the E Building, gauged the impact of rubber rather than wood water bars, worried with the Accessibility Committee where to allow the occasional drinking fountain along the perimeter trails. He knocked his poppy seed while the team discussed whether they should allow battle reenactors to use biodegradable pellet guns on the sesquicentennial of a Cheyenne massacre. And, with the fecal coliform count in Prospect Creek running high, they were mobilizing pooper-scooper volunteers, but should the volunteers be taught to distinguish dog stuff from coyote, so the latter could be left for the naturalists to ponder? And, if prices got any higher in Brazier Heights, the fire department's insurer wouldn't be able to take the liability on controlled burns. Could they afford to contract out with a private burn squad?

Call the Arsonist, he thought to himself. He halfway looked forward to it. Give the rich folks what they'd paid for. *Wilderness*—Janice's voice again—*doesn't stay inside the view.* The graffiti on the Scap, the Ultimate Frisbee announced, would be painted over with rock-colored paint. It was affordable, achievable, relatively harmless. He said it would make the mountain good as new.

In her executive notebook, under the heading "Private Burn Squad???" the intern had drawn a cartoon fire, little houses surrounded by concentric droplets that resembled only the idea of flames. Real fire was something else. He thought about Janice's stove fires, and memories (as was perfectly natural) morphed into scenes, so he listened to the Ultimate Frisbee outline restoration procedures and saw himself forcing Janice underneath him, holding her down with the fire prod, uncertain of what it was he saw. A memory? A fantasy? An act?

Then he realized. His heart started beating, so hard the lights in the conference room seemed to pulse. Adrenaline surged into his thighs. He couldn't believe how stupid he'd been! How self-pitying and slow! She hadn't dumped him. Janice was no coward—if she'd wanted to dump him, she would have. His leg muscle shuddered, but his head was finally clear. It was an expansion, an invitation. She wanted him to track her. Outside his living room, outside his house. Inside his house, sex was mere domestic habit—for her it was. She was waiting for him—to slide up her bedroom window, to unzip her tent fly, to pounce at her on Bear Meadow Trail.

It scared him, but without fear there could be no courage, without courage there could be no growth. In his life, no one had ever been so generous with him. She saw what had happened to him, working half a lifetime with this team of glorified land-scape architects, fastidious rule-makers. She wanted to restore him. He didn't have her address, but it only took a minute online.

That evening, he showered, groomed, and deodorized. He buckled himself into his car, ignited its engine, rehearsed his paces in his mind. Every time he pushed the gas, the car rolled forward—every time he pulled the wheel, it turned. It was easy. He knew where he was going. The birds in the road always flew off safely when the car got close. More than sex even, he wanted to see her. But he couldn't make the car drive to her house.

It went to the grocery store instead. It happened the next day too; he found himself at the Barnes & Noble, the Ace. It didn't matter that he'd brought the fire poker with him. The car made a slow path around the city and, without stopping, brought him home. His keys trembled as he reached for his door handle. His mouth was too dry to eat his toast.

He didn't know what was wrong with him. He set out one weekend morning and the car drove him well east of Prospect toward Cudsberg, toward the Wildcat Rehabilitation Center in the plains.

He braced himself for a grim scene, a cellblock of cougars and bobcats behind pet-store Plexiglas, but the range he saw as he approached was fenced but otherwise untrammeled. He couldn't see any cats, not while driving, but there were watering holes and bones atop a not un-Serengeti-ish plateau. Somewhere beyond the dense chain-link and razor wire, Jenga might be hunting prairie dogs, maybe even deer, scampering up scrub trees to hide from the same friendly sun that had heated the backs of the buffalo whose hooves once tilled this land.

A tremendous billboard tiger, black panther, and African lion topped the headquarters building where he parked. He should have expected that the criminal rich who purchased cougar cubs would also have leopards and cheetahs and tigers. Inside they wanted twenty-nine dollars for admission. They gave him a map with a maze shaped like a paw and a word search on the back. Another sheet had the headshots and stats of their big-draw cats—Honeycut, Mowgli, Mr. Bean.

Would he be able to see Jenga?

"An elevated walkway extends into the preserve," the girl said. "Please don't throw anything down."

He tried to explain. No, he was not the lion's *owner*, so-called. Just an interested party. "Maybe I should have called ahead, but there must be files tracking the progress of the various . . ."

Eventually a trainer (an un-trainer?) was called—a wide, smiley woman, who told him Jenga was just down the hall, in a kind of solitary confinement because the larger cats were likely to eat him if he were released into the main preserve.

Eat him! What could eat *him*? He watched the trainer's strong butt as she brought him back into the recesses of the sterile building, to a white room divided by a wall of caging.

There was no mountain lion he could see. Within the cage, he saw a shabby tree-house structure, a kiddie pool, a folding chair, and a bluish chicken that clucked and stared confidently back.

He searched his side of the cage as well: a desk, an air horn, a sink with a hose, a dart gun, posters, a wall calendar that this month showed rubber ducks arranged in a chariot-racing scene. Except for the chicken, they were in the room alone.

"Oh, come on, Jenga! Get that butterball!" the trainer yelled and a cat, as if conjured, leapt from the structure's middle platform and reached for the chicken with long arms, arms like an elderly swimmer. The blue chicken squawked and, assisting itself with little wing flaps, ran up the ramp to where the cat had been hidden. In its language, the bird berated the cat, the world, its own sweet meat, while the cat looked about in shame. "Puss, puss," the trainer shook her head. "He fakes it for me, but he doesn't have an ounce of kill."

There was some mistake. This wasn't the lion from his walnut tree. The cat walked back up the ramp after the aggrieved chicken, which hopped off the edge and returned to its spot in front of the folding chair. The cat lay down again, a mongrel creature with mountain-lion teeth and skull, the wonderful heavy tail, but shoulder blades and ribs as long and exposed as a coyote's.

"Svengali would kill him in a second. That's the Bengal, but even the other cougars might kill him. Until we get some piss in him, Jenga's housebound."

Stretched out, the mountain lion looked like a twist of rawhide, hardly worth Svengali's trouble. "At least he has this big room," he said. "Does he ever get to go outside?"

"No, this isn't his room." The trainer pointed at a crate, hardly a raccoon trap, on wheels out in the hall. "This is his rehab for the day." Staffed as they were, there wasn't much that could be done for Jenga. *Jenga.* She kept saying that word. They'd already tried one release, but their fund-raising was dependent on their conversion rate, and they were always in the red. The tiger park brought in decent revenue, but they had to focus rehab efforts on the cats with release potential if they wanted to renew their grants. "We might have a lifer here."

Lifer stung him personally. He swore at the woman—not out loud. As long as he made sure his mouth didn't move, he could think whatever he liked. That was the deal, that was civil. Aloud, they spoke of Jenga, but in the silence beneath that word stalked the true lion, who would never submit to a name. The large animal in the room was supposed to make everything real and present, but the nameless lion was far larger than Jenga. Rainey kept up his side of the conversation fluently, but he might have been dreaming. In fact he was. A man wilder than himself was putting *her*, face first, in the raccoon cage and . . . he let it unfold, safe inside the quiet of his mind.

Rainey was awoken, some years later, when a windstorm blew down the black walnut where the cat had first appeared. He was in bed and didn't see the wood shuddering and snapping, but he could hear each ringed year cracking in turn, a thunderous slowness, though anything irreversible has its own kind of speed. It was deafening, the noise hidden in that unremarkable wood.

A long limb punched through his bedroom window. The splintered window frame skated away from the house down the slope of the limb. By moonlight, he saw the branch stab into his bedroom, its crazy finger tracing figures in the air. He could hear his shingles sliding from the crushed roof and slapping the patio dust below. The heat of the fall had boiled the tree sap—he could smell it in the strange breeze.

A city forester said it was twig beetle and tree fungus, a combination known as thousand cankers disease. All the black walnuts in Prospect County were catching. Rainey could have spotted it if he'd been paying attention. Half the crown was withered.

The forester told him to have the tree company take the wood to the landfill, so the beetle wouldn't spread, but how was that supposed to work? The landfill was a place. The bug would be restless wherever. Besides, black walnut was a hard, hot-burning wood.

He piled the logs under a tarp. He let them season, purchased a splitting maul. He eradicated the beetles, one stove fire at a time.

The pile got smaller, barely. He tried to measure, by his memories of how high the stack had been, whether the walnut would outlast him, but his memories were as shapeless and fast as the fires he watched.

The graffiti on the Scap was long gone now, painted over, and Prospect Peak looked like it was supposed to again. Maybe it looked even better—bigger, more expensive. Imagine what it would do for home values if they went ahead and painted the whole range. Everyone would wake, draw their blinds, and feel richer somehow, the way love made you feel.

What thing was he spending log by log? Fire was sun brewed out from wood. Wood was hardened air. "You know why we like watching fire?" Janice had said. "That's how all invisible things move. Fire's the one invisible thing we can see." Maybe she'd said that. He still had her copper pot on the stove, to soften the dryness, she'd said. Other than that he couldn't be sure.

Feeding the embers one evening, he saw four thin claw marks running down the grain of an old branch he'd just set into the flames.

The whole commotion was in the slashes: how the great pale cat had stood, or tried to stand, on the branch, enraged from the sting of the dart, how his rage had turned to torpor and the front legs hadn't straightened with the hind; then the liquid collapse of the body, the blind tail searching left and right, and the final tumbling attack on the limb as he fell. It was ugly and chimpish, a lion hanging like dough for the second he slashed the wood, blank eyes mean—then wide with sleep.

Quickly, without thinking, he took the log from the stove. It was hot, but not impossible to hold. The wood had puffed beside the cuts, healed some, but the cankers were there too, dark bruises on the wood, and beneath them, the hidden tunnels by which the beetles spread their disease. Was the cat still in a cage somewhere, confused day and night by the drumsticks dropped through the hatch, the electric lights, the odor eliminators plugged into the wall? Or maybe he was all better now, perfect, restored. Maybe he was wandering Sunshine Canyon, Fourmile

Creek, Bald Mountain, eating squirrels, watching dogs and humans pass by, tasting the puzzled air where the tall black walnuts used to be. Confused in that world too. Life, a foreign land.

He returned the wood, took the spring handles and latched the stove's etched-glass doors, watched the crocuses sharpen against the light. He rubbed his hands together over the copper pot. He couldn't see any steam, but it must be doing something.

THE APRIL THIEF

I.

The First Alaskan Pony Summit took place in February 1993 in a hockey rink in Fairbanks, Alaska. Several hundred hunters, economists, Athabascans, and animal lovers gathered to share their positions regarding the wild long-hair pony population of the Yukon River Valley, and my father was called in to mediate. He described a microphone with a long black cord that stood where the hockey goal would normally stand. Over four days, concerned Alaskans strapped on cleats, tapped across the ice, and held forth while the crowd cheered and hissed and shook handwritten signs. He brought me back a pair of Athabascan knocking sticks and a discarded sign he said he'd picked out of the stands: QUICK HIPPIES, TAKE AWAY MY KIDS BEFORE I TEACH THEM TO HUNT.

My mom was away on a weeklong silent meditation retreat in Taos, and twelve wasn't quite old enough to fend for myself, so while he was in Alaska, I stayed with my aunt and uncle. Every night when he called, they lingered in the kitchen and watched me talk, glancing unsubtly back and forth. They knew something I did not. "How's the hotel?" I'd ask him, "How's the grub?" and they would consult each other's eyes, like kids confirming the details of a fib.

"Here's the lay," he said on the phone after the first day of the summit. "Solve this one."

A millionaire oil driller named George "Believe It or Not" Orwell imports and breeds what eventually amounts to a herd of three hundred Icelandic ponies that he keeps on his sizable ranch outside Fairbanks until, neglected during his final months, they escape and live wild or at least feral on public land. A debacle, but Orwell's ponies attract enough puzzled media attention that wild pony tourism becomes no small industry in the Yukon and Charley Rivers watershed. Meanwhile, large and waste-laying wolf packs start orbiting the shaggy herd. The state, reliant on tourism money, plans to thin the rapidly pupping wolves with some helicopters and large-caliber rifles, but the animal activists get wind and organize an uncharacteristically successful boycott of pony tourism. The state tables all predator control, but now the Athabascans say the wolves are eating the moose that they survive on, the caribou hunters are opting for the thicker Canadian herds, state revenues are way down, and the wild pony population is on the brink.

"Thorny," I said, watching my aunt watch me. My uncle was pulling his ice cream collection—five pints and two quarts—out of the freezer, as he did every night of my stay. "Are there any moms?" I said.

"Moms?"

"You know, 'My babies! My babies! Don't let the wolf eat my babies—'"

"There's a woman who claims she was raised by wolves. There's a pretty good contingent of crazies."

My aunt pretended to work on her crossword. My uncle turned the hot water to the middle where the tap was quietest as he warmed the scoop.

"Whose side are you secretly on?"

"Secretly secretly?"

"Yeah," I said. "Secretly secretly secretly." I could hear two sirens howling—one here in Boulder, one there in Fairbanks. He took a deep breath and joined.

"*Ahwooooooo*—" he sang.

I did it too. "*Ahwooooooo*—" My aunt's and uncle's eyes scanned the room like sprinklers, like they couldn't determine the source of the sound.

"But don't tell," he said. "How're Uncle and Bea treating you?"

"Your brother puts you to shame. It's two chocolates, mint chip, raspberry, Häagen-Dazs coffee, yellow cake, Cherry Garcia, and no vanillas. I got to go."

"That motherfucker. Call you tomorrow."

"You're missing my childhood," I said.

He laughed. "See you Sunday, Wolfboy."

He hadn't been to North Korea or Palestine, but he'd been everywhere else, the great resolver. I had an aboriginal clay flute, a gypsy (I was supposed to say *Roma*) wineskin, a red-ink stamp that supposedly said *Parker* in Chinese. "You know, Parker," my aunt said when I sat down, "it isn't just moms who should worry about children. It's kind of sexist to say that, don't you think so, sweetie?"

"You know me," I said, tucking in. You could do it like jelly bean pairings—chocolate chocolate raspberry, coffee cake, the suicide bite. Every night, my aunt would explain again that she didn't like ice cream.

"He met a woman raised by wolves," I said.

The crossword puzzle where her ice cream should have been looked like a storm cloud, she'd erased it so hard. "Doesn't he always," she said.

Way back in third grade, for a Career Week presentation, my dad had come to my classroom, and my best friend Javier and I helped him do a skit.

"Gimme that orange, Javier. It's the last orange and I want it!"

"No way! I need it! You can't have it!"

"Oh yeah?"

"Yeah!"

"Now, now, what seems to be the trouble, boys?"

Javier, in his shiny soccer shorts, looked like he might spring up, seize the orange, and race from the room—*Hasta naranja, losers!* I could only think about how weird and amazing it was to have my fresh-shaven dad in class, standing back-straight by the lunch bulletin. Ms. Holland was at her desk, snacking slowly on grape tomatoes, eyes glued to him. He had a handsome earnest furrow on his brow—his practiced professionally concerned look—but a grin kept breaking through.

"Mister, I just really want that orange," Javier said.

"Yeah right! The orange is mine!"

The pale navel orange on the stool squinted nervously up. "Don't worry," I wanted to tell it. "It's only a game. Javier and I hate fruit."

Eventually, what he worked us around to was *why*. Why did we want? It's always important to ask why. Javier was trying to make his great-grandma's favorite cake, and he needed some zest. I was supposedly diabetic and needed some sugar. The little grape tomatoes began to understand.

"Okay," I said to my class, "this is the part where it gets really embarrassing, but basically I agree to let Javier have the peel if I can eat the fruit part, and then we both thank my dad for being such a genius."

"*Well*," he said, opening his broad hands. He smoothed the front of his shirt and told us he'd had nothing to do with it. That was the beauty of it. We'd found our own way. The neutral third party was just there to—

"Such a *modest* genius," said Ms. Holland. "What a *wonderful* pleasure having you. What do we say, everyone?" She faced him, not the class. "Should we have Mr. Samuels again?"

"No, no," he said, "the pleasure's all mine," and he walked out with the orange clasped in his palm.

Why was a pretty good trick to have up your sleeve. Normally, when my dad was gone on his trips—which, according to the giant desk-pad calendar my mom kept on the wall of their bathroom and marked with red stickers every day he was away, was about fifty percent of the time—it was just me and her around the house, and things would have been pretty quiet around there without *why*.

"What are you doing up there, Mom?"

"I'm sitting."

"Why?"

Technically she was a Rolfer, but she spent most of her time meditating up in her loft. Whatever architect designed our house had drawn one bedroom with a twelve-year-old in mind—barely enough floor space to fit a dresser and a guitar case, then a long ladder leading up to a spacious, blue-carpeted loft with two half-moon windows—but my mom had claimed the room for herself and I had been given the home office with the French doors.

"It relaxes me."

"*Why* does it relax you?"

"That's a very complicated question," she'd say after a pause.

"Aren't you bored?"

"Sometimes."

"Well, then how come . . ." And so on, until I'd climbed up her ladder and lotus-positioned myself opposite her, a mantra of my own fiddling my lips. *Om oat oat o-pples and bononos . . . Om eat eat ee-pples and beeneenees . . .* until she finally gave up.

"Parker, please. It's hard to levitate with you watching."

I did a double take, but levitation would have been totally wasted on her. She was tall already and no cajoling could get her on the Gravitron.

❊   ❊   ❊

My dad ran a little late leaving the Pony Summit, but he called at seven thirty to say he was at the Denver airport and headed straight for me. I made my aunt and uncle eat without me. "How did everything go?" my uncle asked him, gray voiced, trying to huddle with him by the door, but my dad made sure that I could hear: "Great. Lots of work still to be done, but we made some progress."

"Oh," my uncle said.

Our house, when we got there, was dark and cold, as if emptiness had accreted over the week. He dropped our suitcases by the door and stepped across the hall to the bathroom.

"Brr," he said, peeing with the door open. "Crank the stat. Stat. Put it on something irresponsible. Presents now or presents later? What do you want for dinner?"

"Gross, Dad. Close the door."

"Better hurry if you want to do swords. I'm losing stream."

When he opened the fridge, white light blasted the kitchen. Stark nothing. It was eight forty-five P.M. "Your mom didn't leave us much, did she?"

"I'm calling Child Services," I said.

"Wait. I'll bet you two Athabascan knocking sticks I can have dinner ready by nine."

His trick was catfish. He put the electric frying pan on low, tightened his laces, and sped the four blocks to the supermarket. I was the lemon and ice cream guy. We met at checkout. Vroom, vroom. Bread, bread. Fry, fry. Nine oh five.

"So who won?" I asked when we sat. "Ponywise."

"But you see, my son, there is no win."

"Far out," I said. "So that means we get to pot-shoot wolves from helicopters?"

Catfish fried gold with a wedge of lemon, no napkins, no knives. I couldn't remember ever having dinner with just him. When he was gone, dinner conversation consisted of me telling my mom about Mr. Kutschke's repeated misuse of *comprise*, and when he was back, they mostly talked about me. Had my gym teacher cooled it since their phone call? Were Javier and I doing buddy costumes again this year? Was I interested in youth fencing at the rec center? The Lipinski girls were taking it. It could get depressing.

He pulled the pad of his thumb across the scruff on his jawbone, as if to measure the length he'd traveled coming home, and stared down at a shaggy, drained lemon. "It's hard. The helicopters are grounded for now, but they might be fighting about it forever," he said. "It's just acrimony up or acrimony down."

After dinner I got the ice cream and he brought out the knocking sticks and the sign. It was hasty, big black letters on poster board.

"Quick hippies, take away my kids before I teach them to hunt?"

"Isn't it hilarious?" he said.

"I don't get it. The kids are going to hunt the hippies?"

"No, no. It's like, Don't tell me how to live."

"It's missing a comma. Hippies are neither speedy nor smart."

He looked disappointed. "Your mom thought it was funny."

"She talked? She's not supposed to talk!"

"We talked on the phone. She's going to stay another few days," he said. He pushed his fingertip into the frost on the ice cream tub and plowed a path down the side. "She's working things out," he said and tasted the frost on his nail.

"I'm highly suspicious," I said.

"They can make phone calls, Parker."

"I don't care, the sign isn't funny. It doesn't even mean anything."

Love was harder to figure out, but I definitely *liked* my dad more than my mom. She was very tall and had excellent posture. I'd been looking up at her my whole life and the growth charts indicated I always would. When he stood straight, my dad was almost as tall, but he didn't have a thing about never stooping. With her, it was like one of the six perfections was being violated when she bent over to kiss me on the head—but then I'd feel benedicted for half an hour. When I told her a joke—I needed someone to practice them on—she made sure to grace my punch line with her smile, a smile too beautiful to designate anything but real pleasure. Still, her happiness was that her son was in a joke-telling phase, look at him, and not that the scarecrow had received an award for being out standing in his field.

And when I asked her, stupidly, if she knew any jokes, she said, "Oh no, honey. I couldn't involve my sense of humor with anything like that."

Once, after Javier and I made her take us to see *Blank Check*, I asked her some plot-clarifying questions on the way home and realized she had managed to sit through the whole movie without watching it. Not even the premise had gotten through.

"What were you doing?" I was embarrassed.

"Impressed?" she said. "I have a rich inner life."

At her Taos meditation retreat, they were supposed to be silent for the whole week, but I didn't think that'd be hard for her. It seemed like I'd seen her do it before, while my dad was off teaching active listening to Bulgarians: me sportscasting the acing of my homework and her at the other end of the dining room table quietly attending to her inners. It would have been simplifying to tell myself, as I sometimes did, that my mom was just distracted by the rigors of spiritual upkeep, but what I actually believed was scarier: she allowed herself to be deaf to my jokes and pre-algebra wizardry and one-man badinage because she saw these as nothing more than early experiments in personality conducted by the real Parker, a boy I'd never met but whom she'd known far longer than she'd known me. Whom, in fact, she loved more than me. However delightful I could be, his potential dwarfed mine. And yet I could tell she was anxious for him, increasingly so, for reasons I couldn't discern.

She would ask me about my "novel," as I allowed myself to designate the mystery story that was now nearly fifteen pages long. For some reason, its progress interested her more than the exquisiteness of my science fair projects or my mock-ups for this year's egg-drop lander. I wondered why. Maybe I had a head for plot? I would update her on my detective's latest findings, often going beyond what I had actually written down. Occasionally she'd surprise me with something remarkable—her tip, for instance, that, if plot ever called for it, a body could be disposed of or a treasure chest hidden beneath a tree. All you needed to do was find a big fallen tree with some of the roots still buried, dump the body in the pried-up dirt, and then cut clear through the trunk and the stump would swing back up and hide the corpse. "Old family recipe," she winked—I didn't even know she could wink. Mostly though, she'd ask questions, not about the actual mystery, which I supposed she didn't want to spoil for herself, but about my detective character. They were strange, even clueless, questions, but I didn't mind. "Has he ever had a case he couldn't solve? How's he handle it when he's not ingenious enough?"

After a few days, my psychic powers started telling me that my mom was never coming back.

"She told you that?" Javier said.

"She didn't tell me anything. She's supposedly at a silent meditation retreat somewhere."

"Your family is weird," he said. "I love them."

He had just bought another gerbil, a lady gerbil, so we could go into business, and we were on his carpet in front of the cage, trying to get production rolling. Javier was an animal expert. He'd put himself in the hospital in second grade with salmonella, from kissing his turtle too much. He had the gerbils, the turtle, a garter snake we caught at my aunt and uncle's house, and a dog named Sid with a fur disease that made her breed impossible to distinguish. He claimed she was husky/wolf/poodle. She was there to watch the show too. At my house, we never had any pets.

"Are you sure that's the right order?" I asked. We were propping them together but they wouldn't stick. "Which one is the girl again?"

"Sheila," he said. He was distracted. He dropped the gerbils and turned to me. "Okay, why are you messing with me? She's probably just in nirvana, okay? You lose track of time when you're in nirvana."

Javier's previous animal venture had been a sidewalk show starring Sid, whose principal tricks were escaping from an over-turned laundry basket and expressing "shame" on command by covering her eyes. Javier had taught her the shame trick by putting Scotch tape on her nose and crying, "For shame, Sidney!" when she pawed to get it off. Sid stared vexedly at the gerbils. In a low crouch, nose against the tiny bars, she looked like she couldn't make up her mind what she wanted worse, gerbil friends or gerbil lunch.

"Maybe they can't, you know, with Sid watching," I said. Her tail was whapping my feet excitedly.

"You really have to start watching TV," Javier said. "Mortal danger always turns it on. Which reminds me—" He pulled up the leg of his wind pants and pointed at the hairs on his calf. "All the way around. I'm telling you, dude, the beast awakes."

"You know how I knew when Oma died? How sometimes you know something but you don't know how you know it? And get this. My dad bought *two* lamb chops and he put them in the *freezer*."

"Your mom really likes lamb chops." Javier sighed dramatically and stood up. He was back in a minute with a piece of computer paper. He wrote *Binding Legal Agreement* across the top in heavy pencil and underlined it, looking at me.

"Okay," he said. "What's the very worst thing it could be? Your dad paid Nazi bikers to kill her?"

"Yeah," I said. "That."

He continued writing: *This piece of paper entitles Parker Samuels to 50% ownership of Sid until his mom comes back home. If Nazi bikers killed her, he can have Sid 100%.* Then he signed it with his fifteen-second signature.

"You're crazy. I can't take your dog."

He handed me the paper. "You don't have to take her. Sometimes when I feel sad, I think, *I have a dog*, and it makes me feel better." The wind pants were still bunched above his knee. "If someone mugs you, you can say, 'Mister, please, I own a dog.'"

"I'm not sad," I said. "And I could say that anyway." I folded it up with our secret fold and slid it into my jeans.

"Actually," he said, "in my experience, you're a so-so liar." He picked up the gerbils again and rubbed them like tinder sticks. Sid had a pink-gray fold of her side meat in her teeth and was itching it so hard a froth was forming on her chin. "But, oh," Javier said, "if *my* mom dies and *I* get really sad, then you have to give her back. It's only fair."

"You know what I'd kill for?" my dad said that night, easing another filet of catfish into golden oil. "A little six-string. You still playing guitar?"

"I practice," I said, not exactly a lie. "I practice when you're gone."

The oil popped and he rushed a finger to his mouth. "New rule. Sing for your supper."

So I strummed out my one song in the dining room backed by sizzling catfish, my crackling vinyl. I would have practiced more if my guitar teacher didn't always talk about all the girls that guitar skills would win me. Even my E7 chord was clumsy, but I could keep the beat going, stomp my imagined cowboy boots, and bellow fine.

It's wrong to say we were breaking Mom's rules—they weren't rules because there's no need to legislate the way things always are—but if she'd walked in the following rules would have been instantly instated: no eight-thirty dinners, no discarded sock balls on the kitchen floor, no having the same dinner three times in a week, no high-decibel singing, no in-progress Risk matches left on the dining-room table. Probably others. No singing for your supper.

He ripped a double handful of romaine in half and threw it in a bowl, then joined in on "just to watch him die," and when I got to "that's what tortures me," a kitchen drawer slid open and a harmonica wailed. He carried the next verse, slid it back, and shook some bacon bits onto the salad. I yowled through the final lines, and he clapped with two forks on the edge of the salad bowl, then dropped them in.

I could picture her mere shadow, like Maleficent's, wrecking the party before she even entered the room. And yet, if our party was fragile enough to be squashed by a shadow, maybe Dad and I weren't the bachelor hearties we pretended. Were sock balls supposed to be fun? The whole house smelled like canola smoke. Besides, Mom's wasn't a chilly shadow: it had warm notes—Assam, sandalwood, samba. Dad wiped his mouth and bowed, his only acknowledgment that this was a show.

"You keep a harmonica in the kitchen?"

"And one in my car. Good work walking that bass line."

"There's a harmonica in our car?"

"*Our* car? What's wrong with your bike? Want some early breakfast?"

It was something like that every night. He'd spin a flake of catfish on his fork as an assayer would spin a stone, "Not pale, not brown, twenty karat at least." If I suggested some variation, he'd say, "Catfish puts whiskers on your cheeks," and I'd do my best version of Mom's humorless smile. After ice cream, he'd say, "Christ, Parker, it's ten thirty," like he'd just noticed. I could be worried, I could wonder what had happened to her and why I was being bribed, but I wasn't going to poop the party by feeling sad. I'd seen her calmly adding red stickers to the desk calendar in their bathroom, never saying it aloud, just displaying the evidence in case he wanted to see for himself: Was he a bad dad, a workaholic, an absentee? But here he was, more availably himself than ever—precisely because she was gone. It was riotous and tenuous and would be over as soon as she came home. But that only made me miss her more.

"Mom's okay, right?" I said when we slid over to the map where we were racing each other to conquer the world.

"I'd tell you, wouldn't I?" he said.

Monday, Javier was tardy to World Cultures. "I think I figured it out!" he whispered when he came in.

"What did you figure out?"

"Parker," said Mr. Mracek, *"sheket b'vakasha."* We were in the middle of Monday Newsreel. By the time he'd shushed you in three languages, it was detention.

I got out a piece of paper, wrote *What did you figure out?* and folded it with our secret fold.

I talked to my dad and he thinks he knows the problem, he wrote back. *I just don't know what to do about it yet.*

Mr. Mracek spent his evenings recording three news channels with three VCRs and over the weekends compiled his notion of the highlights onto a single tape to play in our Monday class. Most kids thought it was dull, but we didn't have a TV, so I had to take what I could get. There was something about Bill Clinton's inaugural speech cribbing from JFK's, something about *Dateline NBC* apologizing for rigging test-drives to light on fire—there wasn't going to be a quiz or anything.

Well?????? I wrote, the question marks hastening into exclamation points. My worst theory was coma: He hadn't really talked to her, just to a highway patrolman and some doctors. He was waiting till things were more certain before he told me the whole story. Probably they were moving her up from Taos in an ambulance, so she could recover at home. My dad might have talked to Javier's. He slid the note back.

It read, *My dad thinks Goldbond and Sheila are neutered.*

"Parker and Javier." Mr. Mracek knelt between us with an elbow on each of our desks. "I gather you don't care about the plight of the Alaskan pony?"

The TV at the front of the class swept over a small hockey rink, full of large men in tough work coats, then settled on Gale, my dad's yellow-bearded partner at Collaborative Solutions. "Gale Young, a 'mediator,' was hired to facilitate the summit," the newscaster said. I craned my neck, as if I might look around the rink and find my dad, but only Gale was there.

The video cut to some stock footage of Icelandic ponies swishing their bangs through the snowy pines, grinding down the chunky snow. A chubby man with a bean-shaped goatee and sunburned cheeks spoke a few nervous sentences about controlling the caribou population. A woman with a fleece vest and what looked like a talking stick shouted about cruelty while a small crowd clapped behind her. My dad was nowhere to be seen.

I looked at Javier. He shrugged. "It's quite a complex situation," Gale said.

A month or two earlier, Javier and I had been babysitting each other at my house while my mom and his parents were at parents' night. Javier took the mutual babysitting very seriously and forbade us from using the pizza knife, or any knife, on our Tombstone. Instead he took the scissors out of the pen jar and brought their inky blades down on the cheese, up through the crust, and like that jammed his knuckles in the boiling sauce.

The burns weren't bad, but he thought he should probably put on aloe and Band-Aids just to establish our responsibility as sitters, so we began rummaging around the kitchen, then the bathroom, then my parents' bathroom, opening cabinets and drawers.

"You don't know where your own aloe vera is?"

"I don't know where anything is."

He sat down on the toilet, shaking his head. "You don't even know where your aloe vera is?" Then he pointed up at my mom's stickered calendar. "What's this?"

I explained her tally of Dad's days away. He shook his head again, but a grin crept out from somewhere in his brain.

"How often do you hear them?" he said.

"How often do I hear them what?"

"I bet you she's denying him relations." I could see the grin light his eyes.

"Don't be dumb."

"Are you sure you don't know where *anything* is?"

"What?" I said.

"If she's denying him relations . . ."

"I told you, he doesn't have any."

"I told *you*," he said. "Every dad has some. You just haven't found it."

"No," I said. "Babysitter says no," but he was already heading back into their bedroom.

We checked all the places Javier had hidden his own magazines—under the drawer lining in the dresser and under the bottom drawer—but we couldn't find anything. Javier went through the underwear, behind the bookcase, pulled up on the corners of the rugs. We never found anything like the ostentatiously lit glossies of sphere-breasted women that Javier's dad kept in a three-ring binder in his gym bag. I declared a victory, and we went back to the kitchen and ate the mangled, waxy-looking pie.

"Told you, Samuels men just aren't into it."

But we did find something that neither of us had made anything of, at least not until Monday Reel. At the far back of the file drawer in my dad's desk, we'd seen the telltale staples of a magazine binding peeking out of a manila folder.

"What's this, what's this?" Javier said.

But it was just a mail-order catalog called *International Gifts*—Chinese name stamps, Maori whistles, Athabascan knocking sticks.

"Calm down about the catalog," Javier said on the way to second-period Art. "Maybe they just didn't put your dad on TV. It doesn't mean he wasn't there. Where else would he be?"

"I don't know," I said.

"Do you think he was hiring the biker killers?"

"Be serious for a second." There were pictures of him in Bulgaria and China. I was sure he'd at least been there. "Why wouldn't they put him on TV?"

"Maybe he was pooping or something. Or maybe he's CIA. They don't want to blow his cover."

"Athabascans probably don't even play the knocking stick. Isn't it all tundra?"

"Okay, do you want me to loan you Wrigley too?"

"Is that your hermit crab?" I knew it was his snake. "I think I'll need a two-thirds share."

After school, I walked down the Thirteenth Street hill from the middle school to the Collaborative Solutions training center. There was always a basket of Nutri-Grain bars next to the coffee-maker, and my dad had said he'd leave two quarters for a soda hidden inside the first *o* of the Collaborative Solutions lettering on the wall. I could do my homework and have my snack in one of the breakout rooms while he finished up day one of his medi-ation training.

I was deep in thought and planned to dwell there for the afternoon, but as soon as I cracked my Crush and opened up my purple *Cuaderno de Actividades*, my dad stuck his head into the room. "Parker, yo," he said.

"Dad, yo."

He had a smirky glow about him from people laughing at his jokes and writing down his ideas all day. "Big favor. The young lady for the role-play didn't show up. You wanna help us out? Twenty bucks."

All I needed to do was play a grouchy high school kid who hadn't been going to school. Gale, the co-trainer, would play my dad, and my dad would play the mediation-savvy school counselor.

"*Ya voy,*" I said. "What's my diabetes?"

He glanced at the Crush and the Nutri-Grain. "Your what?"

"My secret motivation."

"I don't know. You fucking hate fucking school. You can make that part up. The crowd is waiting."

He led me out toward a little table where Gale was sitting, the smudges on his glasses visible across the room. If you were going to put one of them on TV, I thought. The conference room was beige all over, walls paneled with taut rectangles of a soft cloth that (I knew, I'd tried) Velcro hooks would stick to. Forty-some pale, well-intentioned trainees hovered readily over their legal pads. I knew people traveled from all over to go to these trainings, but they all looked basically the same: kind eyed in too much sweater, overly multivitamined.

He introduced me and the role-play to the trainees. "Let's pay attention to how we break out of win-lose thinking. Ready, Gale?"

"Dad's ready."

"Ready, truant?"

"Whatever," I said, slouching into my chair.

"Good." Just like a real school counselor, my dad flopped his hands palms up: "So, you tell me. What's up?"

"Well," said Gale, "I'm just really worried that Parker here hasn't been going to school—and on top of that, that he's been lying to me about it."

"I never lied about school being bullcrap," I said.

"And what is it that frustrates you about our school?" said my dad.

"Mostly the bullcrap."

"Go on."

"*You* go on. You go on and on and on." A couple laughs— disappointing crowd.

"You mean you feel bored during your lessons?"

"Bored doesn't begin to describe it," I said to Gale. "Everyone here treats me like a child. It's not about learning, it's about learning to follow rules. Can't I be an adult and make my own decisions?"

"So that's your *mature* decision? Skipping school?" Gale said.

"That's right." I scuffed my feet on the ground.

A hand went up. "Yes, Clarice," my dad said. He smoothed the front of his shirt.

A pretty woman with eyes so blue they looked dopey lowered her hand. "So I notice they've already revealed a shared value. They both want Parker to be mature."

"Beautiful. And how could we make use of this? Thoughts? Yes, Clarice."

"Now you can reframe the truancy in terms of maturity, as a common problem?" She waited till my dad nodded, then smiled back at him.

"Could you reframe it for us?" he said.

"I'll try. Let's see, can you both describe what you think maturity means to you?" she said slowly, a finger on her neck.

"Very nice," said my dad. "So? Gale? Maturity?"

"How about going to school, for starters."

"And *why*?" he said, looking for emphasis at the nodding class. "Why is attending school mature?"

"Responsibilities," Gale said and gulped from a bottle of water. "Parker has to learn to attend to his responsibilities—"

"How about *you, Dad*?" I said to Gale, watching for a flinch. "Does anyone take attendance on *you*? I never ask you if you were where you say you went. How do I know you went to, you know, work, when you say you went to work?" I could have kept going, but I saw everything I needed. Gale's tired eye skin leaked a white sweat as he desperately, silently consulted my dad.

"But I do, when I can, I always . . . I always am at . . ." I looked away at the complimentary muffins shining back at the office lights.

My dad calmly, professionally took over. "The question, Parker, was what does maturity mean to you." He was as poised as ever, but I had him anyway. Slickness was a thin defense, and

defense was pretty much admission. He hadn't been to Alaska.
If I couldn't see it in his eyes, I could see it in Gale's. He'd lied,
and I could begin to reason why. "So," he asked again, "can you
define maturity for us?"

"I don't know," I said.

"Do you have mature reasons for not going to school?"

"Maybe not one hundred percent mature." Let's wrap this up,
I thought. Forty eager peacemakers were nodding and smiling
to assure us three we were doing a great job. *Thank you*, their
eye contact said. *What a pleasure it is to learn.*

II.

My "novel"—if you really pressed I'd tell you—was called
Marshall Slickfoot: Case of the April Thief. Marshall Slickfoot
lived in fluorescent Miami (where I'd never been), not London,
played jazz saxophone, not violin, was friends with Javier Castro,
not Dr. Watson, but it didn't take a supersleuth to discern my
template. I'd established these preliminaries, but neither I nor
Slickfoot could figure out how the month of April had vamoosed
from everyone's calendars—in retrospect an ambitious first
mystery for what was meant to be an extensive serial. It was, I
felt, a riddle worthy of the great Slickfoot—all of Miami toweled
out of their showers to discover they'd gone straight from March
to May!—but, at moments, I feared it was a little much for me,
and I was prone to occasional frustrations.

Frustration meant, for instance, attacking my notebook with
the stapler, then ripping its pages to flakes, then taping them
together and copying my shreds back into the notebook with
penitent tears in my eyes. It was an odd and embarrassing

ritual, but it succeeded every time in transforming disgust at what I had created into reverence for what I had destroyed. Even in the throes of artistic tantrum, I knew I was exaggerating my despair, embellishing it with undue spittle, as if to hurry up the reciprocal self-admiration that should be on the way. It was a good trick, though it did slow my progress.

For some reason, I held it together better when my dad was home, but after frustrations of a certain magnitude, my mom would broach a mention. "I see we're out of tape again?"

"Not so. I have some invisible tape right here."

It would never be during a frustration. It would be the next day, the manuscript rehabilitated, me at the table after dinner, my Pre-Algebra and World Cultures textbooks splayed around me, a bowl of ice cream on top of a notebook. A few days before she left for Taos, she settled at the table and said, "Hey, tell me about your novel for a second." She sat and leaned over her elbows, her Ashkenazi curls hiding her thin-boned fists, and eyed me across my buffet of homework. "Should we talk about it? How's the novel coming?"

"Excellently well, madam."

She waited.

"Well, you see, the mayor thinks it's a masterful April Fool's joke, and maybe it is, but Slickfoot senses there's blood or money on the line somehow, and since Tax Day is in April, he disguises himself as a Libertarian roulette gambler and infiltrates the—"

"—the oil-rig casino. But why do you think you get so *involved* in the story?"

I knew what she was after. She thought I was avoiding whatever preadolescent resentments I felt toward my absentee father by taking refuge in my brain and maybe stomach. My good-student award from the Optimists' Club, the thickening life-saver that hung above the waistband of my jeans, my stalled mystery serial—behind everything was the ineluctable pain of the onset years. Her own grim Manhattan childhood had made a doctrine of teenage misery, according to which I wasn't just struggling to write my story—I was *struggling to write my story*. But it was obviously untrue. I knew who I was and could pretty well guess who I would be: I wasn't the kind to invent gloves that translated sign language into text or solve prime-number conjectures, but I was pretty sure I was a genius for my age bracket, and genius, unlike looks or athleticism, was good for everything. I planned to remain a kid for some years yet, but I felt serene confidence that adulthood, when it came, would be a cinch. That was *my* story. So, sure, it sucked I hadn't yet figured out who stole April or how, but, as my art teacher's Albert Einstein poster said, no worthy problem is solved by the same level of consciousness that created it. Outsmarting Aunt Bea at mancala was one thing, outsmarting myself was quite another.

"We could *buy* confetti, but an environmentalist makes his own." Nothing, not a smile. "Frustration just proves it's a good mystery," I said.

"But Parker." She picked for a second at a rice clump dried into the place mat. "Okay, so what if you can't solve it?"

"Psst, Mom—fiction, not real—I can just choose a culprit."

"But nothing you've come up with yet is good enough?"

"Because, as a practical matter, what I like to do is estab-lish the first three solutions that occur to me as red herrings. Then—"

"Or maybe you think anything that occurs to you must not be brilliant enough?" My face must have evinced a feeling because now she went for it—despite herself, I could see. "Because maybe what the story is really about isn't April's disappearance. Maybe it's about someone clever enough to solve any problem, no matter how unfair?"

Other people's children were fair game for parlor headshrinking, but best practice was to preserve the human mystery of your own. I attempted to convey this in a look, but something must have been lost in translation because she nodded with the gentle smugness of a parent who has said the right thing. She looked at me and then, still looking at me, looked at nothing. "There are going to be some things that don't make sense."

I moved to shrug but found myself waiting for the crouton in my throat to soften. There was nothing to cry about, and I'd officially resigned from crying anyway, but her tone of voice had tricked my autonomics.

"Why does Slickfoot even want to solve the April problem?" she said, picking up my ice cream bowl. "No one's hurt?" Her tone was bright with maternal self-congratulation, our session was wrapping.

"It's what he does."

"Why did he become a detective?"

"We get into that in the third volume," I said. Only a few wet crumbs of crouton remained, and I could handle those. "It's sort of a Batman thing."

"He was orphaned?"

"Wow. Very good, Mom."

"So that's the case behind the case," she said, all significant again. "Who took his mom and dad away."

As we exited the Collaborative Solutions garage, my dad paid me my twenty dollars for the role-play. He reached over and tucked the bill into the *cuaderno* on my lap. He made some crack about unreported income, but I could hear his brain's cassette wheels turning as he replayed the tape and tried to think what I did and didn't know.

I knew what I knew. He hadn't been in Alaska, and now Mom wasn't coming home. I wasn't stupid. I could string it together. Who needed magazines when they had Clarice or whoever? *Clarices.* He drove a block studying his gauges, assuring himself of my ignorance while I reviewed: *There's a woman here who was raised by wolves,* he'd said for her to overhear. Maybe he'd told Mom when he called Taos. Or maybe she'd caught him and fled to the Zen center and he was supposed to end it and he hadn't. Whichever it was, she wasn't coming home now, because of him.

I found the facts of it completely gross and unthinkable and so allowed myself not to think them. But I had to admit Slickfoot himself would be proud of how I'd penetrated this one. I dulled my shock with a picture of myself, Perceptivity Samuels: I imagined kicking back in Slickfoot's Eames lounger with a well-earned ham croissant.

"I'm not sure what you meant," my dad said slowly after a silent block, "but diabetes is a disease where you can't regulate your blood sugar. It doesn't mean secret motivation. Maybe you meant *agenda.*"

"My bad," I said. I remembered how Ms. Holland had stared at him during the orange skit. "I'm so spacey sometimes, you know?" I clapped the purple *cuaderno* closed around my cash.

"You were great. Who knows what happened to our usual truant. We might have a gig for you. Take our act on the road."

"No thanks."

"But someday you should come with. Wouldn't you like to see beautiful Alaska?"

So, I thought, the act is still on. "Did you see any penguins?"

He looked over, askance. "Wrong hemisphere, buddy. You know that."

"Oops. And where's the rumored harmonica?" I asked.

He dug through the console and handed me a little metal wafer. I blew out a dusty jolting bray. "You don't lie," I said.

"Nope." *Nope*—Perceptivity examined the syllable for subtext.

Nope was a soapy bubble. Its denial floated there, casual, coolheaded, certain, then swallowed itself with a terminal pop. *Nope.* Did he mean "nope, I don't lie" or "nope, I do" or both, since "I don't lie" is either true or a circular flouting of truth? I stared at the Hohner harmonica, its two screws and ten airways and console grime—it was really there. I couldn't get my head around it. All this time, everywhere he went, he'd been playing harmonica?

I had to clear my brain. An image of my mother came to me, the adobe chapel where she waited on sore sitz bones while my dad played his Hohner for Clarice. I saw her, my mom, with her daily grains of Zen rice and cabbage, trapped in contemplative silence, able to do nothing but sift feelings. I had to get her home.

In front of the municipal building, women in black on one side of the sidewalk shook keys at a couple of families on the other side waving Israeli flags. The feeble protest/counterprotest had been happening for years. Maybe my mom thought she was threatening him, making him taste her absence. Maybe she thought it was working. My dad honked encouragingly at the protesters and both parties cheered.

"How do you do it?" I asked him. I blew through the harmonica again—a wreckage of lonesome trains.

Nope. "You got to pinch your lips in. I'll teach you. Pinch your lips and hit just that middle note."

One is never powerless. So says the Collaborative Solutions handbook. Power is not a possession but a relation. It's not deltoid mass, not cash in the bank or guns in the rack. Power is transacted, silently, in shared routines and assumed codes of conduct, in the half-conscious consequences that never come to pass. "Even your dog has power over you," the handbook says. "Just think of all you do for him and what would happen if you did not." Parties in conflict should creatively and thoroughly identify their sources of power.

I could throw a fit, melt down or fake a meltdown, threaten to fling myself from the Volkswagen unless he quit everything and brought Mom home. But I felt too tired. Fits were an attrition tactic, and I wasn't much for cardio. I suspected I could still hit tantrum pitch with some reaching, but then what? Then exhaustion and a cry headache and no other card to play. Besides, my parents were obviously trying hard to spare me the tantrum: they'd connived to remove themselves to unknown locations, so that I would witness no stage of the unfolding cataclysm. They were concerned, apparently, that a boy who would punch himself in the head because his mystery novel wasn't cooperating couldn't be exposed to real-world marital strifes. My power, then, the power the handbook would have me "harvest," came from my presumed ignorance. So long as I remained fragile and clueless, their concern would be manipulatable. As soon as I let on that I knew what they wanted me not to, my power would be gone.

Javier and I had invented the secret fold in elementary school so that, even if someone learned to forge his or my handwriting, we'd be able to spot an impostor note—*Dear Javier, I hate you. Go to hell. Signed, Parker*—but no one had ever attempted anything like that. The fold was an adapted tabletop-football fold, but you had to know the right sequence of tucks and turns—when to roll the triangle into the paper, when to flip it over to the back.

I'd left the binding legal agreement on top of my dresser, and when we got home, I saw that someone had finally tried to infiltrate our friendship. The creases were wrong, the final flap untucked. At first I felt embarrassed—Nazi bikers? I didn't want my dad to think I was stupid. But already the tripwires and pull strings of a plan were revealing their mechanism to my mind.

"Going on my run!" he yelled out over a toilet flush. That was the routine: work, run, around eight we did our nightly catfish and ice cream errand.

"'Kay, get fit. I'm going to eat cocktail peanuts and obliterate my homework." I waited by the upstairs window till he'd swished around the corner. Then I called Javier to fill him in.

"Your whole life is a lie!" Javier said.

"Not really. Once she comes home, it doesn't even affect me really. Not directly. It's like a neighborhood crime."

"Who do you think it is?"

"I don't care. Someone in the same fire precinct, I think, but it doesn't matter who. He goes on lots of trips, it might be lots of people."

"Wow. Of course you can have Sid for a while. I got you, Parker brother. You cry it out with Sidney."

"Were you listening?" Crying was not the plan. "Just bring her over around eight thirty."

When I was getting the ice cream restock that night, I grabbed two freezer bags of corn dogs.

"Seriously?" my dad said at checkout, glancing up from his furtive review of celebrity news.

"They're my favorite."

"Whatever. No they're not."

They were Sid's favorite, except she couldn't digest them. The ingredients list on the back of the bags was as long and wide as a dollar bill.

Javier was waiting with her in our driveway when we got home. He sat on the glum little cement wall that ran up to our garage, kicking a pebble back and forth between his toes. Sid sat in front of him, tracking the little stone, her head wagging as fast as her tail.

"Hey, Javi," my dad said, looking at me. "Walking the dog?"

"Just dropping her off," Javier said. He stood, and Sid watched over her head as he handed me the leash.

"Oh?"

"Yeah, we decided Sid's both of ours for a while." He gave me a hard shoulder squeeze.

My dad looked at me, eyebrows bemusedly peaked. "How come?"

"No reason. We're just really trusting friends."

"I see. Well, come in and have some catfish."

"No thanks. I've been feeling pretty sick to my stomach about something this evening." I cut him a look.

"Are you sure?" It was kind of fun just watching them talk, Javier like some junior knight looking up courageously at his ogre, trying to seem stern despite his round butt and round calves and round cheeks. He'd blow it if he didn't leave soon.

"All right. Bye, Javier," I said. He gave me a solemn nod and walked off without his dog.

My dad shrugged, hoisted the grocery bag a little higher, and led the way in. He did not say, "Weren't you going to tell me about this?" or "How long will Sid be staying?" or "You know your mom doesn't like pets." He just furrowed up his face and found the kitchen. I dragged Sid in the door, unclicked her leash, and she bounced off across the tile. By the time I'd set out a bowl of water, nuked two corn dogs, and yanked out their sticks, my dad's face and dialogue were again smooth.

"Always wanted a dog," he said. "Really makes a so-called house a so-called home."

Steam was still coming off the plate on the floor, but the corn dogs were gone.

"Exactly," I said. "Me too." And I waited for the foulness to begin.

Sid played her part brilliantly over the next few days, poor thing, lurked and flopped shamelessly beneath her cloud. For shame, Sidney. Something was rotten at the Samuelses'.

My dad brought home a bag of kibble—the smallest bag at the store—but I kept Sid surreptitiously supplied with corn dogs and pepperoni rounds. At night, I smeared a little of the bacon grease from the gross can in the fridge onto the foot posts of my parents' bed, so that Sid would retire to my dad's room and he'd spend his nights with her stings, listening to her tongue working on the bed post. I did the pooper-scooping, but planted fresh stray heaps in the shadows by the backyard gate where my dad started and finished his runs. The rest I dumped loose in the garbage bin. I enlarged Sid's presence by talking about her and to her. I made him look at her grossnesses: *Dad, is this a tick? Dad, I can feel a tumor on Sid's belly. Dad, look at this cool thing Sid's fur disease is doing.* And I doted and broadcast the solace her ugly love gave me. "Sid," I said, with Vicks under my nose as we fought over one of his work socks, "can you believe my mom's been gone for two whole weeks? She must hate me."

"Here's the lay," I told Javier at lunch. "Three days of Sid, and Dad's wearing down. He's asked when she's going back to your house twice, and I'm pretty sure he'll step in her poop today."

"How is this supposed to work again?"

I didn't get what was so hard to understand, but I explained again: My dad had read our agreement and so knew that Sid was half mine *only until* my mom returned. Via Sid, I was applying external coercive pressure in the form of dog talk, dog poop, dog flatus, dog fur. If he really wanted to get rid of Sid, all he had to do was end his whatevering and beg my mom to come home. Most crucially, he'd never know my diabetes.

"He was cheating on your mom." Javier shook his head, nudged his triangular popsicle up, and nursed the final inches. "How could anyone cheat on your mom?"

"Shut up. She's just tall."

"He's a liar. That's so weird. Do you hate him? You should probably hate him for at least a while."

The lunchroom gabble kept a steady boil. Two tables over, Eddie Mason sat by himself packing the whole hot lunch into his milk carton. He did this every lunch and then in some self-shaming ritual walked around the cafeteria with it, peddling Eddie's Portable Lunches. He'd been a wacko since kindergarten. Our mothers sang backup together in the synagogue and were often mistaken for sisters, or at least Eddie's mom liked to say so. I hated Eddie, not my dad. I looked at my tray. I never ate hot lunch, and it wasn't sitting with me much better than the corn dogs sat with Sid. "Why? What's it going to do to hate him?"

"You're not even angry?"

"I guess not." I peeled the paper from my popsicle and poured some of the red melt onto my tray, put the big fake-strawberry prism to my lips.

"Parker, no!" Eddie yelled. Everyone looked up—at him and then at me. "Don't eat that! It's poison!"

"Don't be weird, Eddie," Javier yelled back.

"Your diabetes, Parker! Your *diabetes*!"

"He doesn't have diabetes! We weren't talking to you!"

"Shut up," I whispered. The pizza line had turned around. Eddie wasn't making fun of me. He liked to be the butt of his own jokes.

"Nothing regulates your insulin like—why nothing, no, nothing, cures all like an Eddie's Portable Lunch!"

People were returning to their Shark Bites, but Javier couldn't let it go. "Don't be mean, Eddie! He's having a bad day!"

"It's two dollars, just two cash dollars for an Eddie's Portable Lunch!"

"Parker is healthy!" Javier said. "Don't be a jerk about it!"

After school, we walked silently to Javier's house. The Boulder sky was perfect, as it seemed always to be. Through the windows of the hospital gift shop, I could see all the cheerful balloons and the cheap, somber spritzes of flower.

"No one took it that way," he said finally. "You overthink everything too much."

"What do you mean? You called me fat in front of the whole seventh grade."

"You're not fat! You're healthy."

"Just shut up."

There was a helicopter parked on the roof of the adjoining hospital building. Some mangled mountaineer or hypothermic skier had been scooped out of the Rockies and flown in. I stopped to watch the pilot Windex his windshields, and Javier swung an arm over my shoulder.

"Hey. I love you, Parker."

"Just give me a minute," I said.

"Want me to tell the helicopter man? Hey! Helicopter man! I love Parker, even though he's extremely fat!"

"Oh, cut it out."

But we forgot all about it once we got to Javier's. As soon as he unlatched the basement door, we heard the strange, insistent sound. It sounded like a VCR guzzling magnetic tape. Javier recognized it right away: the squeaky mewing of gerbil babies blindly drawing milk. There were four little gnocchis, still matted in their slick packaging. Their urgent nuzzling pushed Sheila through the wood chips like a football coach on a sled.

"Way to go, Goldbond!" Javier said. The old rodent stood to the side examining the fluff on the tip of his tail. He seemed pensive about the crowd that had infiltrated his cage. "You dish that gerbil jizz! I knew you couldn't be neutered! How much do you think we can charge? I need fifty-five bucks for a bearded dragon."

You could see in their tiny stances that until quite recently they'd been spheres. Javier petted each one on the neck wrinkle, whispering trial names too quietly for me to hear.

"Can we name one Goebbels?" I said.

"Look at your handsome babies, Goldbond." Once he got going he could mutter to his creatures for hours. "I hope you're proud."

"Don't you think that was kind of quick?" I said. "You only brought the girl gerbil home a week and a half ago. Do gerbils gestate that fast?"

"Gerbils pretty much do everything fast."

"No way," I said. "Dude, think about it. That's why you couldn't get them to do it—Sheila *came* pregnant. Goldbond isn't the dad."

Javier pulled his hand out of the cage and stared at me and then at his old gerbil shivering beside the large pink family attached to his intended mate. "So who *is* the dad?"

"I don't know. Some pet-store stud."

He gave me his best cold look.

"A big bronco gerbil she used to spunk with."

"What's your problem?"

"I'm just saying. Goldbond better eat those babies before the babies eat him."

While Javier tended to the litter, I went to his room and made the stupid Machiavelli diorama Mr. Kutschke had assigned. I dumped Javier's new soccer cleats on the floor and used the handsome Adidas box to stage a few diabolical-looking power seekers—a prince and a president and a rutting buck. It was Friday, the final day of the Collaborative Solutions training program. The newly minted mediators would go out for tacos and drinks. I was supposed to hang out here until six P.M., do my homework, and walk home. I didn't see the point in getting attached to Pierogi, Larva, and Polyp or whoever if we were going to sell them anyway.

Going through Javier's backpack for a glue stick, I found a decorated Altoids tin. Someone had rubbed the silver foil of many carefully peeled gum wrappers onto it and planted green and blue stick-on earrings into the shape of a J.

Javier hadn't mentioned this to me. Through his open door, I heard him humming songs to his new pets. I opened the Altoids tin silently. Inside was a school picture of Carrie Kabela and a candy necklace with a single candy left.

I helped myself.

I thought about it on my walk back home, my crappy diorama catching in the wind: the dog-fart approach wasn't going to work.

I walked home through North Boulder Park where dogs padded after flying plastic discs. Ribbons of silver spit trailed from their mouths and snapped into their own eyes as they leapt and turned. They were elegant and brainless as the frisbees skimming on mountain air. They sprung and curled themselves into seahorses, tried to clamp their teeth into the discs. Half the time, miraculously, they could. The other half, the frisbees bounced off their fangs. No matter how much gas I pumped out of Sid, it might not be enough to make my dad quit his whatevering. With Sid, I had applied force, but force invites force, the Collaborative Solutions handbook says—thus the endless volleys of lawyers, compelling and enjoining, whereas the wise mediator summons a power greater than force: he appeals to the deep values shared by all disputants—honesty, fairness, well-being. That, my dad would add, was how you really fucked somebody over.

I got home at five forty-five. My dad was still out with his new mediators at the salsa bar, showing off his Spanish ("*Pico de gallo*—the curse of the rooster") and making his same lame jokes: "*Esta salsa*"—dipping his chip in the centerpiece cactus—"*es muy picante para mí.*" I'd gone out with his training groups before. They'd laugh at anything.

I gave Sid a pat and climbed up into my mom's meditation loft. Her crystals were in the little bowl my dad had supposedly brought from Shanghai. I held a clear one up to the little loft window so the light came through and I could see the fairy or whatever trapped inside. My mom didn't really believe in crystals, obviously. As near as I could determine she believed in humility. She believed in *I'm no better than the idiots who do believe in crystals.* I kissed the fairy. I still had the powdery taste of Carrie's necklace in my mouth.

Mom's mini shrine—a board propped up on blocks beneath the loft window as if to be karate-chopped—had some old silver thimbles, a glass *hamsa* balanced on her siddur, a picture of me. The picture of me was supposed to be a picture of her and my dad, but I'd leapt in front like a flying squirrel when Aunt Bea clicked the shutter. You could see their four legs, close together, behind and beneath the hurtling child.

At the bottom of the loft ladder, Sid was whining, her dog whine the same as a human whine, but perfected, its pitch wrung for every drip of desperation, like she really believed life and death depended on my coming down there and scratching her behind the ear. Did wild dogs whine? Or was Sid's needy squeal adapted just for me? Her snout's closest approximation of my *why, why, why?*

"Because it relaxes me!" I said. She hung her head, peeked up sadly, and spiraled down to the floor. Her final flop released a heavy lungful out her dog nose—*sigh*—and the little peals resumed. I opened up my mom's siddur and pretended the Hebrew listed off her rules—*thou shalt not eat catfish four times in one week, thou shalt leave no discarded sock balls on the kitchen floor.* I tried to be impervious to Sid, Talmudic, but I found her whining impossibly persuasive. She could have barked an hour and I wouldn't have budged. But her *why, why, why* somehow infiltrated me.

Because I need to think.

Because I need a new plan.

Because things are super weird right now.

Because my dad's being weird about why my mom is gone.

Because he doesn't want to admit he's doing something.

Because that's not who he is supposedly.

So in his silence, my dad was admitting something—to himself if not aloud. Beyond their desire for certain substantive outcomes—custody, cash, et cetera—all disputants want what the Collaborative Solutions handbook calls "identity chits," confirmations that you really are who you think you are. Many parties will happily handshake over a settlement that leaves them nothing but assurance that they're not an asshole. My newfangled buddy-dad/roommate was not an asshole. He was a good-dude dad who would never snub a dog in need of a scratch, who was teaching his son to play kitchen harmonica and conjure dinners from thin air. The noble savagery of bachelorhood, that was his precious chit, never mind what it overlooked.

When he got home, I was at the table shuffling cards, the chips already split into stacks.

"Hey, family," he said.

"Teach me poker," I said.

He looked around. "Okay. Is Javier here? It's not really a two-person game."

"Don't get me started about Javier right now," I said, making my voice weary and rolling my eyes.

"Trouble in paradise?" He sat down and reached for the pack.

"Hold on," I said. "I've been practicing my shuffle." I showed him my riffle and my bridge.

"The Riverboat Gambler over here," he said. "Here's what we do." He started dealing out four hands. "You play yours, I'll play mine, and Josh and Michaela here will always call."

"Who?"

"Josh and Michaela." He gestured at the two empty chairs. "Split the chips."

"Shouldn't we have cigars or something?"

"And be Saint Bernards? What's going on with Javi?"

"The great resolver springs to action," I said.

"Josh and Michaela will call on everything. It'll give you a chance to learn my bluff." He wrote the hands in sequence— high card, pair, two pair, all the way through five of a kind—on the back of a grocery receipt and dealt out the first round of seven-card stud. He held his down cards tight to his chest so his invisible neighbors couldn't see. Sid settled down beside the table, dragged a paw over her ear. A clump of fur slid off and stuck to her pad. "Ante up for everyone, will you?"

"Okay, here it is," I said. "I need you to lie to Javier for me."

"Queen high bets," he said, keeping his eyes down. "That's you. Make your gambit."

I slid two reds. "The reason Sid is even here, Javier came up with this joint custody thing out of the blue to keep me and him, like, bound together. I think he's worried I'm growing up faster than he is and that I want cooler, better friends. He cooked up this whole ridiculous thing. I don't even want to tell you about it—he said he read about biker gangs planning hate crimes and I'd need Sid for protection—but that's the problem right there. I mean, how childish is that?"

"Pair of jacks showing for Mickey," he said and glanced up only as high as his cards. "So then you *do* want cooler, more sophisticated friends?"

"Here's the thing. I already have them. This eighth-grade girl from the debate team invited me to join, but what do I tell Javier? It would kill him." Leaning against the half wall that separated the kitchen from the dining room was the sign Gale must have brought back from Fairbanks and given to my dad: QUICK HIPPIES, TAKE AWAY MY KIDS BEFORE I TEACH THEM TO HUNT. "I was thinking maybe you could tell him that now I have to go to Hebrew school on Tuesdays *and* Wednesdays."

"Inside straight potential over here with Josh. I got squat—or do I? Final card, down and dirty."

"Would you be willing to do that for me?" I said. "I know *technically* you'd be a liar, but it's okay to lie a little bit, right? As long as he doesn't know, you're not hurting anybody."

He looked up and caught my eyes. "Maybe you underestimate Javier. I don't see him objecting to you joining debate. He does soccer, doesn't he?"

"Please, Dad. A little lie to keep the peace? 'Sorry Parker can't hang out on Tuesdays, Javier. He has more Hebrew school. It's really important.' Doesn't the real world run on this stuff? He won't find out, and even if he does, is it such a big thing for him to know you're a liar?"

He pursed his lips and wiggled them to clean the scuzz off his teeth. "Hate to tell you this, little two pair, but I got my flush. I bet two big blues and a red."

"You think I'm wrong?"

"One red, two blues to see my flush," he said. He was poker faced.

"What is that? Twenty-five cents?"

"Twenty-five thousand. Victory or defeat. Call, reraise, or fold."

I walked Sid back over to Javier's that night to return the dog and bring him up to speed. When I knocked on his basement door, he slipped outside and shut the door behind him. He and Sid were very happy to see each other. He put his head to hers and rolled it back and forth against the twin bumps above her eyes. "Why'd you close the door?" I said. "You got a secret visitor?"

He stood. "I can't let the cold air in. It'll hurt the babies."

"Can't we talk in there?"

"I don't want Sid to come in, either. She might try to eat them."

"Sid can wait in the yard. Let me in."

"I would really appreciate it if you would take care of Sid for another couple days. She'll get lonesome if she sleeps outside."

He had his arms crossed over his nipples to keep out the cold, and he stood blocking the door, stern as a cartoon bull.

"Okay. That works perfect, actually. I've got to tell you the new plan. Can I come in?"

"I don't want to be part of your plots, Parker."

"You don't have to do anything. All it is is—okay, basically the idea now is a values-based appeal to his sense of himself as a role model. I think if—"

"Maybe your mom shouldn't come home, did you think about that? Maybe she'd be better off without your cheater dad."

Sid's leash was still looped over my watch. She flopped down between our toes, her old shoulder blades collapsing under her frayed hide. No one had asked her what *she* thought.

"How are the pups?" I said.

"I think you were right. Goldbond tried to eat one. I think Goldbond is really upset."

"I told you."

He sighed and scratched his dog. "I got to go," he said. "Just chill out a little bit with the evil-genius stuff, okay? And be nice to our dog."

I worked hard on my dad—this was supposed to be about debate club, after all—but he proved extremely wily. I'd explain the situation to him, adding on dramatic details telling by telling: No, Javier couldn't join the team with me—there was a GPA cutoff. No, he couldn't handle the truth, at least not without a big to-do—the last time I sat at another lunch table, he'd ripped up the Incredible Hulk hologram I wanted to trade him for, ripped it to pieces. No, I wasn't willing to forgo debate club—if he really wanted to know, the eighth-grade girl who'd recruited me, she was maybe kind of *interested* in me. Yes, Hebrew school was the perfect excuse! I hadn't decided to be half New Age Jewish just like Javier hadn't decided to be an every-other-Easter

Catholic. And so on. He wouldn't lie for me, but he also wouldn't say, "No, Parker, lying to your best friend is wrong."

I gave up sneaking corn dogs to Sid and doting on her. I tried now to make known my aggrieved indifference to the dog. I acknowledged her only with annoyance—*So look who's still here. How's it feel to be a pawn in a game, Sid?*—and would only scratch her when my dad wasn't looking.

"Dad, let's just lie and tell Javier you're having an allergic reaction to Sid, and she has to go home."

If I could get him to take a stand against dishonesty, then what? Like a spell, everything would lift? The good guys would again be good guys and so would have to act like them? "When are you going to teach me how to cheat?" I asked during our poker lessons. "Should I tuck this throwaway king into my sleeve for later?" No inner battle of the conscience ever broke through his glad-dad demeanor. Its resilience proved I was on the right track—maybe. Or maybe, beyond the teachable values, a new adult morality for which there was no instruction lay waiting. Maybe honesty wasn't an ultimate value, and whatevering and prolonged silent retreats were part of a sufficient marriage, or at least theirs. Maybe right and wrong themselves were subject to negotiation. "If you're so ready for mature friendships, then *you* handle this," he said.

We weren't making much progress in our harmonica lessons either. I could pinch my mouth into the right aperture now and blow or suck a single note, and I could, with many errors and no rhythm, find my way through "Row, Row, Row Your Boat," but it would be a long time before I was harping along to Johnny Cash.

I practiced at the dinner table between mouthfuls of spaghetti or catfish, aimed for that middle C while my dad coached. "What you need to help Javier understand," he said, "is that it's not about ditching him at all—keep your cheeks loose. Separate the people from the problem, right? It's not about him, it's about wanting to learn debate. Less spit."

"But isn't that kind of a lie too? It *is* about him." I helped myself to another massive orange whorl of noodles.

"Well, I definitely wouldn't put it that way. Use that left hand for rhythm, and try making a *we-you* motion with your lips. Once you get the hang of things, the fun part is *bending* your notes."

That week's Monday Reel featured a history of the Brazilian soccer team, a local heroes piece on a quadriplegic karaoke host at the Denver VFW, and a panel of pundits speculating on Clinton's ambitions for a Middle East peace conference.

Javier passed me a note. *Did you eat my candy?*

I almost laughed. *What candy?*

From Carrie K.

I drew a few hearts and passed it back.

Parker—did you go into my backpack and eat the candy necklace?

I needed it for my diabetes. I drew a little fat man, folded it, and slid it to him.

He lifted up enough to read this bottom line and flung the note, like a throwing star, at my neck.

"Hey!" Mr. Mracek stood up at his desk. "That's it!" He separated us and gave Javier a lunch detention.

Javier didn't talk to me in Art and was gone at lunch, so I called that night to apologize. I sat on the edge of my bed in the dark and listened to the springs react nervously under me.

I didn't know why I'd eaten the tangerine candy ring. It was stupid, but I didn't know what else to do when I saw it there on top of Carrie Kabela's little pink face. I'd had to pick it up and then once I'd picked it up I'd had to smell it and taste it on my tongue, and the next thing I knew I'd cracked it with my tooth and had to hide the evidence. "You probably want your dog back," I said.

"Two died today," he said.

"Two gerbils? I'm really sorry. I mean I'm sorry about everything. I don't know what's wrong with me sometimes."

"Gusto and Trampy."

I laughed. "I'm sorry, I'm sorry. It's just you always—"

I could hear him breathing sullenly. "Parker," he said. "Will you give me your opinion on something?"

I could hear my dad in the hall—"Gone running, kiddo."

"Do you like Carrie?" Javier said.

"No, I don't *like* her."

"No, I mean, do you think she's nice? I just want my first, you know, I want her to be—nice."

My stomach gurgled. The buttons on my shirt pulled apart and through the gaps I could see the blubber folds of my hunched belly. "You're asking me?"

"You're smart about people. Do you think I should, you know"—he groaned—"*go out* with her?"

What did I know? One morning at seven eleven, I'd been running after the seven ten bus and Carrie Kabela's dad had pulled over and picked me up. He didn't know me. She must have told him to, but she didn't turn around and talk to me as he drove us the rest of the way to school. She just looked out the window and let me puff—which maybe was the nicer thing to do. In fifth grade, she'd folded a thousand cranes for Ms. Mantito's husband who had Lou Gehrig's. She was probably as nice as they came.

"She talks a lot of shit," I said. "One time she called me a curly Jew."

"Really?" he said.

I needed to fall asleep. "Javier, my dad's calling me," I said. "I got to go."

The house was getting dusky and balled-up socks were everywhere. I could hear the dull jingle of Sid's collar coming down the hall. She stopped at my door and stared at me with those eyes made brighter by the dark—a ragged, shrunken poodle-wolf. "What are you looking at, Sid?" I said, and she trotted over to me and put her chin on my knee. I combed her hair outward with my fingers, following the dandruff-pink part along her spine. She held me in those eyes. Her guts were functional again, post–gas attack. She seemed happy enough to stay like that in the dark, so we sat for a long time, regarding each other, her black nostrils wavering in and out, her breaths pressing down atop my thigh. What the hell was she supposed to do? Help me? *Why did I do that?* I asked her—*When is my mom coming home? What's wrong with me?*—but she couldn't help me. She couldn't do anything about anything, but she sat there for a long time, dumb thing, her loose mouth leaking into my jeans, and didn't look away. She was no genius, but she tried.

The next morning, Tuesday morning, I said I was sick. Cunning was low.

"Stay-home sick?" my dad said. He was in the kitchen pouring my cereal and Sid's kibble, already in his professional costume, the thin sweater narrowing neatly along his back. "Symptoms?"

"You don't want me to get into that," I said. I was in my pajama bottoms and his old 5K Fun Run T-shirt.

"I think it's Debate Club Tuesday, and you don't want to deal." He offered me a choice of bowls, cocoa bombs vs. kibble. "Don't you think I should make you?"

"Dad, I'm butt sick. Come on."

"You just got out of bed. You haven't even peed. Just tell him the best edition of the truth. You guys can handle it." I took my bombs. He poured his own bowl and settled in over the comics, dripping on *Hi and Lois* as he chewed.

"I'll just say I got Hebrew school, but you got to hold your end if he asks."

"You don't need to do that."

The milk in my bowl was already an oily cocoa pink. "So Dad never lies?"

"I didn't say that," he said.

The Collaborate Solutions handbook didn't have a section on deceit, though of course it was a means of conflict resolution—probably the most popular and maybe, when the chips were in, the best. Alaska could kill and collect their wolves and say a parvovirus caused it. The hunters and Athabascans would have their caribou herds, and, none the wiser, the animal people, instead of boycotting, could get their kicks raising money for the afflicted Alaskan wolf. Told well, lies cleaned up after themselves. They not only achieved a resolution, they obscured it altogether. Maybe the received judgment that *lying is bad* hadn't taken selection bias into account: the lies that out might do some damage, but of lies that don't, what could we say? They were moral unknowables and for all I knew they buttressed the world.

I posed with Mom's siddur on my lap while my dad drove me to school. "Got my props," I said.

"Hmm," he said, checking his eyebrows in the mirror.

Rabbi Jaspers, who led my Wednesday Crossing the River classes, liked to tell us, between his sips from a giant Dunkin' Donuts iced coffee, that the essence of becoming a bar mitzvah was accepting the work of *tikkun olam*, repairing the world. Gwen Davis had raised three thousand dollars for the red panda, which wasn't even a real panda. My big project was I was supposed to be teaching computer skills at the mental health center clubhouse, but this wasn't Eagle Scouts: the point, Rabbi Jaspers said, was that all our works and efforts contribute to *tikkun olam*, especially the little stuff. The cosmos needed patching up. Kids were exempt, but once I was an adult, I was supposed to go around smudging on spackle with every little deed.

"God lies," I told my dad when he stopped at our spot, a discreet half block from Casey Middle. "Genesis eighteen. He tells Abraham that Sarah's laughing because she thinks *she's* too old to have a baby, but, if you read what she says, she's laughing that *Abraham* is too old. God's like, 'No, no one's making fun of your old-man dong.' A little peacekeeping fib, right there."

"So if *he* does it . . ."

"Exactly."

"And this is how many verses after he drowns everybody and razes Gomorrah?"

The problem—one problem—was that there was no debate team, not on Tuesdays or any day, but I told him I'd go to debate and I'd see him when we both got home, around five thirty or six. That left me with an afternoon to kill—presumably with Javier.

Javier had been relocated to the back of Mr. Mracek's class, and the Snack Foods of the World presentations weren't enough cover for long-distance note passing. By the time I got to him in Art he had plans.

"What do you mean you have plans?"

He sat at the tall drafting table and studied his runny elephant herd. "I have plans."

"With *Carrie*?" I hated it, but I was relieved my lie hadn't worked.

"No," he said. "Matt Zabka invited me to the kickboxing dojo."

"Matty Zabka?"

"Yeah, I helped him with his lawn-mowing service this weekend. He's got a drivable mower. He does like thirty lawns." Javier blew on his elephants. "That's how he bought his drum kit. I told him I want a bearded dragon and he—"

"So you're mowing lawns this afternoon?"

"No, kickboxing. He's a blue belt or something."

Across the art room, Eddie Mason sat alone with his chin jammed against his sternum, water-coloring the T-shirt on his chest. He looked up at me with a pervy grin and splayed the brush hairs around his nipple.

"Look," I said, "I didn't want to bring it up like this, but Sid sneezed up some blood this morning when we were on our way out the door."

Javier jumped off his stool. "Is she okay?" The stool tottered slowly, then rapidly, and went still.

"My dad's taking her to the vet right now, but you should probably come over after school to check on her." My eyes were down. The art room floor was miraculously clean.

"How much blood was it?"

"Probably it's just a nosebleed or something. We'll find out."

"We should call. What if she's—"

"She's gonna be okay, okay? You can trust me. Just come with me after school."

The weird sleepiness passed more easily this time. In Math, Ms. Gilpin asked me to explain the extra credit problem, and there I was, suddenly in front of the class, drawing a little diagram of the three hunters who paid thirty dollars, ten bucks each, for a twenty-five-dollar room at the inn and the barmaid who stiffed them their change. I hadn't looked at the problem yet, but I figured I would just solve it at the board. It seemed simple enough. *If the hunters each got a dollar back and the barmaid kept two for herself, their $27 plus her $2 makes $29. They started with $30. Where is the missing dollar?*

"It's simple," I said. "The missing dollar is . . . wait a sec, I had this."

"Someone help Parker out," Ms. Gilpin said. "Gwen?"

"Sorry," I said. "I think I just had a mini seizure or something. The missing dollar is, uh . . ."

"Bring back the gold standard!" Eddie Mason said.

Eventually Gwen relieved me at the board and silently rewrote the problem. *Their $27 minus her $2 makes $25.* There was no missing dollar. She flicked the chalk down its gutter.

"That's right," Ms. Gilpin said. "The trick's built into the setup. Sometimes the hardest part is just getting the *question* right."

Javier was waiting at my locker when seventh period got out, eyes looking pink and salty. He said Matty Zabka totally understood. He wanted to go directly to Sid—no stopping for asiago bagels like we usually did on Tuesdays. I tried to assure him everything was going to be all right, but he didn't want to hear it.

We walked in silence past the hospital and park. It was March still, but Boulder was bright and warm. It might have been May already. Lawns, apparently, were already getting mowed. "It was just one sneeze," I said. "She's probably allergic to something."

"I know," Javier said. "Cats and dogs can be allergic to people. We're so stupid we think it's just us allergic to them."

"You think she's allergic to me?"

"It doesn't matter. But can we be quiet though? I'm praying."

I told him I'd pray too. We didn't race. We fit perfectly beside each other on the sidewalk. Our paces matched. Both of us clasped our hands behind beneath our backpacks, and I tried to pray, but I didn't know how. The scrap Hebrew I was learning meant nothing to me. I didn't know how the Hail Mary went after "full of grace." *Hail Mary, full of grace, how does your garden grow?* I didn't know what to pray for anyway—Sid was fine. A minivan with a lacrosse sticker on the back drove by, windows full of laughing girls. *Don't worry, buddy*, said God. *They're not laughing at you.*

Yeah right.

Okay, fine, He said. *A little bit at you.*

Hey, question, I said. *Prayer? Do I just read off my wish list? If you want.*

An honorary doctorate before I leave high school, Mom back home, undiscovered sleeper-agent kung fu . . . like that?

Why not? But you know, little tip, sometimes the hardest part is getting the question right.

We were silent the whole mile home, but when we got to my house and I opened the door expecting Sid's paws clicking across the hardwood and tile, I heard instead the familiar, exotic, paralyzing sounds of sex.

We looked to each other, frozen in the open doorway, silently confirming what the sounds meant.

Rapid grunty murmuring. A low human howl. Aching upholstery.

Run.

"Fuck!" I whispered. "Let's go!"

"What about Sid?"

"Sid's okay. Let's go."

The sounds were close. The living room couch, I thought with horror. Through the huffing, I could hear the mournful rise and fall of a female vowel. The afternoon light seemed to pulse along with it, or else some aural hypnosis dilated my eyes. I didn't want to see her. I didn't want to know the face.

I pushed Javier back out the front door and eased it closed behind me.

"Just let me call Sid and see if she's here."

"They'll notice."

"I'll be quiet."

"No," I said.

"Sid! Come here, Sid!"

"Shut up!" I whispered, but he wouldn't. I tried to put my hand over his mouth, but he jumped away and called again.

"Sidney! Come on, Sid!"

"Listen," I said. "Stop, listen. I made everything up. Sid's fine. She didn't go to the vet. Can we just go to your house and you can take her later?"

He stood there puzzled. His backpack hung in his arm. "Why?"

"Because I don't want to listen to that or see—"

"No, idiot. Why'd you—"

"Because I'm dumb and evil and fat."

"You're not fat."

"Shut up," I said. "They'll hear you."

"Okay, great," he said. "Let's meet her already." He rang the button by the door.

I lunged and shoved him away from the door, and he fell on the porch bench, which scraped loudly across the planks.

I should have run, or something, but before I could think, he recovered, threw a hug around me from behind, and began hammering like a woodpecker on the bell. I leaned back into him and jumped and we both fell with a thud to the porch. I rushed to find my breath and flip over to pin his arms under my knees, but he squirreled out from under me and rang the bell again. I grabbed his feet and the welcome mat slid under him, and his long body collapsed onto the dusty planks.

I was on him again, trying to bounce and crack his ribs with my knees, when we heard the doorknob turn.

We froze like busted lovers and watched the door swing in. My mother stepped onto the porch.

III.

"Dear me, Slickfoot!" said the veterinarian sidekick. "You mean to tell me that the entire city of Miami has skipped directly from March to May! It's unthinkable!"

"It's quite thinkable, Dr. Castro. You have thought it already." He motored them through the late spring heat in his all-new silver convertible Chevrolet Impala. *"What evades my thinking for now is how this deception was perpetrated."* Slickfoot counted again: it was the ninety-first day since New Year's and yet, according to everyone's calendars, already May.

"What if every thought I've ever had in my whole life is wrong! What if I've never had one true thought my whole life!"

"Never worry, my dear Dr. Castro," Slickfoot replied. "You see, if you were wrong about everything, then even your wrong-about-everything supposition would be wrong! Therefore it is disproved by contradiction."

"I'm confused," the good veterinarian said, staring into his hands.

"Yes—a more accurate statement. We are confused. Is it truly April? Truly May? Or are calendar designations lies to begin with? Has a hoax been perpetrated? Or have we been permitted a glimpse at the deep deceptions that constitute reality itself!" They raced on, toward the rancho of George "Believe It or Not" Orwell, the millionaire Icelandic pony breeder. He had been reported dead.

I tried out a calendar manufacturers' ploy, a deceleration in the rotation of the earth, a computer virus, a collectively repressed memory, a teasing capricious god, and shredded them all—but quietly, privately, without a frustration. April was gone. It just was. I couldn't figure it out.

"Open the freezer, buddy," my uncle said when I arrived. It was only the gourmet stuff, fifty dollars' worth, at least. He had them displayed in sections: chocolate-base, fruit-base, other.

"What a treat to have you back so soon," said my aunt.

"Just a few days," my mom said again. "We'll see you soon." They had explained it to me many times, meticulously evasive. *We just need a few days. It's just what married people have to sometimes do.* Not only did they feel no need to explain to me the secret undercurrents of our family life, they also, from her first moment home, cheerily colluded to assure me that nothing had been wrong. Maybe nothing was wrong. Maybe if they could fool me, they could fool themselves. Maybe it was both.

My aunt and uncle were delighted with everything. I tried refusing ice cream just to spite them—then gave in to ice cream to spite myself. When my aunt tried to get me to read her the crossword clues over breakfast, I grumbled along.

"Mailbox capacity?"

"Mailbox capacity? How many letters?" she said.

"Aunt Bea, that's it! You're a wizard!"

Yuks.

My pee was bloody, but I didn't tell anyone. I'd come down hard on Javier, when we'd fallen back on the porch, and his knee had knocked into my kidney. I also had a burn from where his sweater had scraped across my neck. He didn't have a bruise or a scratch, not that I could see glancing across Mr. Mracek's room or peeking up from my drawing in Art.

Maybe I was right about the Clarices. Or maybe it was a secret open marriage. Maybe she needed to go off and get hers. Maybe there was group sex or gay sex or they spent their weeks away in drag. Maybe I was a poisonous thing to be around and she needed to go detoxify. Maybe she was on drugs. Maybe it was rehab. Maybe they both were. Maybe it was nothing. Was that possible? That the whole thing was actually nothing? The Collaborative Solutions handbook says that during a crucial stage of resolution mediators must help disputants determine new, shared narratives of their conflict. No single party possesses the whole truth, and so the story of a conflict must ultimately be told together. By asking *why*, disputants expand, and join, their narratives, and these expanded, joined narratives become the basis of the peace.

The story they told me after my four-day ice-cream binge was this: it could be a little "scary" and "hard" to be in love sometimes, and they both had developed ways of "not dealing" with "how much they loved" each other, but they were going to be more courageous now. This was on the living room couch. I didn't want to touch it at all, but obliviously they asked me to come sit between them, and I did.

I could have asked—mistresses? prostitutes? group sex? drug sex? secret families? KGB? The more scandalous and heart-stopping, the more comforting, frankly, it would be. Perversions would imply a normal, and for that reason pervertible, Samuels home life. But it was worse than that. They reached across my lap and kneaded each other's hands and offered a resolution that obscured what had been resolved. The world had been repaired, expertly, behind my back, and beneath its restored surface was the real hurt world I couldn't see. It seemed like a nice family they were talking about, but I wasn't part of it. They might not have been either. They kissed each other's knuckles and assured us all over again.

Back home, there were signs of Sid everywhere. I'd find a thick clump of her diseased fur sitting in my slipper or on the foot of my bed, and I'd miss the poor crumbling dog. You could pet the long white clumps with a single finger, but they would fall apart after a few strokes, their invisible grit sticking to your hands. My dad did the vacuuming, my mom went room to room with a bundle of burning sage, but even still I'd find a whiff of Sid in the air, a streak of dog nose on the glass door, a few scattered claw marks in the molding along the living room floor. The binding legal agreement sat on my dresser, expired, beside my Athabascan knocking sticks.

They asked me about it at dinner, a cranberry roast chicken thing they made together, kissily competing to pronounce cañihua, the rare old New World grain they'd bought in a little canvas bag. "Haven't seen much of Javi lately," my dad said, dabbing his lips with one of the heavy holiday napkins we now used every night. "You guys need a mediator?"

"We're fine."

"I miss him," my mom said. "The afternoons aren't the same without all the nonsense." She laughed. Her new laugh was having a wildfire debut. I had to admit I really didn't know her, this giggler who would get up in the middle of dinner and attempt a Russian kicking dance with my dad just because he kept calling her soup *the borscht*. She would laugh at my jokes now, too swept up in her happiness to bother with whether or not they were funny. Literally I couldn't recognize her—her new expressions didn't match the lines of her face. "You never told me how Javi's mutt ended up staying here," she said.

"He loaned her because—" I stopped. Taos, Nazis, corn dogs, candy, a made-up bloody sneeze. I couldn't get my head around it. What the hell kind of stupid story was life turning out to be? "I don't know," I said. "I'm sorry. I know it's no pets allowed."

I didn't know and didn't really care where he sat in the cafeteria. I'd stopped eating lunch. I'd sit on someone's bike on the bike rack in front of the school and flick my baby carrots into Thirteenth Street. You'd think a squirrel or something would've come and gathered them, but the carrots just sat there for the whole twenty-minute lunch period. They didn't even get hit by cars, and when they did, nothing happened. He came up to me a few times in the halls, but I turned away, and after a few rounds he stopped trying.

My dad didn't travel that spring, not until May. All spring, he hung new hammocks and marinated eggplant and brought home yuppie wine toys, pourers and stoppers and a two-pound corkscrew that came in its own little black box. It turned out he could cook from a cookbook. Anyone could.

"Play us a song," they'd say, a few glasses in, and make up band names for me. *Live from the dining room table, it's Parker Sams! It's Parker Sam and the Caseworkers.* Eventually, I snipped my B string with a nail clippers—*Bum luck, lovers. No show tonight.* They playacted their regrets well beyond my ego needs. Some nights, I could climb up into her loft and slump for hours; they'd never notice I was gone, so dizzy was their meantime love.

But in May, the Second Alaskan Pony Summit came. My dad kicked his wheelie suitcase aside and kissed her for a long time by the door. I didn't watch, but I could hear her shoulder blades on the wall. "Miss you already," he said, et cetera, the whole show.

I don't know if she looked scared and hollow-eyed, or strong and sure, or what, once he was gone. I didn't look. All week, I tried to stay in a different room.

Maybe it wasn't a crisis, his going, I didn't know, but I knew that what the first Pony Summit couldn't solve, the second wouldn't either. Wolves' lives, ponies' lives, natives' lives, cash: no lasting peace or understanding would be found. At best, short-term and provisional pony policies would temporarily contain a conflict essential to the character and economy of Alaska. Wolves would kill, ponies or caribou, as many as they could, forever. The wild state would need to somehow sell *and* keep its wilderness. Natives, hunters, hippies, crazies, why should it ever cease? Nothing had been solved. He'd be back there again before long.

For a little while I'd had Clarices to picture. The conferences, the plates of calamari in the hotel bars. His little jokes, his belt buckle falling to floor after floor. But I didn't know what to imagine anymore. I pictured Alaska: the giant white mountains and choked paths of ice, the monstrous fish in monstrous rivers, the quaking caribou plains. It didn't stand for anything. It was a real place, and that May I'm fairly sure he really went. I pictured him lifting off our gray Denver runway and flying there. His window seat, his Diet Coke, the vast moss of spring tundra, the white and dangerous peaks. I imagined the wolf packs cowering under the sound of his plane, the hundred lone bears that looked up as he flew, new black mud gushing up between their toes. The hunters teaching their kids when to launch buckshot and when to wait.

Beautiful Alaska. Someday you should come with.

Around the time of the Second Pony Summit, Javier finally stopped me. An empty afternoon: I was walking after school along the chain-link on my way to nothing and he ran up in his shin guards and cleats. "Yo, PS," he said.

He had grass stains on his knees and elbows. His legs and arms looked strong, even sharp. I didn't stop walking, but he kept up across the fence.

"How's your momma doing?"

"Fuck off."

"No, really. I mean, how is she? How's your family?"

"Spooky. Delusional. How's yours?"

He jumped onto the fence, cleat toes poking through, and stuck there as I walked. "I have something for you," he said.

It was a good move: somehow I couldn't keep walking now that he was fixed. I stopped and faced him.

"It's not here," he said.

"What is it? An annulment?"

"Don't be dumb. It's a gerbil. What else could it be?"

"They lived?"

"Two of them." He let his toes ski down to the grass, and the whole fence shook. His big eyes poked at me through the diamonds. "I picked one out for you."

Behind him, the team was running and passing in some complex, weaving formation, a bright white ball moving with them in smooth diagonal lines. He glanced over his shoulder at them. "I've gotta go. Come over. I have an extra little cage."

Overhead, a helicopter beat toward the hospital, held up on dry whisked air. We both looked up, and I tried to imagine its view: us, the fence, the shuttling soccer drill, my mother in her loft, Sid snapping at the butterflies in Javier's yard.

I shook my head. "What if I kill it?"

He nodded. "Well, duh," he said, smiling. "You gotta be careful. You might."

SOLIDARITY FOREVER

'd spent the afternoon lying on the kitchen floor drawing
mazes, my aunt's skirts fanning me as she stepped to pat the
thawing fish or tear a sheet of foil. The radio repeated the news:
Boris Yeltsin was on top of a tank, stamping his fists and ending
the Soviet Union. I was only nine, but I knew what it meant. The
grit on the linoleum pushed the nib of my pen and wobbled the
halls of my maze, beneath which, beneath Aunt Rebecca and
me, my uncle hunched at his basement table working on his
equations. "Bart, come listen to this!" my aunt yelled down the
stairs, but he didn't come. "Go fetch your uncle," she told me, a
grin unsuppressed on her cheeks.

The stairs were pocked concrete, steep and the color of brain.
Uncle Bart capped his highlighter, slid his graph paper to the
left and his almanacs to the right, found his glasses, pressed the
two-button sequence that turned off his calculator, and said,
"There. Now what breaks our concentration?"

We climbed. His dry palm scuffed against the rail. I knew
two squares of linoleum that turned the radio to static when I
stood tall, and I thought in that way I could stop the news from
arriving, but neither of them worked.

My uncle nodded at the broadcast and said nothing, as if he'd known all along this was how a true revolution must proceed.

"Where are you going?" she asked as he turned back to the stairs.

"To work," he said. "I have the gist."

Three hours later, when she stomped on the vent in the kitchen floor to summon him to dinner, he emerged from the staircase, smiling. "I have made a major breakthrough," he announced. "A critical insight! But there is work to do and no time to waste. I may have to sacrifice a few meals."

His plan, he explained as we ate, was to dispense with three out of every four meals. He would eat tonight and then work until not this next but the following breakfast. "I'm making outstanding progress," he said, smiling over his piece of fish. "I've caught the scent of it. Everything else is interruption."

"Well!" said my aunt. "A brilliant plan!"

"Won't you be hungry?" I asked. I saw how eagerly she slapped the vent with her house slippers, three times a day, her few fistfuls of curls bobbing along her neck. She did not have a gift for cooking, or even much interest in food, but as my uncle's own equations demonstrated, a party's power is determined by their material conditions, not their principle commitments, and I could see the pleasure she found in summoning her husband to the table. Except for mealtimes and bedtime and me, she was alone.

"I'm hungry to work," he told me.

"And I suppose you'll want triple your dinner then," she said. "I should run and buy you two more filets?"

"Three more," I corrected.

"Very good, boychik," he said, winking. "But fervor is my dinner now."

She looked to me. I kept my head down, but I knew the look. I tidied my fish bones, stacked them in my napkin. "I'm against taking sides," I said.

The table was a circle, so it didn't matter where we sat, we were all next to each other, but I always sat between her knife and his fork. The chair opposite me held nobody, just old pamphlets—*The State of the Union* and *Labor's Labors Lost*.

"Do you see what you're doing to him?" she said. "It is an issue of love."

"Nobody is doing anything to me. I'm not in the middle and I'm not on a side."

"Focus is very important right now," he said. "We can discuss it further at breakfast. On Wednesday."

She pushed back her chair, took my plate, and scraped the fish into Margaret Thatcher's bowl, which sat on the open oven door atop the charred streaks of grease where the dog could reach her kibble and scraps without cricking her spine. The enormous gray animal stumbled into the kitchen and worked at the crumbling fish, her blind nose pushed left and right by the heat.

"It goes dinner, skip three, breakfast, skip three, lunch," I said. "Dinner, breakfast, lunch." I was trying to break one of the fish bones on my napkin, but it wouldn't snap.

"A balanced diet," she said.

He stood and his napkin fell from his lap.

"Wait," she said. "Jacob, is there anything you'd like to say to your uncle before he disappears for you-do-the-math days? What you asked about the radio broadcast?"

He stopped and smiled at me impatiently. I didn't look at him. I didn't want him to know what I had said.

"He asked is communism over," she said. I could hear the gloating in her voice and did not look up.

"Communism is *not*—" But he calmed himself. "History will not cease," he said. "Nor shall work." And he was gone.

We all believed in the importance of Uncle Bart's work—he was, as I understood it then, mapping the progress of Marxism and proving by math that it would prevail. When he was a young man, my aunt liked to tell me, manufacturers of missiles and computer missile systems had tried to recruit him, but instead he had devoted himself to the cause. I was not permitted to disturb my uncle, not even to show him how dividing by zero made the pocket calculator display our middle initial, but on rare evenings he would bring some graphs and equations upstairs and slap them on the table in a triumphant sweat. They were cryptic to me, but I imagined his math coaxing history forward toward the revolution, after which his attention would be free.

I knew, though, that Uncle Bart's work was not actually progressing so well. While Aunt Rebecca cooked or knitted or walked her dog, I would lie, weak with summer, on the kitchen linoleum and listen to him through the vent: "Yes, Bartholomäus, very true, yes, but this tells us nothing!" Or "The thousandth time! Do you have some affection for the mistake!" It had been no different the afternoon Yeltsin mounted his tank and Uncle Bart announced his critical insight. I could hear his papers crumpling. "It does not hold! It does not hold! It does not hold!"

We all three looked like communists. Bart was strong, but not in the American way: I'd seen him carry our chest freezer up the stairs by himself when it was choked heavy with frost, but his body stayed lean and small as a drawer hammer. Big veins bound his hands and muscle to his heart. He never got angry because when he got angry the might of history raged in him. He had split our single table leaf with his fists, which could stamp, I'm sure, twice as hard as Yeltsin's. Bart's father, who had been in Buchenwald when Bart was a boy, had emerged a communist, so communism was locked in our bones, his and mine. Rebecca was a communist too, but by choice. She wore no makeup and no jewelry except a long pin through her hair, which I assumed was a weapon of the revolution. Someday, I figured, she would ram it through the president's eye. She was stocky and swift, her scribble of hard curls bounding to keep up with her as she hefted her pots across the counter. "We'll never get equal pieces till we all own the pie," she said, but I didn't need it explained.

Our basement was stocked with six months of food—mandarin oranges, navy beans, and mustards—five-gallon buckets of flour and oats, the chest freezer where we kept our soup meat and the plastic bag with the stock certificates Bart's equations had told him to buy. Three walls of nonperishables peered over Bart bent at his small table, his pencil tracing indices of class power as they rose and fell across his yellow graphs and illustrated how the struggle would progress. We stored food in the basement because, according to Bart's equations, there would be a restabilizing period after the revolution during which food distribution and agriculture itself would need to adjust to the new economy, and he wanted the Meirs at least to be prepared. We were—and had been for a long time.

There too awaiting the revolution was a six-month supply of my aunt's hormone pills. She was a survivor of uterine cancer, and a cache of spare estrogen rested in tall orange pill bottles beside our jams to preserve her smooth cheeks for our utopia. After my uncle had descended again to his basement, my aunt put a tight hand on the counter and looked around her kitchen. The greasy radio, the open oven, the pan of ruined foil. Her eyes settled finally on the red pill waiting on her plate. She took one with every meal. "Tell me about your cancer," I said. I knew it calmed her to talk.

She filled a glass and watched the trapped air slowly rise from it. "Cancer? I destroyed cancer."

"But that's for your missing ovaries?"

"Your uncle likes me dollish."

"Explain it to me again," I said, and she did, as I dried the dishes and put the kettle on for our story-time tea, how before I was born she got very sick and they took out her uterus, where the baby grows, which was called a hysterectomy, and her ovaries, which was called an oophorectomy. "I lost my oomph is the delicate way your uncle puts it." She laid a hand across her lost oomph as the kettle yowled.

I liked to hear the story of her cancer because it proved she was not my mother. I knew she wasn't—my mom had been Bart's half sister, who died before I could remember—but the red pills proved it was true: she provided for me in every way a mother might, but she was not my mother. I was not sure—I am still not sure—what the difference might have been, but I knew our loyalty, like hers and Bart's, was chosen. There were old pictures of Bart and her from their courtship, their arms locked in front of factories and courthouses, lying foot to foot to block bulldozers. I loved her too and thought I always would, but it was only a promise we'd made.

That night, story done, tea gone, I tried to count myself to sleep. To a hundred by ones, to two hundred by twos, and so forth, like my uncle had taught me long ago, but it only woke me up. Marked off in fives, a count beats with a brighter snare—twenty, twenty-five, thirty, thirty-five, like Yelstin stamping his thigh—and the rhythm grows louder and more assured as the stride is lengthened. "Yes, boychik," Bart had said when I showed him I could count by tens and twenties. "Hundreds! Thousands! But can you count by halves? Can you count by thirds or tenths or hundredths?" And a despair opened in me: the confidence that had carried me to a thousand washed out between zero and a half, as if along that channel a thousand drains, and drains within drains, had been unplugged. "It's okay, Jakey," my aunt had said. "Jacob, it's nothing," caring but not understanding or caring to understand my fright. Ear to the dark, I knew what had come unstopped beneath our house. *It does not hold, it does not hold, it does not hold.*

The next morning as she oversaw our oats, I decided I would show my aunt my linoleum patterns. My uncle had not emerged.

The linoleum was a grid of small brown and white squares with grimy tan borders, and so far I'd discovered seventeen ways of seeing the kitchen floor. Each new way earned a wish, and I'd saved all seventeen wishes. There was the basic way, just little squares everywhere. Next, Fours, and then Nines, border squares wrapped around a center square, and Graveyard, a field of plus signs everywhere. Daisies, Diamonds, Chain Links, and Tic-Tac-Toes. Those were the easy ones. I could turn one into the next with my eyes or make the Nines twinkle by shifting the center square. Waffles, Up-Stairs, Down-Stairs, Pumpkin Teeth, Pyramids. The hardest to see were the swastikas, but I could do it if I focused: Good Swastikas and Bad Swastikas, twisted into one another. I could feel the difference between them.

"Want to see something?" I asked her. She was sorting old mail, glancing at her newsletters and coupons in the oat steam before placing them in their stack.

She looked at me with my skinny legs crossed on the tile. "Is it mouse craps? I swear—"

Drawing with my finger, I showed her the first few patterns, the easy ones.

"Daisies?" she said. "What do you mean daisies? I'm losing my stomach."

"I know!" Nausea was part of it. I was delighted she understood. "Can I tell you a secret?"

"You used to tell me all your secrets."

"Secretly, I think that when I finally look at it right, in the right way, secretly I think that I'll fall through." I was whispering. "It'll open, and I'll fall in between."

"Jesus," she said. "Tell me you don't really think that." She resumed snapping the mail into piles while the oatmeal hissed.

"Maybe I think it but don't *really* think it."

"Jesus Christ," she said. She handed me my pile, which was the junk-mail pile.

"There are swastikas too," I said. "You can't see them, I bet, but there are swastikas on your own kitchen floor."

She looked at the floor for the length of a sigh to see if it would do anything, her eyes pinched, as if she'd suspected swastikas all along. Then she turned back to the popping gruel. "You used to have such nice secrets," she said.

"I did?"

She looked at me and my stack of furniture coupons. "You used to say, 'Do you want to know a secret?' and I'd say, 'Of course,' and you'd say, 'Come here—'" She tapped her wrinkling lips and leaned in toward the oatmeal to hear its secret. "'I love you, Aunt Rebecca,'" she whispered.

"Why was it a secret?"

"It was *our* secret. You used to have such nice secrets. Now you're getting too smart."

"I know," I said. "I still love you though."

"*Still?*" she said, scooping my bowl. "Still! You weasel. God praise your perseverance."

I decided I liked it that she didn't understand. I didn't understand it either. When I knew a pattern, I could fix it in my mind and it would spread across the floor. Everywhere I looked, Daisies would bloom. The linoleum ended where the living room carpet began, but from where I sat, I saw the lines extending invisibly through the empty doorway, parting the carpet nubs into strips and squares. If my eyes were better trained I could have counted how many Graveyards it was from the sink to the couch or the closet or to the mailboxes outside across the street. It frightened me how a grid would extend forever. I told myself maybe it couldn't spread outside walls or couldn't cross streets, but a grid would reach through any line I tried to draw around it, until I had to admit that everyplace, no matter how long my life or where it took me, even across oceans, I would always stand on some coordinate of my aunt's beige kitchen floor.

But I thought if I could learn the right shape, it would break the grid. It happened already for brief instants with the larger shapes I knew. I'd flex my eyes and focus all my mind on a five-by-five, but the square would begin to shift and slide, and I'd get lost. That was how it felt—like the floor twitched under me and somehow I slid with it, through a secret space that had to be outside of what the grid could touch.

I spent whole afternoons trying to enter that secret space and watching it slip away. The encyclopedia said linoleum was squeezed oil and rosin and wood flour, and I felt I had in my power ways of seeing that would turn the floor again into a gauze of clear amber and dust. When I found the right pattern in the tiles, maybe its shapes would skate away from each other, maybe between the keys of lines and squares new light would flood my eyes, and I would be able to slip past the floor into the secret other space.

Every pattern scattered differently. I'd clench my eyes to clear them, lie down as low as I could beneath my aunt and her radio, and listen to my uncle struggling underground.

I spent a lot of time thinking about that other place and trying to get there. In dreams, whole territories you've never seen are somehow known to you: it was like that—except before the dream. If I'd been there before, I couldn't remember it, but I could remember remembering it—a memory told to a memory, but not to me. Maybe it was only inches away, on the inside or other side of everything, if I could only penetrate my senses, the inner thing this world was wrapped onto. Or maybe I was in it already, unable to tell because my eyes threw up sights that fooled me blind.

There was no name for it. It was private, I didn't need a name. Call it the There, my There. It wasn't an imaginary world because I didn't let myself imagine it. It was big, perhaps endless, but mine—others' too perhaps, but even so my own in a way that this world couldn't be. Whatever it was, I couldn't get there. I'd found no stable entrance, but I was looking: at the back of our cabinets, through the tears in our carpet, through the kitchen floor.

Rebecca and I missed no meals. "Lunch, Jacob!" she would call loud enough for him to hear. "A little lunch for the lumpen."

When Wednesday's breakfast finally came, my uncle still did not climb the concrete stairs. My aunt stared at her bowl till a crust cooled over her oats.

"Ask me how I feel," she said. August was almost out. After Labor Day, school would start and she would be alone during the days.

"How do you feel?"

She had stepped out of her slipper and was scratching Margaret Thatcher with her toes. Even the dog looked like a communist, shrouded, ragged, aggrieved. "Someday there will be folk ballads. 'Brave Bart the Breakfast-Skipper.'"

"Should I bring him his bowl?"

"You see? A loving boy deserves to be loved back."

"Breakfast is the most important meal," I said.

"And these are your breakfast years. I won't pretend I don't worry."

"I'll just bring it to him."

"No, Jacob. Let him bluff." The oats were cold and clotted solid anyway.

At last she halved a grapefruit for us to share. It had always been a problem at breakfasts what to do with the fourth half of grapefruit. Mathematically, it was better now, but I knew not to mention math.

"I guess there's food in the basement if he needs," I said.

"No," she said. "He wouldn't dare."

An important dispute was underway at the Coors factory, which was a short bus trip from our house, and most days after breakfast, my aunt and I gathered our picket signs and stood outside the cement brewery turrets, shouting labor anthems at the trucks that rolled past. The workers weren't rallying—they didn't even have a union—so for the meantime they relied on us to broadcast their oppression.

"If you start feeling sorry for yourself, think of the brewery kids. Work at Coors and *contractually* you neglect your children, the swing shifts they run. Your uncle is neglectful by mere disposition."

She would shake her sign beside the main drive while I marched mine back and forth on the factory's endless sidewalk and executed my about-faces. I tried to believe that it wasn't me marching, but the earth, like a giant ball, rolling beneath me. There was a place, a secret coordinate, where I was still.

"Why don't you stay over here?" she said. "Is it so boring by me?"

"I like to march."

"You look ridiculous. Come sing with me. One more chorus, then some lunch."

I rolled her toward me, pulling the earth back under my toes. It worked for a couple steps: I reached a cracked white sneaker forward, planted it, and rolled the square of sidewalk underneath behind me. Then, as always, the wind and sound broke through, and I was in the air again. I skipped to her, flapping my sign, and we sang:

> When the union's inspiration through the workers' blood
> shall run,
> There can be no power greater anywhere beneath the sun;
> Yet what force on earth is weaker than the feeble strength
> of one,
> But the union makes us strong.

After protest, we borrowed newspapers from the bagel franchise. "A person should read at least three newspapers a day," she said. "Chomsky reads twenty-five."

I read the comics on the bus. The three papers all serialized the same strips: Dagwood, late for the same workday, crashed into the same mailman, scattered the same mail. At home, a note was waiting on the counter: *Babushka, I have dulled my appetite and sharpened my focus. Till bed, your B.*

She dropped the day-old bagels beside the note.

"How do you feel?" I said. She didn't answer till I'd repeated it twice.

"Please, Jacob," she said. "Don't make a monkey of me."

When the three of us finally met again, my aunt announced over crumbling cheese sandwiches that alongside my uncle's hunger strike she would be undertaking an auxiliary boycott of her own. For as long as he could do without his meals, she could spare us the expense of her hormone pills.

It didn't make sense to me. "Isn't it medicine?" I said.

"And do you know what will happen?" she said, looking at him. "I will grow a beard, as thick as Karl Marx's."

I tried to reason out how this would help and whether there was something I should now give up too. My uncle looked confused himself. He studied her and she stared back twice as hard. "Will you really grow a beard?" I said.

"No," he said, and she said, "Yes indeed." I touched my face and looked at hers. It didn't seem any more impossible than a beard coming out of my face.

"You know, Jacob, I was a very shiny penny once, and your uncle, he clung to me, like no one else should even look. I am happy to keep myself girlish for a husband who sits down to breakfast with me. But if you treat us like old rags, well then—"

"Will the cancer come back?" I said.

"No," he said again, and she said, "We will see."

She would take her pill when and only when he ate with us. She seemed unconcerned, almost eager to turn ugly, but I could see the sleepy cancer cells emerging again from wherever they'd been hidden, and I made surreptitious tallies on my uncle's graph paper after each meal in case someday the doctor would need to know—pills taken, pills skipped, two rows of lines on his yellow grids. *I kept track*, I would tell the worried doctor. *She took forty-one pills and skipped a hundred twenty-three.*

Thank you, Jacob. This is indispensable. With this, we can surely devise a cure.

It was equally a tally of the meals my uncle missed, and if my aunt found it, I knew she'd flap it in his face, as she had the report card that said I struggled making friends. So I hid my records by turning them into mazes. The tallies marked off corridors, which I extended down the page, the pills taken forking and turning to meet the pills skipped. Each week's ledger covered a new sheet, which I'd hide with the pamphlets on the empty chair. *It's all right here, doctor. Let me show you how to decode.*

After our Labor Day protest at the Coors brewery, fourth grade began, and I looked for more clues there. There were sheets of graph paper stacked in baskets. The recycled pages were rough and tan yellow and would compress a little when I pinched them. All the same patterns were here.

"Can anyone tell me what's wrong with this map?" Ms. Muldoon said on the first day of school. The bottom edge curled up because the map had been rolled all summer. Her hand floated over the big purplish pancreas in the upper right. "No one? This here, the Ukraine, declared independence from the USSR two days ago." She wore a headband and a floppy cotton dress, and was young: old enough to teach fourth grade, but too young to be our mother. I wondered if she was a shiny penny.

"Tonight, tell your parents about the Ukraine. This year we're going to share what we learn." I pictured my uncle, right then at his own desk, holding his skull over his almanacs with two fingers and a thumb. *Neither the map nor the Soviet Union is wrong!* he would have shouted, and split the desk between his fists. The map swung as Ms. Muldoon stroked the Ukraine with her small bright hand. Then she gave it a tug, and the obsolete world let out a little scream and rolled itself away.

"Jakey," my aunt said when I was home from school. "Pork chops. Go get some mustard from the basement."

"But that's for the revolution," I said.

"If the thinker objects, tell him to come up and discuss it with me."

I worried about disturbing him, but he didn't seem upset to see me. "Hello, boychik," he said. "So you've come to join the underground?"

"I guess. Rebecca said she needs some mustard."

"Oh, and don't you think she has plenty enough mustard?"

"I don't know. She said she needs some."

"Always listen to your aunt, Jacob. The yellow? Or the bourgeois?"

"It's for pork chops."

"The bourgeois." He handed me a jar. "Tell her I'll give her some more mustard later."

"Okay." I stayed watching him.

"Well?"

"School started today," I said.

"The fourth grade. A big poop now."

"Almost. Except for the fifth graders."

"What does one learn in the fourth grade? Anything revolutionary?"

"Probably. Ms. Muldoon is really nice. She's dynamic."

He laughed, which meant I earned a wish. "Is that so?"

"I think it is. We're going to make noodles from dough."

"They prepare you for a life of meaning, I see. Come tell me when you've learned something to serve our cause."

I said nothing about the Ukraine. Upstairs, my aunt was peeling potatoes over the sink, tempting the knife with her thumb. "Will this cut the mustard?" I asked.

"Isn't your uncle funny," she said. "Any other messages? Did he object?"

I put the jar on the counter and stood on the step stool to kiss her cheek. "Smells wonderful, Rebecca."

"Nice try, weasel."

"Never mind." I sat on the floor.

"He didn't object? He must be hungry. Did he look hungry?"

"He said he'd give you some more mustard later."

"And what do you think that means?"

"I don't know. It's about sex, right?"

She laughed into the sink. "Let's hope not," she said.

At dinner, her knife cut through her pork chop in two strokes while mine had to work back and forth. That was how I knew she was angry. "Delicious," I said after a while, patting my belly. It was. I studied the scorched mustard, its broiled brown, the craters where it had bubbled away, and, guiltily, I tasted what was waiting in it. A hope, a promise, a revolution—I didn't know what it was or whether it had expired, whether it was dangerous for me to eat. Maybe she tasted it too. In factories, identical jars were filling with identical mustard, hundreds every minute, conveyed on toward infinity, but no mustard would ever be this mustard again, and we were eating it alone.

She sent me to the basement every afternoon, for a can of black olives or tomato soup, a few cups of flour or a box of matches. It was her putsch. I knew what she was doing.

"Your book light needs triple-As," she said at bedtime. "Will you run down?"

"It's on."

"It's dim."

"We could turn on the lamp."

"Two geniuses! The lamp won't fix your batteries."

"They're for the revolution."

"A revolution comes, you'll take them back from your book light. Hurry up."

I waited for my uncle to refuse, to look up from his table with cold rage in his eyes and hiss, *You want that we should starve?!* a thousand years of suffering in his voice. But he did not. He was starving now. There were moments when his flesh would disappear and only his skeleton would be there beneath the bald bulb, his arms clutching at his ribs. "Has the dynamic noodle taught you anything revolutionary today?" the skeleton would say, joking or else pleading for help.

I took the batteries to her in my room and she sat there rubbing them with a thumb. Rebecca was changing too. The natural pink that clung to her cheeks when she laughed or yelled was now always there, even when her face was cold. And whiskers were starting to poke through, on her chin and upper lip. I knew she had noticed them because as she sat there clutching the batteries she ran her empty hand absently across her face until she realized what she was doing and looked to see if I was watching.

"What are you smiling at, weasel?"

"I wasn't smiling," I said. I wasn't. It was a cancer symptom for all I knew.

"Someday you'll find it unforgivable what your uncle's doing."

"I forgive him."

"You can't. You don't even know what he's done yet," she said, falling quiet.

"I think you can forgive anything if you want to."

She rubbed my knee as if to say the idea had been tried before. "When you were a baby, he worried about you constantly. *This thigh has three creases, and this one only two, babushka*— you had more doctor's appointments than me." After a few attempts she got the batteries oriented, and the book lamp put lumpy shadows on her face. She looked at me and whatever she saw made her sad. I didn't know why I made her sad, and I didn't like it. Her crumb brown eyes were wet and gleaming, and she said nothing.

"I'm okay," I said. "Stop it. I'm okay."

When I woke that night in the heat and the dark, my aunt was still there with me, sleeping against me in my little bed. She'd filled the room with her breath, her heat and body smell. The whole room sank toward where her red nightgown weighed on the mattress springs. She looked peaceful, unarmed, her chin nosing against my blanket, but I knew it was another stratagem, her sleeping there. Through the gaps in my dreams, I could remember she'd slept in my bed before.

She was up before me in the morning and said nothing, and the next night she was back in her own bed. But it was enough. Her humidity stuck in the heat. She'd flushed and sweated, and clutched me. Alone in the dark, I stared at my upside-down map of the world, the ivory whistle that had escaped with Bart from Germany, the hanging spaceship I'd made from coffee cans and foil—all of it had her skin cells, her smell. There was no way to wash it off. But I'd let her hold me. Most of us don't learn what that's like until we're older—to be held by sleeping arms, arms that can't pull or lift but still can hold.

My mazes began to assume a similar shape. I wanted to know what it meant.

Every day I drew three new paths, one from the top of the page if he had eaten and she had taken her pill, otherwise from the bottom, turning my pencil and turning the graph paper on the kitchen floor until the pencil tip was dizzy and lost inside its labyrinths and I had to pick up the sheet to see which side was up. So I didn't understand why the same spiral fingerprint emerged in maze after maze. I knew it had something to do with the ratio I was illustrating—one to three, the buried fraction my mazes mapped and hid. One to three, two to six, three to nine, twelve, thirty-six, till I could be lost inside something small and simple as a third. The paths that guided my finger turned and twisted and covered every square as they rooted about methodlessly for some way off their page. I traced each path, but they didn't lead to anything that I could see. Then I hid them among my uncle's old papers where they wouldn't be found.

"And this, *this*, is your crucial insight!" I heard my uncle through the kitchen vent as I drew. "Chasing your clever tail!"

"We're learning about the sperm and the egg this year," I announced late that fall, when he appeared for breakfast one morning. I reasoned if there was anything revolutionary in the fourth-grade curriculum, anything to serve the cause, this was it. I watched my uncle's forehead, but the wrinkles didn't rise.

"You already know all that," my aunt said.

"Did you know there are a million sperms on the tip of a pencil and only one of them is you?"

"Please, Jacob. Don't be gross."

Steam rose from the boiled eggs my aunt set before us in bowls. Over the months of his meal strike, my uncle's arms had become thin as his wrists. He tried to saw through a shell, but the knife slipped, plinked the bowl, and fell. "Give me that," she said.

"Is one out of a million a miracle?"

"From a probabilistic point of view, it's impossible that any of us exist."

She took his bowl from him; the dog squealed under her toe. "I exist. Jacob exists."

I was worried she wouldn't give it back to him, but at the counter she sheared caps off his eggs with a breadknife and opened their soft-boiled curds into the bowl. He reached up for his breakfast, lowered it safely, and began chasing the mysterious soup with his spoon. "One microscopically improbable event divided by all the chaos of biology and history and cosmology. One over the infinite—the chance of your existence is indistinguishable from zero."

"This explains it, does it?" she said. She had not sat back down. "Here I am. Here I am except I don't exist?" If she left him, as she sometimes threatened when she was in this tone of voice, I knew I would have to go with her. He knew it too, and all he had to do to stop her was eat.

"Is it sort of like my dad?" They turned to each other, then to me. "How I don't have a dad, except I had to have one. So he exists and also doesn't? Are we like that?"

"Wonderful," she said, but she didn't storm away. "Do you see what you're doing to him? I'm the one who deals with it when he gets upset. I can't just say, Jacob, you don't exist."

"I'm not upset," I said. I wasn't.

"Yes, Rebecca, what would we do without your equilibrations?"

"And how long do you think you could make it without me? A week? A month?"

He had stopped eating and listened. A film began to wrinkle atop his yolk. I understood what it meant, one over the infinite. I was the one and, just as I'd suspected, the infinite was right there, right beneath me all this time.

"It would be a loss beyond my powers of grieving," he said. "Don't tease me with these things."

"You'll come upstairs, and Jacob and I will be halfway to—" But she couldn't even come up with a place.

"Halfway to nowhere!" I said. I felt I had determined something. One sperm and one egg met in the numerator, where they hovered over every other world that might have been.

"Shush," she said. "Don't joke. It's not a game."

She was there again when I woke that night. My right arm was under hers. She held my hand in a little pit of heat made by her breath and chest. I tugged on my arm, but she slept tight. The room was too hot, and her smell was thick over everything. I leaned up to see her face. She looked calm and unburdened. I dared myself to wet the bed, but I couldn't. I would have wished myself There, with all my wishes, but I knew it wouldn't work. I didn't know why I comforted her, but I did. There was peace for her there. It wasn't my choice.

I heard them sometimes, off in the dark, never mind his frailty or the whiskers she grew. I knew what they were doing, but not why. They couldn't have kids. Why would they do that if they couldn't have kids? It didn't sound like pleasure. It sounded like desperation and work. But I sensed it wasn't the one sperm and one egg that mattered, it wasn't the top of the fraction where this world lived—it was the underside of the fraction, the infinite that held up the actual. Their bed, their walls, our floor—the fraction line extended through every aching surface, and beneath it was the There they were trying, through each other, to touch.

I hated the sound of it, but I listened because I needed to learn. I gave myself a wish for enduring it. Then I'd play with my wishes till it was through. I had sixty-three saved up, one hundred twenty-four if I wished for the wishes to double, since it cost a wish to double them, two hundred forty-six if I doubled them again. I think I knew a million were no better than one. I could keep wishing for wishes, until I had so many their number could only be felt at, but then? Approximately endless wishes, one approximate wish. What was I gathering, then? Wishing is not prayer, though the stakes are the same. It's a game, and it is played alone.

Then, almost as if I'd wished for it, it was my junior year of college and I was having sex on a pillow-topped mattress in an apartment in Bozeman, Montana, a thousand miles from our brewery town. I was as far as scholarships and our remaining stock certificates could send me, in the embrace of a lissome rich girl with a mole rising and falling on the crux of her hip. It was late morning and light, and whatever remote and secret world I had wished for seemed very close to here where I was. Fast approaching, I closed my eyes, I opened my eyes, I tried to see it, but with only that brief distance to travel and four thighs clapping me on, I flew right past.

Her name was Beth. She was on her semester abroad. She'd left another boy in London, with whom she had an understanding, an understanding I had been allowed to join, according to terms. First of all, I was not allowed to love her.

She swung off of me, smiling. "Who were you thinking about? You had your eyes squinched up like you were trying to squeeze them out of your head."

"Nobody," I said. "It's just an old habit."

"Oh?" It was a Sunday morning, the blinds' shadows warped and broke atop her crumpled sheets. She lay down, heedless of how her soft breasts slipped against me.

"It's nothing, I promise."

"Fine, never mind it, I'm hungry," she said. She pulled away, disappeared and peed, and was back in a minute with a plate of toaster waffles, which she laid between us on the sheets. "Say it," she said, crushing a sector of waffle in her cheek.

"I think I can go again."

"Bravo, but say it first."

"I have to say it every time? I have no feelings for you."

"Thank you," she said, brushing out her eyelashes. She reached over the waffles, their Graveyards, Daisies, Tic-Tac-Toes, and pulled me toward her, toward the fine, bare down on her jaw, where my lips by instinct shaped a kiss. "Now, damn it, what were you thinking?"

"It's private."

"Aha. Of course it is." She set the plate at the foot of the bed and slid my hand high over her thigh. "Do you believe in intimacy or not?"

She was rich and nimble hearted, able to negotiate with love. She'd done all this before, cavorted with the natives, caught a plane. She could trust herself—it struck such lovely terror in me. She'd found me early that fall and wasted no time. A campus play, a lecture, a study date, I came up with anything I could—we went together, went home together, woke up together, no feelings. She kept an electric kettle by her bed. The chipped blue mug was mine. I was all acceptance, I knew my part, I just wanted to play it well.

I went to her classes more often than my own. I cooked for her in her kitchen while she was at the campus gym, kept boxer shorts in my backpack so she wouldn't feel like I was moving in. I wrote her history papers, I brought her fancy teas.

But she asked me two more times that morning and once that evening beside a wine bottle on her living room floor and again the next morning while we were supposed to be in class—*What were you thinking about?*

"I close my eyes and think of England."

"Not funny. Now you have to say."

I didn't know if it was what was best or worst in me. "I was expanding fractions," I said.

"Oh god." She rolled toward me. "You disgusting child. Aren't you supposed to think about a football match for that?"

"Traditionally, baseball."

"Shall I ask Ollie? Maybe football works better." I couldn't imagine this man. Some kind of perfumed banker, I supposed. Red freckles on his pecs. I could never have done it and knew therefore that I didn't deserve it, this season of reckless affection.

"Are you jealous?" I said.

"Of his girls?"

"No, no, of my fractions."

"Oh, I don't delude myself I measure up to fractions."

"Few do."

"So hard on yourself, Jacob. You're a good three out of four."

"Quit flirting," I said. "I need to teach you some maths."

She planted another skew kiss and rolled against me so my hand draped her hip and her shoulder blades caught the light. "All right, then. Talk fractions to me."

I breathed through the hair over her ear and tried, for the first time since I'd shown my aunt the linoleum patterns, to explain. Imagine you don't know how to add fractions. A third plus a fifth. They're not like terms. It's like trying to add two apples without knowing the word *apple* or the word *fruit* or the word *thing*. What good does it do to know *two*? Two what? I ran my hand over her ribs, her hip, its mole. The apples' shapes are different, their colors, their sizes, tastes, but that all disappears as soon as we make them two of a kind. The second apple turns the first to a thing there can always be another of—abstracted, single, a unit.

"A unit?" she said.

A thing supplied by the mind, not nature, and therefore in endless supply. As soon as you have two apples, you can have infinite apples, each with no identity of its own. Only its commodity dimensions remain visible, the rest of the apple is gone. At first there's nothing invisible about a fraction. A third is like the apples. You can have one third, two thirds, however many thirds, no differences among them. But what happens when it's a third and a fifth?

"Search me—" She slid my hand, her planchette.

What joins a third and a fifth together finally is not a trick of subdivision—that a fifth could be three-fifteenths—but the inner spaciousness that subdivision unveils. A fifth might be two tenths, ten fiftieths, two hundred pieces of a thousand. An infinite space was there all along.

"Slow it down," she said. "Go slow."

Division turned the count inward, toward an inner space that gave all things a common inner measure. I lay the counting numbers on her with my fingertips, an infinite sequence of ones. One touch, a second, a third, so numerable only when they were abstracted, indistinct. That is what I learned from fractions, I said. I drew ones on her, told her each, if you felt your way into it, was endless. Every stroke a dozen touches, every touch a thousand nerves, every nerve channeling a million electric lights made of life the same as mine. For a second I thought she understood.

"So you want to be the numerator this time?"

"You'll never get it," I said.

"But don't worry, I'll never care."

There are certain lonely pleasures that partners cannot share and others that won't be found elsewhere or again. I told myself I wouldn't tell her about Boris Yeltsin, the hunger strike, history's equations, my aunt hiding in my bed. I stopped talking and let her breathe. When we were done, I professed again I had no feelings. We decided to skip afternoon classes to hike, then didn't hike. We stayed inside. She took another endless shower. I sat on the rug and worked my problem set, drawing the figures with a finger in the pile. It helped me think. The rug's giant red flowers and fronds turned and repeated at perfect intervals. In the evenness, I could sense the gridded backing beneath. I could sense it also in how the carpet pile bent as I traced my math. The texture of it sent a pleasing overwhelming feeling up my finger, as if my nerves could feel the buried order in the nap. She eyed me dividing and deriving as she toweled her way from bathroom to bedroom, but I wouldn't tell her about the kitchen floor I'd tried to tumble through, though all she would have had to say was fall.

I ran the twelve blocks home to Bart after Ms. Muldoon's fraction lesson. *This* at last was revolutionary knowledge, I thought—a new way to split the pie. "What do we need from the basement today?" I said at the back door.

"Don't yell," said my aunt. "What's for snack?"

"No snack."

"Right," she said. "Of course. Pardon me. Who needs snack?"

I remember the fantasy as clearly as what actually followed: *This*, I say, *is how to make the pie.* He seats himself on a bucket of wheat flour and offers me his chair.

And this is how to zoom into the pieces so they can be compared.

From each according to his ability, to each according to his need!

It's called common denominators!

Common denominators? A revolutionary principle! The missing key! Now, a simple calculation and we step into our promised world. Jacob, my boy! But first—Rebecca!—our bellies need a feast!

"Bart?" I said again in the dark of the stairs. "Hello? Uncle Bart?"

An uncapped highlighter lay in the light at the base.

His face, when I found him, was hovering over the table, pulling against the coil of his spine. His scalp had a dry cut, as if he'd smashed his head into his glasses, and his blank eyes were intent on the dry brown drops on his graph. He was so thin, a snipped marionette, wrists straining his shoulders toward the floor. When he looked up, there was terror in his eyes. His words were sludgy and loose: "You? I told you to leave me be, babush-ka."

He looked like skin pinned onto bone. "Uncle Bart?"

But a monster surfaced in his face. "What have you done to me?" he slurred. Spit strung down his chin. "Waste of a whore!

Blood leech! There is not far enough away! Go and go die and die twice!"

Based on the scans Dr. Kemal believed it was not my uncle's first stroke, but there was no way to know how many there had been. A fig of brain had been hit beyond recovery. It wasn't clear how bad the loss would be.

"He's been on a terrible diet," my aunt told the doctors. "He won't sit down to meals." In the bright hospital light, her whiskers shined like gold. "He's an unreasonable man, please talk with him. I've tried."

We moved from room to room through the fluorescent hallways, turning at right angles, dragging our toes on the thin violet carpet of the waiting rooms. I held her hand tight. I did not tell her what I'd heard.

In a basket next to the waiting room couch was a book of puzzles: There once was a carver of chess pieces who made an exquisite chess set for the emperor and asked only to be paid in rice—one grain for the first piece, set on the first square, two for the next, then four, doubling and redoubling in this way until the set was complete. The emperor was happy to pay so little for the figurines, and promised he would double the grain of rice across all sixty-four squares. *Was the emperor right to be so pleased?*

"He would owe him nine billion billion grains!" I told my uncle when he woke. It was more than any empire could hold.

"A good subversive, this chess-piece maker," he said. "But who will have to count the grains?"

"He will?"

"Good boy."

"Let your uncle rest, Jacob."

"The revolution was incomplete?"

He laughed. "The revolution was incomplete." It made a hundred wishes. I could feel how few they were.

We left him there that night, and my aunt climbed again into my bed, even though he wasn't there to spite. Within, I watched the chess-piece carver's rice double—thirty-two, sixty-four, one twenty-eight—until the dark of my mind was bright with it, and then I doubled it again, and again, beyond any count, and when she rolled over and tried to talk to me, I hid inside the grain where she wouldn't find me. Her whiskers tickled my forehead, but I couldn't let her know I was awake. She gasped and shook, but I didn't open my eyes. I split every grain of rice in two and then in two again, halves, quarters, eighths, until I'd made dust from dust, and the air in me was light enough to breathe.

He couldn't read maps or charts or his own graphs, though the equations themselves still made some sense to him, I think. His balance came back slowly, but he wobbled in a new way. He never fell but seemed always a little unsure of how the room fit around him, and looked both ways crossing the kitchen to his chair, and even after he'd regained some weight, he wobbled as he had at his most frail.

He ate. Many times a day, he took our salad bowl of Jell-O from the fridge and reduced it by another spoonful. "Observe my gusto," he said when he'd scraped his plate.

My aunt cried in the bathroom as she plucked out her whiskers. "What have you done with my old gray crone?" he said when we converged for Sunday lunch. She blushed. It looked like blush, but we could see it was also a wound.

"How's your discovery?" I asked him.

"My graphs have all turned nauseous," he said. "My brain, my embolus, Dr. Kemal is eloquent on the point, but I look at my figures, my pads and pads of graphs, and I get dizzy."

"You were a brilliant mathematician," said my aunt, kissing his skull. "It's an absolute tragedy, for us and for communism."

"We've entered a time," he said, "when it means very little to be a communist. Maybe it will mean something again someday. One can hope."

There was a great flayed fish left over from dinner on the table, its dead eye shining up, wide enough to spy us all.

"You know," he said, patting the empty chair, "I made a fascinating discovery today, going through my pamphlets here. I found some graphs or figures that I can't recall. The fanciest lines, trickier than a Kandinsky, twisted into labyrinths, I would say." He winked at me. "Do you have any idea what these labyrinths could be, babushka?"

"You were so brilliant," she said. "You can't remember it, you poor dear." She set down her fork and stroked his arm with her fingers. "That was your model for the future, the fight."

"Well, it was a dazzling future if that is so," he said. "But for the moment, I am glad to be here."

It was a good decade for the Coors Brewing Company and a bad decade for the left. The Coors family, through their forty-million-dollar Castle Rock Foundation, became a major bankroller of the American Enterprise Institute, the Cato Institute, and the

Heritage Foundation, which Joe Coors himself founded and steered. Coors was the fastest-growing beer company in America, the nation's number-three supplier, and our beer plant expanded into the largest in the world. "Liberation is at hand," Dick Armey, the new House majority leader, wrote in the Heritage Foundation's *Policy Review*. "A paradigm-shattering revolution has just taken place . . . This revolution has been so sudden and sweeping that few in Washington have yet grasped its full meaning. But when the true significance of the 1980s freedom revolution sinks in, politics, culture—indeed the entire human outlook—will change. History is now on the side of freedom."

"You shouldn't drink that," I told Beth one night. We were at a big American house party, so she could anthropologize and bum cigarettes. All around us, the silver cans flashed.

"Boychik, boychik," she said. "You really want to be against beer?" It was December already. In a week, she'd be back in England, and we were finally hitting our stride. She leaned in, locked eyes. "In fact—" She slid through elbows to the fridge and returned with a second silver can.

"I can't."

"Jacob," she said, cracking it open, "do yourself some favors. Cheers me. To America, land of the brave." The dazzling future dazzled in the diamond bracelet swaying from her wrist, the diamond earrings studded through her tongue-shy ears. Communism flexed briefly in the muscles of my jaws.

But I took the can. I had several, I'll confess, and their effects did not improve their taste, but I did accumulate a short-lived freedom. "Take me home," I said, pulling the cigarette from her mouth. "I'm having no feelings for you."

"Math class?"

"Advanced." And we marched ourselves to her apartment, singing union songs.

My aunt called the next day. She was raving. "I didn't want to disrupt you, Jacob. I thought it could wait. It's going to be hardest on you, poor thing."

I stood in my room, my face an inch from the bare white wall. "The cancer?" I said.

"I thought I could tell you once you were home. Jacob, I'm overrun. Come home, can you come today?"

I didn't understand—she was going to die today? "It's finals week," I said.

"Finals week!" she said. "What if it is?"

I said I would come right away. I just had to investigate the Greyhound schedule. But I knew how she could get. "You sound good. When did you—" But it was my uncle on the phone now.

"What have we ever asked of you! The woman who raised you! You are a runaway? You will come home at once!"

"I just need a day or two to make arrangements. I'll lose my scholarship."

"Scholarship!" he boomed. "His scholarship!"

"Is she okay?"

But it was her again, "I'm fine, I'm well. It's him you'll kill." I could hear his rage behind her, storming against the kitchen walls. "You're right, take your exams, we can't disturb. But did you have to rankle? How am I going to pacify him?" But she didn't go pacify him. She told me about the pain with her bowel movements and the blood in her stool, the sequence of doctors and tests. "It's as old as you are, Jacob. It's been nibbling in me two decades."

I have tried sometimes to blame Beth, but it was not her fault. I told her nothing (she would have bought me a plane ticket and sent me away) and told myself I was willing to be wrong, that there would be five weeks between semesters to visit and make things right.

I took my finals. I cannot say I studied hard. I rode with Beth in her cab to the airport. "Well," she said, "high fives for a happy adventure. Don't forget me too soon." I went straight to the Greyhound depot and waited with my duffel while the driver put on chains.

Inside the bus station, a man was begging. He'd set a training toilet out for change, *Cash Only* written in marker on the seat. The bone of his neck lay on the wall, the rest of him slumped in a child-birthing pose, his green socks fallen to his heels. I tried to hand him the sandwich I'd packed, and he pointed to the seat. I dropped it through. "Read, asshole," he said, but I didn't take it back.

Then the bus door opened and bundled families helped one another up the dark steps. I watched through the window as passengers took last pulls on their cigarettes and the driver tossed their backpacks in the cargo hold. I didn't get on.

The driver looked twice, clamped down the luggage doors. The PA system announced the departure again. My heart jumped, and I did not stand up.

The bus pulled away into the black snow. All I could see in the depot window was the scrape of old stickers on the glass.

A double-wide across the street advertised Coors and Kokanee. Inside, a man with a Woody Woodpecker tattoo was punching keno in the warmth. It was twelve hours till the next bus, and when I saw how easy twelve could pass, I wondered why not twenty-four.

Drinkers sing about forgetting, but I didn't forget where I was supposed to be. The panic was only stronger drink by drink. I looked at the keno flashing and remembered the wishes—a hundred, two? I had them still, if not the count. I could've wished her better, could've wished to be there. I bought another beer and pushed some numbers, watched them all strike out.

The poker machines, the mussy deer heads on the wall, the lightening street, the fluorescent beer—it was not where I belonged: a roadhouse booth at noon, a table, a wall. Like a sleepwalker, I watched these outer surfaces for signs of another place. Once my despair was perfected, and it must be nearly, I supposed I would break through.

I do this still, as if I might find my aunt again or find something half recalled. I stand in my kitchen, look at my skin and imagine the darkness bending inside me, look at the air itself, which likewise we never see. Don't we all try, eyes crossed on nothing, to see the air before light obscures it? We walk out of the bar and stand on a street wetted black by rain and look left, right, uptown, downtown, put a hand on the parking meter and steady ourselves while the polar star skids in the night like a scar on the eye, and we feel a private seasickness we cannot beat. She fell in the kitchen, choked by a clot in her lung. And where was I?

I fed my cash to a game called Bingo Gold Rush and learned what my lucky numbers were worth.

Bart and I didn't talk much that month. I needed him to rage at me, but he couldn't manage it. He could hardly bring his water to his mouth. The best we could do was to sit at the old kitchen table late into the night, doing our work together. I had a few papers overdue.

I thought he wouldn't make it. A woman from the Peace and Justice Center came to the door with an aspen wreath and he held it like he had no clue. "Aspens share their root systems," she said, trying to explain. I assumed the grief would kill him, but he got up every morning and set the timer for our eggs. I had to drag myself out of bed when I heard the little bell. I knew he wouldn't call for me to come. I could see already decades passing in that way, tolled off by that little bell, until he was too deaf to hear its tiny ring. We buried her and defrosted a soup she had made.

"Turkey broth?" I said, but I didn't tell him how she and I used to stop and buy turkey necks after protest, turkey necks and a box of story-time tea.

He stirred the carrots through the broth. "I can't remember which kaddish it is I ought to do."

Three weeks ago, I went to visit my uncle. He invited me. We had fallen out of the habit of holiday visits. I am not sure when.

"Jacob?" he said into his phone, though we had already been talking for some minutes.

"Still here."

"Do they give you a day off for the villain Columbus?"

"They call it Indigenous Peoples' Day."

"So now we can feel good about it. This is even worse."

"It's just a Monday. Tuesday is prep."

"Do you know what they do on the Kristallnacht anniversary? Have I told you? In Germany?"

"They celebrate the wall coming down."

"Because it was the same day. Why lament when you can celebrate? So you know everything now. Why don't you come see me?"

"Well, sure, but—"

"Yes, *well, sure, but* first you protest politely, and I offer to pay; you say that's not the point, I say, 'Of course not, the point is I haven't seen my boychik in many months,' and you say, 'Enough with the guilt! How long can a family trade on guilt?' and I say, 'Most families don't need to.' 'Christ almighty!' you say and acquiesce."

"Christ almighty, I acquiesce."

"Good," he said.

"But you're paying."

He was not well. He was hidden inside a pale yellow sweater that once had fit him like armor. The old V-neck hung all weekend from his collarbones, got in the way when he watered his potted plants.

He lives now in an old low-income high-rise. We spent the weekend at his high window, watching traffic at the car wash beneath through the brown glass. He had four folding chairs in a row and we played a slow game of leapfrog with them so we could stay in the patch of sun. He called it his sandbox.

We talked and talked, as if it were natural for us. He had many questions, and suspicions, about my school and the politics of charter-school funding, and it was hard to turn the conversation back to him.

"You're eighty-two?"

"And you're a math teacher?"

"Eighty-three."

"I'm a spring goose. I'm—"

"Please," I said. I tried to give him permission.

"Okay, spoilsport, you can see. I'm a puppet of myself now, I know. It's a bone thing."

"Is it bad?"

"Not so bad I can't enjoy an episode of denial."

A plate of nuts and a bronze cracker warmed in the sun patch—Brazil nuts, walnuts, hazelnuts, cracked shells mixed in with the rest. I could smell their exotic dusts in the sunlight. He leaned forward and thumbed at an almond, forgetting for a moment it needed a nutcracker.

"The revolution," I said. "International socialism. All that. What do you make of it now?"

"From his seventh-story vantage?" He cracked the nut and picked at the meat, blew a flake of its skin off his nail. "I still believe in a classless world, but I won't see it. Neither will you. Seems likely we'll destroy ourselves before the conditions for it—" He handed me the nut. "There are too many of us, but you should have a child even so. Find someone, be a pa-pa."

"Why?"

He considered it as if it were history's great question. "Because you know how to love." Then, before I could disagree, he asked, "Do you think about our family often?"

"Of course," I said.

"Not just the three of us. Our people. History, hope."

"I guess I don't feel too connected to anything like that," I said.

"But you must. It's you. Most days there's death every way I look, but the future is our future too. Jacob, my child, you are a great and penetrating joy."

THE CLOWN

The clown counted his murders as he drove the new couple to the house on Rocking Horse Lane. Not few. The Lexus needed air again, according to the little orange light, the man in his passenger seat was offering original commentary on the Clintons, and behind the clown's left eye a toothache and an earache were collaborating. Not few at all, and some of the murders had been admirably painful, admirably patient. Outside the Lexus it was seventy-two degrees in October, and inside the Lexus, according to a different screen, it was also seventy-two degrees, the car's climate system blowing hard even so. The clown hated the Lexus and was wearing a blazer he'd bought to match it. In the backseat, the woman, very pregnant, was picking her teeth with the aid of her phone. The clown's mouth—thirsty—tasted like waffle fries and crispy chicken sandwich, and so did all the rest of him. Salt, grease, a synthetic drive-thru savor—he was likely composed of it by now. No matter how many times he sucked the straw the soda was still out.

"We hate to leave the downtown," the man, Seamus, was saying again. "Our apartment is five minutes from Pinche Taco, five minutes from Cerebral Brewing, like two minutes from Über Dog, but how fast I got her pregnant, we're going to need rooms."

"Congratulations," said the clown, shaking his ice. Any kind of knife murder, some hooks, some rod-and-fire stuff. One dehydration. He tried to recognize himself, his life and effort, in the résumé, but it was like he'd consigned his life effort to a secret man. What was left ate waffle fries, sold houses, making way for the secret man's return.

But he had a good feeling about this couple. Early thirties, Apple Watches, fecund. He *wanted* to kill them. That was something. The woman, Eliza, was very quiet. All she had said since the place on Ridgeway Row was "Hi, Daddy" when they passed a young tort lawyer's billboard. Seamus was lavishly freckled, in an overlaundered polo probably assigned to lazy weekend wear, curling collar leaning toward the postnuptial paunch.

The houses on Vinci Park and Ridgeway Row, where the air still smelled of other people's lentil soup, had been staged disappointments, unmowed drabnesses after which 404 Rocking Horse would gleam like a mirror. It was the perfect place for Eliza and Seamus; Eliza and Seamus were the perfect pair for it. The clown had been preparing this for a while.

"We're thinking high fours, maybe low fives," Seamus was lowballing already. "They're reviewing me for associate sooner than anyone in company history, so it's not that. I'm just not ready for *the* house yet, you know?"

The clown did know. The man wanted granite counters, sectional couches, a pop-up soccer goal. There was time yet for Japanese fountains. He wanted the yard the kid could mow for iTunes money, not the one that needed a koi specialist. Happiness was not so hard to engineer for the typical, but it did no good to say it. The house on Rocking Horse would speak for him, a three-bedroom with a power study and a crafts room with a guest loft. You had to let the clients spin twice in a living room and recognize themselves. Not just themselves—the selves they knew and also latent selves they just suspected. Only then, when they saw their books in the cases and their mugs in the cabinet, could the murderer emerge from the basement, where he'd been waiting all along.

"Downtown, it's fun and all, but it's not safe for Eliza or the kid. All the money the city has now, you think they'd clean that shit out. Our alleyway, every morning someone's given them all hot coffee and donuts. These bums are glamping."

The clown, forty-eight, amicably divorced, amicably depressed, real-estate licensed, was aware that he was a type too. Apart from murder, his interests were no less predictable than Seamus's. He'd offered lunch after the Ridgeway place—he often took clients out—but now he was thinking about Tums—he loved Tums—about gin, about juice cleanses, about smothering Seamus's face with the wet side of Seamus's scalp. He rarely spoke his mind. He let his thoughts imbue his smile.

He'd set about it in earnest ten years ago, full sails with research and planning, whiteface and greasepaint, professional grade, learned to accentuate a menace, if there was one, already present in his face. The wig had cost a fortune, real hair, bruised strawberry, but it had lasted. The teeth too, cutlery porcelain, filed, stained. Ought to be tax deductible. The nails he made himself with molded tin. It took most of an hour to put it all on, but people did react—more so than they would to rubber stuff, he hoped. "That tall building over there would be your closest hospital, if anything happens," he said. "Terrific obstetrics center, though I'm sure you've already made plans. There's the Whole Foods coming up and here's a mosque, should you be needing one of those. I believe it would be your polling place were you to move before the election."

Seamus grumbled something about voting early. For the rest of Seamus's life, a diminishing proposition, indignation would race cholesterol. He would make a colorful choking victim, but the clown had promised himself patience, intentionality. Cruelty and pain were easy quantities, but murder used to *express* something in him. Take the kings of Greece and Persia who entertained guests with hollow bronze bulls that seemed to bay when wheeled over a fire, when in fact it was condemned queens screaming from inside. It was cruel, it was painful—but it was so kingly too. The court clapping and marveling, pretending they didn't know, while the king spat seeds from his grapes. The Aztecs murdered like Aztecs, the Nazis murdered like Nazis. The clown, meanwhile, had groomed himself to match the Lexus that was supposed to give him credibility regarding other people's homes.

"Been saving this place for a special family," he said, pulling into the driveway. It was true.

During the walk-through, Seamus stuck close by, explaining everything to the clown: "I never liked these kind of light switches. . . . Chessboard, huh? I want to learn some chess strategy, some real chess systems. . . . No disrespect to your grill here, but it's all about the smoker."

Noted. The clown had to remind himself it wasn't about killing Seamus, no matter how urgently he deserved to be murdered. Murder had to come from the inside. The urgency must be in him.

"We're only two crosswalks to Langston Elementary, where Mark Zuckerberg's nephew went to school," he said. "Langston's a recipient of a 2016 tech-arts grant from the George Lucas foundation, the one on NPR." That was enough to provoke several more minutes of opinionation from Seamus. It was an old trick: the more a client heard his own voice in a house, the more he felt the house was his. Eliza, meanwhile, was going around seeing how the toilets flushed.

The clown liked knives, big knives, little knives—but what even was a knife? Something very narrow but no less hard. The set stashed in the crawl space of 404 Rocking Horse had chef's knives, cleavers, a straightedge razor, a few more theatrical things, toothy, curving. Almost every night since the house had been vacant, he'd let himself in, retrieved his things from the crawl space, and, fully kitted out, sharpened his knives, grind by meditative grind. Just last night, he'd sat thickly painted under this floor. Breathe. Intuit the killer already implied by the house. On the iPhone on his knee, his Facebook feed worked the cud of another late-breaking candidate scandal.

Touring the basement ("Here's your water heater. . . . These guys here are for bolting a safe. . . ."), he found one of his fingernails. "Huh? What do you think this is?" He showed the man, but the shrug was a shrug, not a shiver.

Whatever. He'd imagined stashing acids and paralyzing agents down there too—imagined how shocked and impressed Eliza and Seamus would be if they woke to find themselves prepped for a chemical flaying or immobilized beneath a swinging blade. He wished he could do something like that, but it was too much contraption. The engineering and constructing, the procurement of regulated chemicals—it was beyond him. He was a knife clown. He could never pretend to be what he was not.

Eliza said the house was perfect. Seamus, saving face, said they'd "have to do a little thinking through." The deciders, the clown imagined, were Eliza and her billboard dad. "Well, I think you're perfect for it," the clown said. They were. Their smug veneer would rip right through. The clown expected to hear from them Monday or Tuesday at the worst. He would throw in a moving service if the sale called for it, and they'd be dead before Thanksgiving. He promised it to himself the way he'd promised Owen ski camp, which now he would actually be able to pay for. A thing to look forward to, as the boy's therapist had suggested. Something the best version of you, if not you yourself, would want to do.

After he returned Seamus and Eliza to the RE/MAX lot, the clown accepted a Friday nachos invitation. Usually, a birthday or two had accumulated during the week. This time Lauren had made her first sale since licensure. "*I'm* going to buy *you* a drink," she said to the clown, poking and sweeping a fingertip accidentally enough across his nipple. She leaned in and whispered behind her nails, "It's a lie . . . you're going to buy *me* a drink."

He doubted she actually wanted to fuck him, but he was pretty sure she wanted him imagining it, so he did imagine it, let it imbue his smile, and told her he'd be there.

He pulled over on his way to Baja's and made notes on the couple in his phone. Arrogance, wealth, an anxious hatefulness, the unconscious rivalry between them. There was some authentic American fearfulness in them perfectly suited to the Rocking Horse property, away in its little suburban circlet of fast-growth trees and prize schools and four-cheese macaroni chains. He worried for a second that someone else might murder them first.

At Baja's, Haru and Leroy hailed him from the corner booth. Lauren didn't even look up from her eye tunnel with Monique, who was telling the story of the movie she'd watched last night. Haru and Leroy were comparing notes on the *BioShock* installment they both were playing. Haru liked spicy food, shoes, and video games. Leroy liked Bernie Sanders, video games, and the Cleveland Cavaliers. Monique liked movies, her husband, and coconut oil. Everybody was a person. And the clown? For his birthday, the office had given him a Starbucks card.

After ten minutes, he proposed a toast: "To virtue!" he said and sat quickly down. Lauren made a wounded scoffing sound, and everyone laughed, and the clown stood up quickly and amended: "To the conquests of Lauren—may they be many."

They shared a smile then, escaping for some seconds the commotion of the nachos. He hadn't been fair. These were real people, not portfolios of interest. He searched her. Lauren had bobbed black hair, wore silver; the purple in her veins made her neck seem almost tattooed. She did have at least one tattoo, some text on her side you could see through the white of her work shirts. She liked Heart, she hated baby carrots. . . . He searched harder. Maybe his own self had become small through a habitual disregard for the uniquenesses of other selves. So he studied her for particularities. At RE/MAX Reservoir Day, Lauren had spat arcs of water through her teeth. She called her car Thumper. She could do fingertip push-ups. For Halloween she was going to be the *Terminator* mom. He waited for a reciprocal sense of selfhood to reveal itself in him, but all he saw was Seamus trailing entrails through his perfect home.

"I don't think I should drive," she said. It was the third or fourth time she had said it, but they'd stayed there drinking beers. The others—Monique with her eyebrows—had long ago waved bye.

"How bad is the Uber from here?" He waved for the bill.

"I don't trust Ubers. Could be anyone," she said. "Could be—"

He waited. "Could be who?"

"A serial fucker." She was drunk. She laughed.

"Really. What's the worst that could happen?"

"Are you kidding?" She chipped off a dot of toasted cheese.

She was right. He apologized. He was just fishing for ideas. He said, "You never told me though. What'd you sell?"

"Four-oh-four Rocking Horse," she said, reviving. She popped up and did her little dance again, tossing invisible cash onto the table.

He supposed now he'd just have to murder her instead. Baja's didn't take American Express, so he put down the Banana

Republic Visa and the cash he had, distractedly trying to make a plan.

She was drunk enough. In the Lexus, he leaned over and kissed her, and she reached almost immediately for his belt. She could barely kiss, all the hurry-up in her hand. "Not here," he said, but she unbuckled him and lifted it out.

Cheese and chips and too many Sam Adams and still that crispy chicken flavor. The Lexus needed air, according to the little orange light, and the woman in the passenger seat was now fellating him like she wanted to get things over with. "Not here," he said again.

"I don't want to go home," she said. "I hate my place."

"But this is a Baja's parking lot."

She laughed, only in order to say, "You make me laugh." Perhaps everyone had done this before, accidentally fucked a coworker on nacho Friday, but did it have to be done as a grim reenactment of the last time? Back in the corner booth, she'd had him defending *James and the Giant Peach*, denouncing nutmeg (not a happy flavor), describing the brazen bulls Greek kings used to kill their queens, now he felt anonymous again. "I better go pee," she said, but she didn't sprint for Thumper. She squatted between two pickup trucks and climbed back in.

He took her to the house on Rocking Horse Lane and let her fall asleep on the couch. In the basement, he retrieved his kit and knives and changed. He listened to the subterranean sounds of the neighborhood as he greased beneath the naked bulb— the switches of preprogrammed sprinklers, the swamp coolers falling back to work, even in October. He glued on the charred eyebrows, sealed the sharp teeth in. He washed the yellow, snake-slit contact lens in saline and eased it on. He combed the wig up, full fry, cinched the big belt tight atop his happy sooted tatters. He slid a few unscabbarded knives through the belt. The nails came last or he'd shred everything in the process.

He approached the couch in squeaking shoes, leaned over the back and watched her sleeping. Now was when the menace should awaken something in him. The secret man was here.

He leaned further, grazed his nails across her face, punctured the couch leather claw by claw next to her ear. He bit down on his gums with his cutlery teeth until a drop of blood rolled over his lips, oiled itself redder on his smile, and fell onto her neck. She didn't wake.

Fine. He had too much beer in him for a chase scene, anyway. He aimed a fingernail for either side of her trachea. He would just rip it forward and hold her down while she drained. Then he'd get a U-Haul, find someplace to torch the couch (a show-house couch might not be missed), torch her, grind her teeth and any stubborn bones, Clorox the living room and the Lexus, and return the van. He'd have to chainsaw the couch to move it by himself. That would be dusty. Sometime in the A.M. you could expect Eliza and her dad to come peeking through the windows. He was supposed to FaceTime with Owen's therapist at noon.

He didn't mind hard work. He hadn't become a murder clown following paths of least resistance.

There were Tums in the glove box. He loved Tums, but he was afraid to go even that far in his suit.

He woke her up at 5 A.M. "I fell asleep," she said. A couch crease had left a rather gorgeous scar along her face.

"Let's get donuts. I'll drive you home."

She blinked at him. "We didn't even—"

"You mean you don't remember? You cooed, you cried . . ."

She yawned, squeezing her eyes to size her headache. "That's fucked up, Dennis."

He apologized. "I took a long shower and slept upstairs. We'll never speak of it again."

It didn't mean he was *never* going to murder her—just because he hadn't murdered her last night. When the morning papers were dropped off at Donut Time, he spread the crossword and watched her make quick work of it and the Jumble.

The sunrise woke up a little rain. Saturday was supposedly a workday, but hooky made things sweet. "I like your face," she said. "It's a real face. Some faces look like you could reach right through them."

He leaned forward and she tested the reality of his scruff. "You shave like a dad," she said.

He thought he understood what she meant by that—she meant she'd finally realized she didn't want and hadn't wanted him. That was okay. A lover you always half suspected was trying to kill you. He'd never killed a friend before.

"I am a dad."

"I know. Riley? Jonas?"

"Owen."

"*Owen*. And you never miss a soccer game?"

The black jelly in a halved donut trembled as a cement mixer drove by. "The soccer games are in San Jose, actually."

"Christmases and campouts?" He looked at her but she was already looking at him. "Your ex won't even let you have a campout? Really? You shave like such a great dad."

"It's not her. Owen never liked me very much," he said. "I thought I'd be a fun dad. Nieces and nephews always liked me. I've got all the Roald Dahls."

She waited.

"He'd get hysterical if his mom tried to leave us alone."

"He didn't grow out of it?"

"He was four when we divorced, and she waited three years before they moved away. My days were impossible. He refused to get out of the car when she brought him over. They've been in California now for seven and a half years."

Lauren's forehead wrinkles were legibly sympathetic. Her eyes, though, were wondering what had scared the kid. "He's old enough to explain himself, isn't he?" she said.

He told her about the therapist he paid for. "Part of me is a little proud of him, for figuring me out so fast. How long did it take you to learn to hate your dad?"

"He said he was voting for Trump and I pretty much declared it." She'd noticed the drop of blood on her collar, was scraping at it casually, unsurprised to find it there. "I couldn't believe him. But I figure I only need to hate him till Hillary wins."

Lauren admitted her plan for the day was to carve pumpkins and decorate her place for Halloween. He should help. When it was time to FaceTime the therapist, she'd leave him alone. "Do you like pumpkins?"

"I like knives," he said.

At the Safeway next to Donut Time, Lauren turned the pumpkins carefully, examining their personalities, she said. She asked him what candy they should get, and he realized his tooth- and earaches were gone. She directed him to a costume store, just opening, where she bought cobwebs and some cartoonish plastic bones, and then to an art supply where she got a large roll of black construction paper. He drove slowly in and out of parking lots so the knife kit in his trunk wouldn't clank.

He followed Thumper from the Baja's lot back to her duplex. The street looked vaguely familiar—maybe he'd bought a kayak off Craigslist somewhere over here?

She brewed them coffees that bore no relation to the Styrofoam stuff from Donut Time. He could feel its strength right through the mug. He leaned back against the counter, savoring, while she, with impressive fluidity, ran a razor over the blackout paper, tracing the profiles of cats and crones. She didn't even draw the line in pencil first. He held the paper to the windows and she taped it on.

She brushed the shreds off the kitchen table and got out a mixing bowl and knives. She looked at him. "I'm going to say it even though I don't think it needs to be said."

"Friends."

"And not the kind who fuck each other."

"Agreed."

"Good." She set down her pumpkin heavily, its thud and her *good* coinciding. "Now, what else is there that friends do?"

Her kitchen had banged-up wood cabinets and wallpaper that reminded him of bed-and-breakfast sheets. The place wasn't her, but you could see how she'd exerted herself against it in little ways, her pretty mixing bowls and denim apron on a peg. Big Boggle was with the cookbooks on the fridge top, a duck skull she must have found on a hike was on the window ledge over the sink. She'd hung a pull-up bar in the doorway and a string of prosperity hens from the bar. She played Bessie Smith and warmed up empanadas she'd made with minced lamb. She had a homemade chimichurri.

He carved his own face onto the pumpkin. She seemed amused. "It's Dennis," he explained.

She looked back and forth. "I suppose it is."

At noon, he sat with his iPad in the Lexus and talked to Dr. Jordie. She was at home, in a living room—he saw an adult son walk behind her with a cereal bowl. She asked how he was in a tone that indicated small talk, not therapeutic concern, and pretended not to observe that he'd hidden himself in a car.

"I might not be able to pay for ski camp after all," he said. "I'm sorry. I haven't told Tina."

"Ski camp might have been ambitious," she said in her Terry Gross voice. "Tina had to promise Owen he wouldn't have to go."

He opened his mouth to say he didn't know what to say and couldn't say even this.

"It's been a rough week," Dr. Jordie said. There was a wobbling view of her chin and blurred arm skin as she scratched something off the laptop screen. "Owen refused to go to school. He refused to eat or shower. Tina was making any deal he'd take."

The clown thought his face looked relaxed in the little frame superimposed on Dr. Jordie, but he felt a sour pain in his saliva glands, as if they were being squeezed. He'd been made to believe Owen wanted to go to ski camp. Now he scrubbed away his image of the boy watching ski videos on his phone and intuiting potential future freedoms. A yipping alpine skier dropping through blue sky—he'd thought maybe Owen had glimpsed his own secret man, and not a bad one. Behind his face, where the therapist couldn't see, the clown scrubbed at the free skier, until the white snow and red Gore-Tex rinsed away except for a few persistent smears.

Meanwhile, he'd missed a few sentences. ". . . got or gave himself a bloody nose and refused to hold it closed," the therapist was saying. "He sat there in English class with blood dripping onto his shirt." She paused for him to react.

"Was it a lot of blood?" the clown said.

"We talked at some length about it. He said he wanted to show them what a freak he is."

"He's not a freak."

She smiled to indicate that the reply to follow would be worth her fee. "That's actually not for us to say, Dennis. He feels like one—but the crucial thing isn't that. It's that he wants to *show* everyone. He wanted his whole class to know who he is."

The clown felt like a dummy for not using Lauren's bedroom as she'd offered. It was finally a little cool out and the windows were fogging up. He'd imagined she didn't really want him to see her room—her unmade sheets, the twisted-up workout clothes flung to the floor. Like the blazer he still had on, his bedroom furnishings were selected to match the Lexus: king mattress made of some proprietary foam, tall vase of reeds in the corner, woodblock prints of some samurai character talking to the breeze. Guests to his bedroom were rare, and left knowing no more than he let them.

Dr. Jordie's son walked by again, this time wearing a towel over his neck. So they had a pool. He imagined the son face-down, afloat on his own bleach-clean blood. "Very intimate in its way," Dr. Jordie was saying. He thanked her and PayPalled the fee.

When he came back into the kitchen, Lauren was the *Terminator* mom. Witches and arched cats made of sunlight shined through the blackout paper into the room. "How did I do?" she said. She had on Linda Hamilton's black tank top, utility belt, and sunglasses, and a water gun. "Sarah Connor, 1995." She did a one-arm pull-up on the bar in the kitchen door and landed looking at him. Maybe she thought he'd gone outside so he could cry, but there was no scrutiny in her eyes, only attention. "I'm going to smear on some greasy war-zone-looking shit later. Do you do Halloween?"

"I was thinking," he said before he could stop himself, "of being a scary clown."

"Classic. For a party or for the kids?"

It felt like the fog from the Lexus was coating his skin. He shouldn't have said anything. Halloween was Monday, any parties would be tonight. She attempted a second one-arm pull-up with no luck. "Do you have your costume yet? You should have got it when we were at the party store."

"I have it," he said. His voice was weird. "From last year."

"Wait a second." She squeezed out another pull-up with two arms and thudded to the floor. "You're not one of those clown prankers, are you? Is this a thing you do every year?"

He instructed his face not to do anything, but she was already grinning and shaking her head. "Holy shit."

"I'll be right back," he said.

Up and down her street were Hillary-Kaine signs, yes on Prop 200, yes on Amendment C, plastic gravestones, broom-crashed witches, jack-o'-lantern leaf bags, Love Trumps Hate. He got the kit from the back of the Lexus and carried it in. He laid it in a kitchen chair and undid the clasps. He set the wig between the pumpkins and showed her his greasepaint and his sponges, his red curtain-cloth pants with their ragged patches, his floorboard-slapping shoes, his shirts with their bloodstains and chipped buttons, his long stained teeth, his yellow metal nails. He didn't look up at her the whole time. He couldn't. He searched for more things to show her, so he could delay meeting her eyes. He unscrewed the contact case, so she could see the jaundiced snake-eye floating in its sterile cup. It scared him how violently it shook.

Finally he had to look up, so anxious now he couldn't pretend otherwise. "I'm glad to know you, Dennis," she said. She laughed. "I've known some geeks, I mean I thought I was a connoisseur . . ." She picked up the wig ("May I?") and pressed it on over her Sarah Connor do. She giggled as she fluffed it up, pulling loose plaster dust from the Rocking Horse basement or else trapped flecks of bone. She Jokered up her smile but couldn't hold it. Her giggling quivered the whole wig. She held one of the jack-o'-lantern knives, classic Bates Motel grip. "So you stalk around like this? People must flip out. I'd straight-up mace you before you could say 'punked.' I hope you're safe out there."

He laughed, but it was not his Lexus laugh. It started sociably enough, a laugh at himself, at how he must look, but it cracked down the middle when it reached his belly and something wet and maniacal blurted out of him. Lauren blinked and put a hand on his shoulder. She looked him in the eye, trying to see if he was crying or what. Whatever it is, let's hear it, she seemed to say. He didn't know what to do.

He started to say something but was laughing again—bilious, hot, disgusting, straight from his gut. It was mirthless and too loud and chicken flavored. She was backing away from him now ("You okay, Dennis?"), the wig sliding off her head.

"Give me the knife," he said.

To his surprise, she did, the safe way, gripping the blade and offering him the handle.

"You said you wanted me to show you," he said. It was the clown's voice, not Dennis's. "I'll show you, then." It terrified him what he was saying. He had to stop for breath between each word. *I'll show you. I'll—show—you.*

All the fun was happening downtown, five minutes from Pinche Taco, five minutes from Cerebral Brewing, about two minutes from Über Dog. There were scarecrows and Wonder Women and Cookie Monsters marauding through the early dark. Med students and waitresses, guised as Amelia Earhart, as swan-Björk, swung arms overhead to taxis, to the songs of passing cars, to friends stepping out of corner liquor stores across the street. A quartet of speeding Harleys ripped a seam in the night.

A foam Hulk fist fell from a balcony and bounced into the road. Everyone was hidden in the clamor, welcomed and exalted by it. The clown felt simultaneous with himself. It couldn't be explained.

The clown and Lauren waited at the crosswalk with two scanty pirates. They eyed him. He was suspiciously uncostumed. The clown wore just his blazer and slacks, his graying temples, but beside him Lauren was to the nines. The happy tatters ill-fit her even better than they ill-fit him. He'd whited her face and drawn a great big ripping smile, almost to her eyes. Her forehead was smaller than his and the charred eyebrows reached up and tangled in the frizz of the wig. The teeth bulged her lips into a psychopathic grin. The tinsel nails made a little music as they walked.

Seamus and Eliza's apartment complex was exactly what he'd imagined, a high cube of condos with mountain bikes on the balconies, fake brick on Tyvek, banners over the office. He could picture the police tape, the office phone ringing, the men encamped in the alley shooing off the sirens and lights.

What he'd tell Owen, if Owen wanted to hear him, was that it was the scariest thing in the world to let yourself be known. You might not be liked. In fact, you wouldn't be. There's plenty in each of us that's unforgivable, he'd say. In a political world, it would always make a kind of sense to hide yourself away. But, he'd say, I want you to know me, even if sometimes you hate what you see. And I hope you'll find a way to let me know you too.

He led Lauren up the courtyard stairs and along the balcony past potted cactuses and airing yoga mats. He gestured for her to listen. Behind the door, Seamus was making original commentary on the Clintons. Lauren seemed nervous. She kept whispering, was she supposed to say something or do something scary? "Do I say trick or treat?" The clown took a deep breath and let it all imbue his smile. He told her relax. It was going to be great. The knife was in his blazer, his heart was in his smile. He knocked and said, "Don't worry. Just keep your eyes on me."

THE RINGMASTER

For a few years in there, ten, he'd worked for a midsize engineering firm called Holt Innovations. He filled his thermos each morning, scraped off the little brown Nissan, and motored out to the technology park off 36. He was a diligent disappointment; the others, his coworkers and supervisors, were less diligent. There was a race to make an LED that gave off strong white light, and he was unsurprised when Holt had lost. He retired and let a decade pass without ever once needing to think about the lazy firm, until a letter portending to change his life forever arrived from their lawyer. He flapped it on the counter while he sorted through the Valpak.

That morning, he had gone downstairs to work on the train and for the first time in his life couldn't. He'd flicked on the hem of Christmas lights and the table lamp and looked over the landscape and the train, car by car, but no addition or adjustment or new detail occurred to him. He got out the pencil razor and the paints and held up the new pieces he'd been shaving under the work light. He looked at the still train again, the dusty children racing after it, the old men watching in their row. It seemed fine the way it was. It didn't want another stowaway hanging on the kitchen car or another snake sleeping in the shrubs. He had run it for a little while, slow, then turned it off, went back upstairs, and got the mail for something to do.

The letter said Holt was finally folding but had managed to cover its debts with the sale of a few prize patents. All remaining unexpired patents owned by the firm would become the exclusive intellectual property of the engineers who'd filed them. In his case, one patent, Patent 6055895, would revert to his possession that month and was his to lease, sell, or bequeath. Please contact Melvin Handke of Handke & Kempf.

He put the letter back in its envelope, tore it in half, and slid it into the recycling with the rest. A worthless and embarrassing thing to own. He popped the lid off the cake in the fridge and cut a square around a curling yellow Y with the cold and gummy knife. The frosting was loud on his teeth. Patent 6055895, sum of his cleverness. His to bequeath. He stooped back downstairs to watch the train, cake wobbling on his palm.

He'd taken his time to build the train. It was standard HO scale, nickel silver rails on a base of fiber ties. Some of it was scratch-built and some was easy kit stuff that he'd tweaked. An N or Z scale would have let him fit more train on the table, but the HO was big enough to detail, and now, decades into it, all the detail work he'd put in snuck up and surprised him. A little brown turtle between two of the ties, a flattened penny painted on the track—he'd done more to every piece than he recalled. So these days it was archaeology: he'd find a campaign pin on one of the clowns, a ruby ring on a tiger's claw, and he'd remember it—or he wouldn't remember it. Mostly what his archaeology turned up was spent time. Years alone in basements gluing plastic shrubs to plaster, planting gray glass pebbles into streams. The unremembered details proved how lost all those years were. Dusting out the elephant car with a can of air, he saw a mousetrap he'd fixed in long ago, but the memory of it was gone, somewhere in the basement dark and the smell of stone.

He'd never thought much about what would happen to the train. Half a dozen pieces were from the set he'd started as a kid, and so he allowed himself to say it was the same set he'd been building, basement to basement, all this time. If it *was* one thing, the same train all his life, then he'd moved it four times: Cincinnati to Golden, twice in Golden, then to Denver in 1990. He wasn't moving again, but maybe it would. He hoped it would. It was the smallest problem in the world.

Nothing was going to happen to him anytime soon, but that was when you hoped it would happen. The lucky ones ate their piece of birthday cake and woke up dead the next morning, seventy-nine and a day. He shouldn't talk like that—it was coming, but that didn't mean it was here.

He clicked the DC down to almost nothing, left his fingers on the dial. He loved a slow train. He loved how a slow train labored. A small black thing wobbled on top of a coal car. He picked it up but couldn't see what it was until he ducked it into the headlight. A bat. And he remembered slowly that he had glued bats inside the tunnel before he'd fixed it in. This one must have fallen just as the train passed through. Little marvels like that. He put it in his pocket and helped himself back up the stairs, warmed his coffee on the stove.

Best odds were that he would slip someday on his way down to the set and knock his hip bone into pieces and never hoist the rest of himself back up, and he'd have to lie there half a week on his bloating yellow legs, wishing he could just reach the switch and have some light. He was indulging himself now. There were no best odds because no one was betting. It was too sure for betting. Every other loner old bachelor had pulled it off before him, and he'd be as good at it as they were.

He had a nephew he knew about in Glenwood who had two kids, a little girl and a little boy who would be about four. The nephew was his stepsister's boy, and he didn't know whether she was even alive, but he looked the nephew up and explained. What did he explain? That he had a train set he'd put some time into that he was hoping to give away maybe inside the family and he thought the little boy . . . He let it hang there till the nephew understood.

"Sure thing," said the nephew. "I remember your trains. I remember one time we stayed with you when we were moving to Salt Lake."

Of course, he said, but he couldn't remember.

"You don't remember? I was nine. I stole a little oil well. My mom made us turn around and drive it back." The nephew laughed.

Sure, he said. The telephone cord was twisted into something it would never get out of.

"The problem is we don't have much space up here. We got four of us and two cats, and I need an office. It's a mess anyways. It's not the sort of thing we could just set up on the rug?"

For crying out loud, the set was plaster. Just to get it up the stairs, they'd have to chisel off the tracks and run a Skil saw through the hills and lake and woody town and moldy-looking orchard. It was his own damn fault for making such a monstrous thing, four folding banquet tables set up side by side. In one of the hills he'd buried, god knows why, a little tin airship that he'd played with as a kid, and through the plastic pond water you could see the sunken steamer chest he'd filled with birdseed and a tiny wooden bell he'd carved. He imagined the train on the rug, the cats disdaining to watch, just three or four cars making a little loop around the laundry, derailing with the tremors of a passing shoe. It was his own fault. He thanked the nephew and said he understood. The nephew told him to take care. He went back down and searched it: the tired train, its traveling circus, the boys running, frozen midstride, the old men, the plastic orchard with its sickly trees. One of the trees had *Chapman* carved into the wood, and he had no idea who Chapman was. You could barely see it, *Chapman*, in a little circle on a little trunk, a snake swallowing its tail. He'd forgot to ask about the nephew's mother. That was shameful, but he didn't call back to ask. Rima, his stepsister, ex-step after her mother left his pa—it was ancient history. They shared a house for a few years when they were kids, that was all.

It wasn't that he wanted to preserve it just so. Rip it up, wrap it around the Christmas tree, he didn't care. It was a toy, so play with it. He just wanted—he didn't know what he wanted. Maybe what he wanted was vain and impossible. He'd been goddamn sentimental and now he'd have to pay. He flicked a plastic apple off its branch, shut off the string of lights.

The first car was the engine car. It was a long pipe of black and it bore the rest along. It said BERKSHIRE 1218 across its back, and in its windows were two men, his engineers. No pilots came in an engine car, but he'd put the waving, running children by the track and he wanted them to catch a wave, or a wink, back from the train, so he'd whittled down two torsos under the fly-tying glass and popped out the roof to fit them in. They were small men and speed made them smaller, but the children gathered there could see them all the same. Their mustaches were painted gray and their levers were gold and the children were good children who might wish to pilot trains. When they waved, the engineers would wink and pluck a grape from a paper bag he'd put in with them and pull the whistle so the kids could hear it blow. One's eyes were brown and blue like a husky's eyes, and the grapes' blue matched, and their size made them a thrilling thing to see. A compass hung from the husky's neck, though the steel rails set the way. The tracks sprayed dust and grit at the children's shins, and the steam that blew the whistle was the same that drove the train, and its greeting was also warning and farewell.

The second car was the coal car and so was the third and the old men might themselves have mined the coal. They sat in a row behind the racing kids and watched, though cataract milk showed in their eyes. Their chairs were true wood and some really folded and one was a rocker glued back on its heels.

What was coal? the old men grumped. Their hair was the same stuff as the tumbleweed. Coal, if you wanted to hear about it, came from the earth's own depths, which was one of only two places things could come from. Coal was ancient buried death, dead ferns and dead fish and even old dead boys and girls, and so it was life itself that pushed the train along. That was what coal was and where it was from, and the only other place a thing could come from was the sky, comets and sunshine, and the old men said nothing hardly ever came from there. His coal was crumbled rubber, and it was old and dry, and he had to oil it to keep it black.

The fourth car was the banner car, trumpeting the cargo of the train. It was a wall of brightly papered wood, ballyhoo for the traveling show, and the children pointed at its every word. It promised DEATH DEFIERS! and the children would point and the old men would shake their heads. It promised HIDEOUS MONSTERS! and BREATHTAKING BEAUTIES! and CATS! and ELEPHANTS! and CLOWNS! and the children ran and pointed and the old men shook their heads.

When the train had passed and the children gathered to recall what they had seen, it seemed the banner car had promised them every feat and creature they could think to name. THE GREATEST SHOW ON EARTH, and it had passed them. The children stared at the empty track in disbelief.

And how, the old men muttered, could one length of wood have promised all of this? Heart-stopping beauties? Earth's strongest man? Twins on a flying trapeze? Only fools could miss the ruse. The only show there was was this one—the dying orchard, the silted pond. The banner car was balsa board, and the circus cut a straight, thin path through the sidelands that were their land, and it would not be stopping here.

The hobby shop he liked best was Jim Mitner's, and Monday morning he called Jim up to ask. Did he know a good kid with an interest in model trains? It was early and cloudless and bright, and he could hear the Burlington line's shy blow.

"Sure," said Jim, "the show must go on. A worthy heir." He said he'd ask around, nice man. "Maybe one of these Warhammer kids is into trains."

He thanked him. He could hear what a quaint old sap he was being, but Jim denied it. "It's marketing, Mick," he said. "Your generation can't keep keeping me afloat."

But then Jim called him back only two days later and said he'd keep looking. "Nothing yet, but I'll keep looking," he said. What was that supposed to mean? It had only been two days. "Mick, the kids all buy robo-wizards and alien-battle-balls. I can't comprehend my own stock anymore. I'll find somebody, it just might take me a stretch."

That was that. Someday a little Casey Jones was going to walk in with an engineer's cap on? When had anything ever—how about you give up on this already?

But he didn't. The yellow pages there in the drawer looked brand-new and strange. He called up the Jefferson County safe house. For the kids living there an interval. Something to keep them occupied, he said.

"Toy, clothes, and food donations are accepted Wednesdays and Sundays," the woman said. "Bring an itemized list if you're going to need a tax receipt."

He tried to make himself understood. Was there someone there he could talk with who would be in charge of setting it up? It wasn't all so straightforward, and he'd like to help with the rebuilding, some of the wire work and so on. It would just be a lot easier if he were there.

"Maybe you'll consider a cash donation," she said.

Itemized list, he sneered when she cut the line. He tried Toys for Tots. The Ronald McDonald House. The Parenting Place at the YWCA. Emergency Family Assistance. He wasn't being stiff—it was dangerous if you didn't set it up right. His voice was sore at the end of it, his elbow too, from leaning on the counter by the phone. Why did it have to be his problem anyway? Someone would notice when the mail piled up. He had one last piece of the Safeway cake and slid the rest into the bin.

He liked the sugar, but mostly he'd bought the cakes each year to torment himself. For seventy-five, he'd gone big, called up old coworkers, none from Holt but a few from the energy lab who he knew would indulge him. Dana Stede and Otto Mosher came over. There's chili in the slow cooker, help yourselves. It was fine. They stayed in the kitchen the whole time, it got dark, they went home. Dana did all the talking for him. They were gracious. He wouldn't put them through it again.

One thing he'd always remember Rima for—he'd had a birthday for himself one of the years she was with them, his ninth, tenth, or eleventh. He took five boys to the horse track, and Rima, six years older than him, came as a chaperone. His friends—if you could call them that, one had broken his nose only a month before—got surly when they found out they weren't allowed to place cash bets. They blamed him, and he thought maybe they were right. Stupid to have thought just horses were a show. Rima, he could remember, was wearing one of her deluxe hats, a fancy little pastry, fashion and a joke on fashion, and she knew better than to come to his defense. She'd just faced off the loudest boy. "What?" he'd said. And she'd oinked twice like a pig and turned back to the track.

He called Jim again.

"How's it, Mick?"

It's nothing about the asking around, he explained right off. He appreciated Jim's looking, and he wasn't going to be a pesterer. He just had a quick question. Had Jim ever carried or heard of a company named Chapman? It was carved into one of his trees and he didn't recall doing it or who Chapman was.

"Nope," said Jim. "It's no insignia. An old sweetheart, maybe? Did you show Miss Mary Chapman some apple-tree shade?" Jim laughed. "You know what I saw in the catalog? Couldn't believe it. A big top. How many years you been working on that circus without ever setting up the show? You want me to order one?"

He told Jim thanks but no, he finally had the train how he wanted it. And Jim said, "Don't talk like that," as if he'd said something grave.

The phone rang again as soon as he set it down—he hadn't moved from the counter at least.

"Good afternoon. Is this Michael Parsons?"

He said that it was.

"Wonderful. This is Melvin Handke, I represent—"

I'm not interested, he said.

"It's not a solicitation call, sir. It's—"

It's RGB looping in light-emitting diodes, he said. I'm not interested.

It didn't seem to sink in far. "Yes, I see you got my letter. Your patent, Patent 6055895, is not presently leased to any, um, ah, companies, but that of course could change at any time. There are patent management services you could consider subscribing to that would—"

It's worthless, he said. The yellow pages were still open on the counter. Beneath CHILDREN'S SERVICES was CHIMNEY CLEANING, under CHIMNEY CLEANING, CHOCOLATE. Then pages and pages of CHURCH.

"Excuse me?"

It's a thing of no worth, he said.

"Yes, but, well, with all due respect, Mr. Parsons, you don't know that. It may have some unforeseen—"

It won't, he said. Please don't contact me about this anymore.

The way time moved these days. Afternoons he boiled his tea on the coil, watched the weather. Autumn air took the kettle vapor up. The huff in the kettle mounted and he shut it off before the scream but tilted it to make a few shrill notes as it lifted off the stove.

He tried to rub the dryness off his hands in the steam, but it was too gentle. He watched it spread. *I'll move twenty thousand tons on that*, a genius had said. A genius—an engine—an engineer. Denver electricity was still sixty percent coal, so his train did run on coal—the old men were right—though the steam was off in a turbine in Commerce City.

The glow drained out of the stove coil, eighty percent nickel, twenty percent chromium, resistance pitched to tear reluctant electrons loose, their sweat enough to boil tea. As a boy, he'd wanted to be either an inventor or a railroad engineer. He'd ended up somewhere between. It wasn't so bad. Holt was a grave-yard, but the renewable energy lab had moved him to Golden, and he'd liked his years there. It was a misnomer, though—*renewable*. From one way of looking, even coal might be renewed, once we all were crushed a million years down underground, and from another way nothing renewed—it all ran on the heat of a dying ember in the sky. Physics, for all its effort, still had no way to measure the time in things: carbon crushed, coal burnt, tea brewed.

When the tea was steeped he went down to the seventy-year train. Once he'd rigged a way for the flag on the caboose to click a clock tower a minute forward when it passed, and with the dial set at 41 the train could tell real time. But he didn't like it. The set should have its own inconvertible time, he decided—the chil-dren running, the turtle clawing over ties.

The test lights that ringed the basement were the only use that Patent 6055895 had ever been put to. His clever little circuits, ten years' work. Instead of racing everyone to find the indium phosphide or oxide that would allow a bright white LED, his brave idea was to have a circuit of red, green, and blue lights inside each diode that would blend to a fresh white. It might have worked, but the emission patterns never matched up. Each nub on the string housed a different experimental circuitry, and the bulbs bled red, green, blue, purple, yellow, but never white. It turned out he'd made Christmas lights, production cost a thousand times what a string from Target ran. They lit the basement well enough. At least he wasn't infringing on Holt's patent now.

He blew the whistle for the children, and the wooden whistle made a true train sound, better than the Burlington line's. More trainlike than a train. His first set, more than seventy years ago, had the Rocky Mountains. That was what the box had said. Now he lived at their foot. As a kid, the whole future was your model world. He was going to be an engineer, and then he was an engineer—the other kind. He was going to see the Rockies, and then he did see the Rockies, and so on. Nothing had disappointed him much, nor was anything much like what it had claimed to be.

He'd been to the circus, in Cincinnati, as a kid, and in truth he wasn't that impressed. It was so much humbler than what had been promised. The six-foot strongman, polyester stretched across his paunch; the tired, wounded elephants; the hokey top hat exclaiming each act—it seemed smaller now than his own miniatures, which at least could fill their world. He'd known how big the real world was and that even giants didn't measure. The elephants were the same as him: small things in a world too vast to occupy.

His elephants' eyes were bright enamel and their eyelashes were cuts of one he'd pulled from his own eye. It was the most childish thing but who could help it: all his life, he'd wanted to be small and with them. A tiny life where he would fit. The frustration of it was part of the marvel of the set. He could see it all, but he'd never been there. He'd always wanted to go.

❖   ❖   ❖

The children had three ways of looking at the train: at the car before them, at the line receding, and at the procession coming nearer. Each was its own joy and each its own terror. The marvel of the arriving train was made double by its immediate retreat, and its disappearance was twice as frightening, for the train continued to approach. The children could not greet the car before them without also waving it farewell, and so there were three ways of looking at the train, and all ways were the same, and then the train was gone and gone forever.

He wished he could see it like that: nothing and nothing and nothing and then a train and then nothing again. Was the last nothing better or worse than the first? All he could see was the loop. That was the problem with the set. All sets. No train in the world ran like that.

The fifth car was the cat car and so was the sixth, and the cats were so huge and fierce and peerless that they could only be bored. They were out of HO scale and hardly two fit to a car, and he supposed they knew they were too big for their island world. They looked so bored. They were always and ostentatiously bored, and their teeth hung bored against their blackened gums. Their boredom was their arrogance and they were entitled to it. What did they have to fear?

Boredom at its worst could gather into rage—the children running trackside hoped it would. Come on, lazies, they said, want a taste? Pounce! I dare you.

Why did they want that? Something in them wanted an attack? But the cats did not bat an eye. They lay in their cars and licked the oiled wood and their hearts rumbled in the darkness of their chests. The children's strides were varied and the fastest froze most credibly, their stillness somehow suited to their speed. He ate his breakfast, he ate his lunch. When the month changed, the calendar pulled the pushpin off the wall.

Dana Stede called and said he had Rockies tickets, did Mick want to come along—it's a Reds game?

That was nice. They'd gone to a few games together when they worked at the energy lab, years ago. This time Dana's son came too, drove them in his big, boxy Honda SUV. The son was in his thirties, tending bar. They got talking. The son kept asking him questions. He didn't think he'd been asked so many questions in his whole life. The son wanted to know if Mick thought he should get married. "You seem like a functional old bachelor to me. You take Pop's side? Should I get spliced?" Well, he said, do you love her? "Mickey," the son said, "I love *them*."

In the fourth inning, the son got up and came back with three more cups of Coors. He hadn't planned on finishing the first one, but now he had to. He could hear himself talking, the rubbery sound of his own voice. When the Reds hit a triple, he made a croak of elation he didn't know he could make. He saw Dana smiling at him and supposed he maybe should be embarrassed, but he didn't pay any attention. The high line of the stadium held a late blue sky aloft, and his team was winning. He hailed the fellow over and bought them each a dog.

"Thanks, Mick," Dana said, "I thought we might all get dinner after, but this'll do."

Thanks, Mick, I thought we might all get dinner after, but this'll do—why did that crush him? It made no sense. He looked at his sneaker toes. He could have had something nice, fettuccini, with Dana and the boy and kept the talk going, but he'd ruined it.

"You all right, buddy?" the son said.

By the time the game was over he was so exhausted he could never have made it past appetizers.

"Take care, old dog," said the son when they dropped him off. "Tough luck about your Reds."

Melvin Handke kept his promise. He hadn't called again.

He thought some certificate might appear in the mail, Patent 6055895 in the flesh, but nothing had come. Maybe there was no document. It was just out there, his intellectual property, wherever it had always been.

He didn't think he'd been unspeakably rude, but he called anyway.

"Hello?" a woman said.

Handke and Kempf? he asked.

"Handke and wife," she said. He'd looked in the residence listings.

I apologize, he said. I'll call the office number.

"I can take a message. What is it?"

He played the words in his head. *Tell him Mick Parsons is sorry about being curt on the phone last month.*

"Go ahead," she said, then, "Mister, I think you know how to help yourself to a yogurt cup." He heard war sounds—bombs and machine guns in a boy's voice—coming through the line. "I'm sorry, what did you say?" she said.

Nothing yet, he said.

"Well? Shoot."

Does your son have an interest in model trains?

"Aw hell," she said. "Look, I'm sorry, but will you take us off your list?"

On his walk to the Safeway one day, he realized he didn't know whether or not he could run. It wasn't the running children that got him thinking. It was two sweaty pink men who waved as they came jogging by. They were both wearing high-tech running shirts without any sleeves. They moved at a pretty good clip. They were talking about a woman named Amy, and their heavy breath made them loud.

"Amy, no! She didn't!"

"I swear to god. Right there in front of everyone. Amy did."

"Goddamn it. What a babe."

He was impressed how easily they moved and talked. From their hair and the veins in their cheeks, he guessed they were in their fifties. He had never been a runner, but his body remembered the thrill of sprinting. He wondered if his ankles were strong enough to push and his knees strong enough to catch. Well, he thought, just try. Run.

But instead of breaking into a jog, he came to a stop. He stood there on the sidewalk in the Colorado blue with his empty canvas grocery bag hanging from his hand. He felt the gas in his legs, but a stiffness surrounded his memory of the old thrill. For a minute he was frozen, as if he'd tricked himself and now was unable to even walk. A black dog watched him from the passenger seat of a passing car. The dog turned its head, tracking him as it passed. When the car was gone, the neighborhood was quiet. Not a leaf blower, not a coasting bike. He could hear nothing. Time hadn't stopped, he could feel it. He stood there fixed in the painted afternoon, searching the sky until the silence gave him a shiver and the shiver let him move on.

When the man in front of the Safeway asked for change, he fished up three quarters and a little bat.

The nephew called. The phone was ringing off the wall these days. He said he and the kids would be in Denver Sunday. Maybe they could come by and say hello. "Lana and Eben would love to meet you. And they'd love to see your train."

He didn't like the tone of it, the pity. They showed up more than an hour after they'd said, the two kids crashing into his house when he opened the door, both wearing Egyptian death masks. "We just came from the King Tut exhibit," the nephew said. "Have you seen it?" The nephew took off his coat, folded it over the back of the armchair, and walked into his kitchen, where he leaned confidently back against the counter. What was he confident of? That he was welcome? That he would be liked? He hadn't seen him in years, why should he be liked? The nephew's face cupped a tight smile, which should have seemed smug, but didn't. He was stubbled and strong. He didn't look like a man who needed a home office. "Lana, Eben," he said, "did you meet your uncle Michael?"

I'm your great-ex-step-uncle, he said. He'd prepared it.

"I know," said the girl. The mask was gone somewhere and she was repinning her hair. He asked and she said she was seven, exhausted by the question. She was beautiful, he thought, and he recognized something shameful in the thought—a sorrow he should not be feeling. The boy was off and running. He asked the nephew how Rima was.

"Alzheimer's," he said. "Mom's in a nursing home in Salt Lake."

He said he was sorry to hear that. And the nephew launched into it—mostly a defense of the nursing-home decision. He could detect no sign of actual sadness on the man. The nephew was doing a lot of nodding in agreement with himself. "Don't worry, she's the same old red-hen prima donna as ever. She tells the nurses a young man is coming to bring her diamonds. They say she's always smiling like she's got some little secret. We don't get to—"

"Daddy, look!" came the shout from the basement.

The seventh car was the elephant car and so were the eighth and ninth, and if he could give the train to his elephants, he would. The elephants were the only ones that seemed to watch him back. Their hides were gray, their tusks were white, but in their black glass eyes the Christmas LEDs flared. They examined every unlucky color as they turned around the room. The elephants knew the set better than he did. The hobo napping on his guitar, the pollywogs tickling the pond, they'd forget no thing lit by his failed lights.

He showed the boy how to switch it on and let him turn the dial and set the speed. "All the way," said the boy, and the train spun at its fastest past the orchard trees.

Now, bothered old stick that he was, he couldn't take his nervous eyes off of their little grabbers.

"Is that a spittoon?" said the girl, poking between the old men's chairs. Cartoons? How did the world still know that word?

The nephew saw him watching her finger. "Don't touch," he told her. He took the striped cap from its nail and plopped it on the boy's head. "Let your sissy have a go."

The boy stepped backward and without looking took his great-ex-step-uncle's hand, as if they were about to cross a street. The little hand was soft and warm. "Put it on its fastest," he told the girl, but she slowed it down and stared in at the cars.

"That one has the tigers in it, Eben. Look, Eben, clowns."

The nephew looked over the children and nodded, a quick self-satisfied dip. "Quite a creation," he said.

"Make it run over my finger, Lana," said the little boy, pulling away his hand.

He remembered some wafer cookies he had and went upstairs to get them. When he returned, the train was still going but the girl had her back to it. "Uncle Michael, where's Eben?" she said smiling.

Of course there was only one place to hide. He told the nephew it probably wasn't so safe for the boy to be under there—all the cords and a box with some sculpting tools—and the nephew said, "Okay, giant underground troll golem, come on out."

The troll didn't like that. There was a bang on the bottom of the set, and the train keeled off its track.

"Hey!" said the nephew, grabbing the boy by his wiggly arm. "That is *not* how we treat other people's things."

A scowl set itself into the little skeleton. The engineer's hat fell off his head.

"That is not how we treat other people's things, Eben," said the girl.

It was fine, the set was always crumbling and getting fixed, he tried to explain, but it was like his voice wasn't there at all. When he offered him a wafer cookie, the boy ran up the stairs and slammed the door. They found him sitting cross-armed on the living room floor behind his Egyptian mask.

But the boy was repaired in no time. He couldn't believe it. The nephew ate a wafer cookie, and went, "Mmm," then louder, "Mmm! *Mmmm!*" until he wound around his son with that hum, and scooped up the child, and rubbed the sound back and forth against his belly, as if he were the yummy thing.

"Daddy!" screamed the little boy, and when the death mask slipped from his face, he was beaming, as if through this ceremony, all hurt and shame had been absolved.

The girl watched skeptically. "May I have a cookie too?" she said.

The repaired boy still did not want one, but when his father asked them, "What do you guys say? Should we come back and play with Uncle Mike's trains again sometime?" they both shouted, "Yeah!" The girl leapt off the ground with an upward punch. The rings on the highboy bounced, and the rhino painting tilted out of plumb, but it didn't matter. He knew he shouldn't but he said it anyway, forget the nephew: Now, I have a question for you. How would you two like to have a train like that at your house?

Their big eyes consulted silently.

You'd have to be very gentle with it, he said.

"We'd probably break it," said the girl.

"Yeah," said the little boy, "I'd probably break it."

That would be okay, he said.

"And sometimes," she said—their father was nodding proudly—"it's more fun to go play with other people's toys."

Here was what he'd always hated about children—how they treated you like a child.

"You can come play Wii," said the little boy.

"At my one friend's house," she said, "there's a trampoline, and at my other's, in the summer, there's a pool."

His own children sprinted just to glimpse the train while they could. The horse smoking a pipe—did you see him! Did you see the king monkey wore a cape! Then they forgot. He knew they forgot because the train looped again, and they ran again, after a sight they'd never seen and thought they'd never see again.

"Hug your uncle," the nephew said, and the little boy and girl hugged him dutifully.

Goodbye, goodbye.

He watched his own door close and heard for the first time in a long time the quiet of his house.

A ticking, a terrestrial purring, something sliding in the pipes. He went to the kitchen, but it was there too. The vent metal flinched. Something was circling in, through the walls around him. He commanded his ears to stop listening. He went to the door to call the nephew back, any pretense, but they were gone. His heart pumped up little jets of blood, flooded, pumped, flooded again, the same old pig-iron blood. He could hear the rust on the pump, the chug of the engine, a creak shifting chamber to chamber through his house. A pleading cold sank through the gray meat of his arms. Where was he?

Then it was over. He was standing in his own doorway. He breathed. He was fine.

He went out to get the mail, but it was Sunday, there was no mail.

The liquor store opened at eleven in the morning. The woman at the register was eating candy cigarettes, watching the black-and-white TV. Liquor-store smell was either the liquor through the bottles or else it was the glue in all the cardboard they broke down. Heavy stock needed extra glue.

Boxes? he asked.

"Pallet in the back," she said.

He took twelve, but it turned out he only needed five. That surprised him. It didn't take any time at all. He boxed the cars away, pried off the tracks and set them in another box. The Skil saw went easily through the plaster world—mmm! *Mmmm!* He cut it into squares and left them on the table under a layer of their own dust.

He taped the boxes closed. JACK DANIEL'S. EVAN WILLIAMS. JIM BEAM. And there it came: *Chapman.* John Chapman: Johnny Appleseed.

He'd made a figure of him, long ago. He could vaguely remember the American saint talking to the children, telling them how every seed became a seedling, and every seedling grew into a tree, and so on. Every tree burst with fruit. Every apple held new seeds. The world is drawn in circles. Every train in time looped round again. He looked for the little tree with the carving, but now he couldn't find it. It was a lie, he thought, an old one. The world did not renew. It was bound from one place to another, a place he wouldn't see.

He shook a little, wrapping the cord around the Skil saw, as if overwhelmed with the relief.

He called the paper. Classifieds. Yes. Well, I'm trying to find a kid, nine, ten, eleven, interested in model trains. Yes. I want to give an old set away. A train set. Free. No, I'd rather not sell it. "One moment please," she said, then it was a manager on the phone: "You're looking for nine-year-olds?"

He had to take out any mention of age to persuade them to run it. No one would call anyway. The bank's executors could figure it out—sell it, take their fee, give the ten dollars to the charities he'd named, save a prairie dog or two. But the phone rang early the next morning. "Yes, I'm calling about the train. Right, right. Perfect. Do you mind if we come over and have a peek?" They didn't even ask what scale.

They knocked just as he was having his sandwich. Two men, hair white, but not as old as him. One in a sweater vest, the other a sweater of similar knit. They told him their names but spoke so fast introductions were over before he could instruct himself to remember. They stood smiling in his doorway, round shaved cheeks and wire glasses. One wore a gold signet ring on his pinky. All right, come in, he said.

They complimented everything in his house, wanted to know if he had any other antiques to salvage. He decided not to offer them a drink.

It's down in my dungeon, he said, and they loved that. He could hear their patience as he gripped his way down the stairs. He still had his napkin tucked in his shirt. It's in those boxes there, he said.

He watched them slice the tape and arrange a half-dozen cars directly on the plaster where they tottered on the dust. "Wow, Mick—Mick, these are wonderful! Look, clowns. Scary! Mick, we can't take this from you."

Only a con man spoke your name twice a sentence. It isn't doing any good here, he said.

"But we couldn't, we just couldn't," said the signet ring. He wished they wouldn't protest. He didn't see the need. Take it, he said. You're doing me a favor. I need it out.

"We—"

I'm glad you'll appreciate it, he said. The landscape is yours too, if you want to stick it back together.

"Gosh. We know a perfect dealer for this. For train stuff. They've got one like this, even bigger, on display."

Wow, he said.

"You should visit."

He said that would be nice.

They all looked at one another. He didn't have anything ready to say. "How long have you been working on this?" the sweater vest asked.

A little while, he said. He wanted to ask about children— nephews or nieces—but he didn't know how. He asked if they needed his help getting it out of the basement.

"Don't you worry about any of that," the signet said. "We'll

take care of it all. Now what kind of batteries does it take? Or
do you just push it by hand?"

There was no caboose. The last car was another engine that
faced the other way around, in case the train needed to edge
back a length or two. It held another engineer who looked back
on the empty track, which pulled away endlessly beneath his
feet. He didn't wave or wink or pull the whistle. He just felt the
weight behind him and stared at what was left after the show
had passed. His eyes were opaque and pasty and his hands
gripped controls he never used, and his engine car had no real
engine that could make the train reverse.

When the train had sped past, the old men would say, Running
late for its wreck, I guess. That was why the circus couldn't stop,
the old men told the kids. They'd miss their wreck. The children
flinched and muttered, but the old men knew the joke was true.
All trains wrecked. All trains fell from their rails, poured from
some trellis, dove into a marsh. The marsh was thick and gray
and clouded by its own cold-boiled fumes. It was bog laid atop
thicker bog laid atop a bog still thicker yet, and the train would
sink, they supposed, forever. The cataracted old men could see
the bog as well as they'd seen the passing train. They could
see the dark inside it. It was one of only two places toward which
all things are bound and the other was the sky and nothing
hardly ever made it there. The circus turned to coal, they said,
and they meant it as a consolation.

When the tiresome gratitudes were finally over and sweater
vest and signet ring were gone, he went back down and looked

at the four white plastic folding tables. Banquet tables. He could have a banquet now.

He looked in close. With the tables uncovered, he could see the red, green, and blue in his lights mottling the surface. He hadn't been able to see it on the landscape, but on the bare surface he could see his failed work: unsteady pebbles of color, a tiny useless fire that would not resolve to white. He dragged a finger through the harlequin dust.

Here he was. He wasn't going to pretend to be surprised. The phone rang a few more times. Thanks for your interest, he said. It's been claimed.

The gray-brown circuitry of the Denver valley . . . the stinking Suncor refinery on the edge of 85 . . . the chalk-straight lines guarding dealerships and tech academies . . . the real world went like this. His little brown Nissan rolled north atop its planet, over the crushed-stone gravel and roof-black asphalt and the mute green land that lay beneath the endless grid. Past the flats of Commerce City, Thornton, Northglenn, sales-tax-purchased Open Space, Foster Reservoir, Mulligan Reservoir, across the highway a great big place called Camping World. Styrofoam football helmets on wagging antennas. Towels pinched in passenger windows to block out sun. Where a county road rose over the highway, two boys were hanging a sign, $10 PUPPIES. A mile marker wore a plastic flower wreath. North of Fort Collins, prairie dogs chirped and chewed on orange flagging tape, and the dirt was loose and tawny. Dry rivers, crooked paths of lime, tire peels scalped off by the road. In Cheyenne, the Nissan turned west across the Union Pacific line, and the highway began to rise and fall with the topography—snow-patched greens, little bug-hunting birds clutching bouncy blades of grass, spilled conifers tousling the hills.

He tried to see the planet passing. He'd forgot how fast the highway struck you blind. His eyes would settle into the distance where the lanes pulled into one. Again and again, he had to shake his eyes off of it. Off of the trucks, off of the billboard breakfast sandwiches hovering next to the road. Every mile of the way, animals had smeared their gel across the blacktop. Something stood for foreground wherever you turned, but the land itself you had to force yourself to see. He pressed his head back and took the shape of the horizon, the wavering ring that coasted with him. It was there if you really focused, an earth and you turning across it. New hills rose ahead as the old ones sank behind. Clouds cast off from oceans flew on in long salutes. Fins of moraine marked the paths of the glaciers, those old dragons, as they shrank back to their caves. It was here, his real landscape, and him inside it, and so what? His eyes kept falling back to the speedometer, the distance, the long line of the road. It was just as hard to imagine: he lived here.

She wouldn't remember him. A rumpled face claiming to be her brother or to once have been. If she did remember him, she wouldn't remember that he'd come. There wasn't any point to it. He didn't know what he'd tell her, but that wouldn't matter. They tramped into my house like little pharaohs, he'd say.

On his way out the door, he'd seen the package from Handke & Kempf, and at a rest stop he had a cup from the thermos and looked inside. A letter said something apologetic—the INSPIRE campaign, CFO's commendable eagerness to return Holt's

patents to the lead engineers, however the board, the liquida-
tion procedures. He smiled, he could hardly be bothered to
skim. Beneath the letter was a piece of wood, varnished to a
plastic brown. A black metal plate had been affixed to the wood
with shop glue. In sharp gold lines at the top of the slab sat the
insignia of the failed engineering firm. Beneath, it read: *Holt
Innovations Honors Michael Parsons, Inventor of Loop-Based
RGB Blending in Light-Emitting Diodes.* On the back, there
was a little hanger and a sticker advertising the plaque shop, a
place called Honorifics Inc.

The box was a high-quality corrugated cardboard mailer with
a good sheet of foam wrap. Behind the foam wrap, the final item
was a packing list with the date, his name, and the product count.
He read it again, amused: MICHAEL PARSONS—ACHIEVEMENT
PLAQUE—1.

He stopped early for the night in western Wyoming, first motel
off the ramp. He stood in the nearly empty lot with his bag and
pointed his binoculars out from the lines of the parking lot. A
clear sky, a strong breeze. The wind dragged a gas station cup
loudly across the asphalt. Two gold hills pushed away from the
hex of roads. Through the binoculars, the sky might be searched
forever.

In his room, he sat on the untouched bed with both feet on
the floor and looked again, without the binoculars now. The
thatch wallpaper, the hard-stuffed chair, the bright brass drawer
pulls. He tried to see the thousand, or ten thousand, people who
had shared this rectangle with him. The watercolor of a garden
trellis, the Velcro square on the remote, the unstained coffee

maker next to the TV. Real life had happened in this modeled room, and there was no sign left.

The bedspread was a patterned chaos of reds and yellows and greens. It looked cheaply dyed and new. Probably fifty thousand beds across the continent were now wearing the same design. He laid his hands on top of it, pulled his palms across, traced the fancy stitches through their curls. He tried to feel the color, and maybe could, its dull fire against his open hands.

Acknowledgments

To Janet Silver, Ariel Lewiton, and Callie Garnett, this book's champions, my endless thanks.

Thank you to the many institutions that supported this work: the James Michener–Copernicus Society of America, Ucross Foundation, Vermont Studio Center, and Cornell College Center for the Literary Arts. Thank you to the Iowa Writers' Workshop, especially Connie Brothers, Kelly Smith, Deb West, and Jan Zenisek, and to the University of Denver, especially Karla Heeps, Laird Hunt, Brian Kiteley, and Selah Saterstrom. Thank you to Karin Schalm and Suzanne and Michael Ziegler for your open doors.

Thanks to the many friends and teachers who read these stories and supported me—especially Kevin Brockmeier, Ethan Canin, Lan Samantha Chang, Peter Orner, Marilynne Robinson, and Wells Tower; Marcus Burke, César Díaz, Carmen Maria Machado, Thirii Myo Kyaw Myint, Ben Mauk, Natalie Rogers, and Tony Tulathimutte. Extra-special thanks to the Mount Rushmore Broom Company of Salmon Ear, Idaho.

Thanks to Christopher Boyer of Kestrel Aerial Photography for his help with "Aerialists"; acknowledgment is also due to Julian Dibbell's *My Tiny Life*. Thanks to sharp readers and editors at *American Short Fiction*, *Guernica*, *Colorado Review*, and *Mid-American Review*. My great gratitude to Sarah Gorham, Kristen Radtke, and everyone at Sarabande Books. The Bloomsbury team—Nancy Miller, Liese Mayer, Laura Phillips, Marie Coolman, Sarah New, Laura Keefe, Nicole Jarvis, Ellen Whitaker, Katya Mezhibovskaya, Caitie Kealy, and Callie Garnett—has been daring, generous, and kind.

Finally, my loving thanks to the Juniper Street Collective, my own family circus, and to the circuses on Francis, North, and West Third Streets too. This book is dedicated, in memory of Carola Mayer and Harry Gray, to my parents, the best parents. It was written beside Ashley Colley, who drew, cut, and screenprinted the circus images and whose intellect and courage saved me more than once.

A Note on the Author

Mark Mayer spent two years at Cornell College's Center for the Literary Arts as the Robert P. Dana Emerging Writer-in-Residence. He has an MFA from the Iowa Writers' Workshop. He lives in Denver.